slags

Also by Emma Jane Unsworth

Animals
Adults

slags

emma jane
unsworth

b

THE BOROUGH PRESS

The Borough Press
An imprint of HarperCollins*Publishers* Ltd
1 London Bridge Street
London SE1 9GF

www.harpercollins.co.uk

HarperCollins*Publishers*
Macken House, 39/40 Mayor Street Upper
Dublin 1, D01 C9W8, Ireland

First published by HarperCollins*Publishers* 2025
1

For Loobs

It is a small thing
to rage in your own bowl

Anne Sexton

I too beneath your moon, almighty Sex,
Go forth at nightfall crying like a cat,
Leaving the lofty tower I laboured at
For birds to foul and boys and girls to vex
With tittering chalk; and you, and the long necks
Of neighbours sitting where their mothers sat
Are well aware of shadowy this and that
In me, that's neither noble nor complex.
Such as I am, however, I have brought
To what it is, this tower; it is my own;
Though it was reared To Beauty, it was wrought
From what I had to build with: honest bone
Is there, and anguish; pride; and burning thought;
And lust is there, and nights not spent alone.

Edna St. Vincent Millay

Somewhere near Watford

All the old party girls were falling. Sarah could feel it on the city streets, in the slow limp of Saturday nights where no one went out any more to pound the pavements with their passion or fury. Sofas were the new bar stools. People didn't salute the sun from jagged rooftops, glass in hand. People jogged instead, at 5 a.m. Across the land, beds were made and slept in. Geese flew overhead, unheard. The clubs and pubs were dying; younger generations preferred coffee and conversation. Everyone was thinking about their gut health, or their crochet, or the state of the economy.

Sarah herself, once a committed party girl, was regularly flirting with sobriety. This time she'd managed a month so far. She had given up drinking in February – nothing so cliched as January, for god's sake – because she was starting to feel unwelcome in her own life. As though her personality was a badly fitting suit she'd inherited from a dead aunt. Night after night, she had sat sober, in front of a candle, forgiving herself, waiting for clarity to hit. A month in, she was ready to cave. It was just so boring. Sarah possessed grit and tenacity like any woman with red hair, but the one thing she couldn't hack was the boredom.

Which was why she was sneaking glances at someone else's

phone, reading the texts of the woman sitting beside her. To be fair, they were excellent texts. Some of the best Sarah had read, in fact. They were a real treat. They *were* a sort of party. They had everything: intrigue, raunch, playfulness – and a plot twist.

I keep thinking of you with Keeley.

I keep thinking of you coming over after and punishing me, tasting her on me.

Have you got a lot on at work?

Yeah we're moving to a bigger office on a higher floor on Monday.

These all sent in succession, barely a thirty-second pause between, the shift in tone leaving its recipient seemingly unaffected. Sex and mundanity, all wrapped up. Sarah was reeling. Unsure whether this unflinching juxtaposition of opposites was evolved or basic. The woman whose phone she was spying on looked barely thirty. She looked like she was coming home from a shift at a department store or jewellery shop. She looked elegant but not rich, keen to shuck off her blouse and trousers and get into her pink onesie with a bowl of noodles. A normal life. A normal life shot through with sexts.

The train was heading out of London, bound for the North. Blocks of flats flicked past in her peripheral vision. The woman next to her skittered through her socials. Checked her bank balance. Ordered a pair of fur-lined Crocs. It wasn't the colour Sarah would have chosen but this wasn't Sarah and it wasn't her life. Or her phone. She was just looking at it. It was Saturday night. This was entertainment.

Ding! A new message arrived on the woman's phone, the alert blooming down blue from the top of the screen. The woman flicked back to her inbox.

That'll be exciting for you and the team xoxo

Sarah sighed. Can we get back to tasting Keeley? It was a silent thought, but the woman seemed to sense it and self-consciously clicked her phone to sleep and placed it face down on the table, turning her head towards Sarah in an accusatory fashion. Sarah closed her eyes and pretended to be asleep. She could probably actually sleep, she was so tired. Should she do a little fake snore? No. It was hard to gauge the volume of such things, and overdoing it would incriminate her instantly. Instead, she resigned herself to a genuine, heartfelt slump.

It was work, Sarah told herself. The lack of an exercise regime. Too many decades of being a caner. But it was more than that, too. She was suffering from a bone-deep exhaustion these days; sometimes so deep she struggled to get out of her chair. What was that? Boredom, was all that Sarah could conclude. Was it the same thing the romantics called ennui? Or 'general malaise'? Maybe it was just a social *fin de siècle*. Sarah hoped she could give it a French name. Things with French names always sounded better. Like her sister.

Sarah would be seeing Juliette the next day. They were going on a trip, and she needed to be on form — they both did. Holidays demanded that of you. Besides, Juliette would be expecting teetotal Sarah to be full of gusto, not dragging her anchor.

Ding! The woman next to her turned her phone over. Sarah squinted and scried, trying to make out the words on the screen without moving her head. Maybe the texters would say goodbye to each other now. But how did you conclude a conversation like that? Sarah wondered. Did you go sexy or mundane, to sign off? Going sexy might be too much of a leap after hugs and kisses and fur-lined Crocs. So, then. Back to work? Business as usual? Depressing. Because sex was important. In her teens, sex had been bravado and bluster, rarely about her own pleasure so much as the social conquest. In her twenties, sex was a power tool, a way to test her carnivorous desires to destroy men and eat their souls. Which would

3

have been fun, if she hadn't secretly doubted her true attractiveness, and found her carefully organised fantasies constantly punctured by the chaos and instability of reality. In her thirties, sex was rife with fertility considerations — was she/did she want to be/could she/ was it too early/too late — the viral questioning of that exhausting epoch. In her early forties, so far she was feeling a desirous ownership of her body seeping back under her bedroom door at night, like light from an old lamp. This was her decade to really take it all back; to sharply skewer everything she wanted carnally, before the following decade's menopause sent her into another chapter of manufactured spite: telling her she was a washed-up crone, soon to be invisible. Her vision was suddenly unfogged by capitalism's weakening of womanhood, and she wanted to snatch the window while it lasted. Sarah didn't know how she felt about her ovaries. But she was definitely looking forward to not having to worry all the time about how she was supposed to feel about them. Sex wasn't about her ovaries. It was the simple, brute charge of *getting her rocks off*. And Sarah had been decidedly unrocked for a long time now. The orbitals of sex — romance, passion, desire — were pleasant and conducive but also very much not the thing. Now that Sarah had given up drinking, sex was all she had left. It was the only source of thrill and escape. For a while, she'd thought that this natural substitute for alcohol would get her through these pale, wan months where her soul wintered and restored itself, healing in tandem with her liver. Citalopram had left her libido in a sulk. But she'd cut the antidepressants down — literally, millimetre by millimetre, shaving them each day to avoid headaches — and now she had been officially unmedicated for three months, she was like a sailor on shore leave. Shame the online dating scene wasn't up to it. A vivid sex life might have been just the thing that saved Sarah from the dullness of her own redemption arc. But there was no one to go out with to find potential hook-ups. Everyone was married off, babied up, tired.

Soon she would be the only one left out of the old crew that used to rail around Manchester's Northern Quarter: Soho for rock stars. If online dating was the best option – sober dates, with people she met online – the era had taken a tragic turn. It wasn't the anonymity that bothered her. The anonymity of the internet was in its own way arousing. Sarah could go for a bot, when the time came. No, it wasn't that – it was the nonchalance. The laziness. Complacency was the real boner-wilter. Sex was nothing if not a case for industry. Sweat. Effort. But maybe the sex she knew, the sex she liked, wasn't relevant any more. Maybe her sex life had a sell-by date, and it was rotting at the back of the fridge, behind the aspirational silken tofu. If this was the case, it was truly the end times. It was, in part, her dystopian mood that had prompted the suggestion of a motorhome trip. And then, to Sarah's surprise, Juliette had jumped at it.

The train slowed on the approach to a station and the woman with the phone started to stand up – Sarah's cue to move and let her pass. She got up and let the woman squeeze with her bags and coat through the narrow gap into the aisle.

'I hope you enjoyed that,' the woman said as she passed.

Before thinking, Sarah replied: 'I enjoyed it more than anything in ages, thank you.'

The woman stopped, stunned. She looked at Sarah's face and, ascertaining that Sarah was being genuine, nodded, before making her way to the doors.

A few people on the train turned to look at Sarah. Sarah did not feel it would be wise, or respectful, to explain.

* * *

The next day, Sarah got up early in her city centre hotel – fresh, like a sober person! There had been no noises in the hotel: no midnight anarchy. No running in the corridors. No smoking in the lifts.

Maybe someone had got up at some point and clunked their door with a suitcase because they were getting an early flight, but it had barely woken her. The deathly hum of the aircon soundtracked her facial cleansing routine.

It was strange to be back in Manchester. For so long it had felt like home, like an ex, and now it was like they had almost forgotten each other. A sadness for lost love percolated into her morning coffee. She looked around at the other people having hotel breakfast. Here they all were, visitors, passing through.

At 9 a.m. she checked out and got a cab to the hire shop. She stood with the man doing the handover on a drizzly forecourt, surrounded by huge white and cream vehicles. She had gone classic: a B-class Hymer, made in the late 80s – boxy lights, an American metal grille on the front, shiny walnut interior, corrugated-metal sides that shone rose gold, big sexy-ass fenders, hubcaps like festive charger plates. It looked cool, but it was small inside. Would she and her sister really be able to spend a week in there together?

'Get your leccy plugged in soon as you park up,' the man said. 'That's the big orange cable,' he went on.

'Right.'

He looked at her. 'You driven anything this big before?'

'An ice-cream van, once. In a sort of chase situation. Also, a tractor. Drunk. On private land.'

'She's a good girl,' he said (yep: *She*), slapping the van's bumper. 'Getting on a bit, but behaves herself if she's handled right,' he added with a wink.

Oh fuck's sake, really, please. As a woman clearly not in her twenties any more, she often had to endure this: men going out of their way to make her still feel sexy. So considerate of them. Sarah had bitten her tongue while he delivered the rest of his macho little handover ceremony: the cartridge toilet, the gas canister, the grey-water release. By the end he was practically doing bench presses with a metal pole on the sofa in the back 'lounge'.

'It's heavy, this, despite the fact it's hollow,' he gasped as he lay on his side, pole aloft, one hand unplugging a grey rubber stopper from the floor. 'You sure you're going to be all right?'

'I'm pretty sure I can handle a foldaway table, yeah, but thanks.'

'Well, it slots into that hole, there. Either end works. Then you just wriggle your top on until it's in good and locked. Takes a bit of coaxing.'

'Oh.' Gross.

'Where you heading anyway? You want it for a week, did you say?'

'Yes. We're heading up to Scotland.'

'In early March! Why?'

'It's my sister's birthday.'

'Be careful. People die up there. Of exposure.'

'We're pretty hardy. I am especially.'

'Prefer Ireland, myself. Better dairy products. You're probably lactose intolerant, aren't you?'

'What would make you think I was lactose intolerant?'

'All the young people are these days.'

'I think a lot of them are just environmentally conscious.' She considered the motorhome and questioned her choice again. 'And I'm not young. People telling me I was too young until they started telling me I was too old has already put me behind on the property ladder. I'm the lost generation.'

He frowned, confused.

'Never mind,' Sarah said. She thanked him, took the keys and got into the cab.

The Hymer was awful to drive. The dog-leg gearstick refused to get into first, which made stopping and starting stressful. Sarah started to wonder whether she should have just gone for something more modern. But she was determined to stick it out. It was important not to be ageist. The unfiltered morning sun blazed through the windscreen. Sarah remembered she didn't have her sunglasses. She'd left them at a man's house, three nights ago. Shit. This was going to be a problem. She wasn't likely to see him again and had been relieved that he hadn't messaged her, so she hadn't even had to ghost him, or be honest. She had simply put their previous chat in her archive, with her drug dealers. So now she just had to look on it as a simple transaction: sex in exchange for her favourite Christian Diors. Had the sex been worth it?

Well.

'Ronnie Hotdogs' was his name.

Scarlet lingerie was his game.

He had, as Sarah had requested on Feeld, kept a pencil behind his ear and his boxers at half mast. She was going through what she could only presume was a carpenter-fetish phase. The scenario in her mind was a small hallway and rushed, illicit coitus – midway through the construction of some sustainable wood shelving. (Sustainable wood because even in her fantasies, the thought of ecological disaster could put her off. The Earth on fire was not erotic.) Ronnie had obliged, to a point. They had used his hallway, the boxer elastic was tangible on her inner thighs, and the pencil was there, nestled in the nook of his left ear's upper cartilage, withstanding their slams with admirable tenacity. The only trouble was, it was an IKEA pencil, one of those short stubby wooden ones you get free by the entrance, and Sarah was distracted by the logo and a thousand depressing memories of university rentals and bulk-buying tealights. She almost couldn't finish. When she eventually did, she had an overwhelming desire for meatballs. Over cocoa and cheese toasties she had questioned his choice of prop, and he had defended himself by saying it was 'the only pencil he had in the house'. Which only vexed Sarah further, since she had spent a hundred quid on red suspenders at Agent

Provocateur. Maybe she really should start doing what her friend Ginny suggested: 'Tell them your fetish is a year's subscription to *Elle Decor* and two bottles of chilled Dom Pérignon' . . . But Sarah knew that was a slippery slope.

She'd get them back, she consoled herself. She would turn up at his house when she got back. Or just, you know, message him. She could see the tortoiseshell Christian Diors on the plant stand by his shoe rack, placed there before she'd gone in for the kill. Damn. She stopped at traffic lights and checked her phone. No new messages. Was he wearing her sunglasses? Would Ronnie Hotdog's next Feeld conquest spot them and take them as a spoil of passion? Unthinkable. They *were* great sunglasses. No, Sarah decided, he would not. He seemed the honourable, organised sort. The day before their date he'd sent her a text asking her to confirm the date YES or NO. Like it was a hair appointment. He was a matter-of-fact person. He would not harbour stolen property. Also, he'd disliked her tattoo. Which meant he might be a moral person, too.

'Is that an eye?' he'd asked, working away behind her.

'It's a hieroglyph,' Sarah said, trying not to lose her focus.

He stopped. 'It's putting me off,' he said. 'I feel like it's watching me.'

It wasn't the first time a man had said this, but Sarah pretended it was. That tattoo was regretful, something she'd had done drunk as a teenager. Sarah despised the term 'tramp stamp', but it was a tramp stamp.

'You should get that lasered,' he said. He'd started to lose his erection.

'Or we could just change position?' Sarah said. 'Give me solutions, not problems, Ronnie.'

You could always rely on the executive chat to get a rise out of them. Missionary it was. Well, Sarah thought, Jesus was the OG carpenter. So that was apt.

* * *

Sarah's mind was pulled into the present as the lights turned to red. She pushed her foot down on the brake and, with effort, the clutch pedal. She yanked the gearstick from fourth to neutral. The motorhome was stubborn, snarling and clunking with every attempt to tame or correct it.

Seeking solace, she reached for her phone and checked her messages (nothing), then her emails. A little notification popped up telling her she had activated automatic replies. Her OOO. She marvelled at her own brazenness. It was the first time she'd done it, but her boss had made her. *Take some time.* He was worried about her, she could tell. He thought she was a maniac. But she was a productive maniac. She worked fifteen-hour days most days, and often late into the evening for American Zooms, and she checked and replied to her emails all weekend, if any came in. She'd told herself for five years that she'd slow down but after the pandemic, she seemed to be speeding up. It might not be a problem. She loved her job, but more than that, Sarah loved doing *a good job.* But she should have boundaries. Boundaries. Like she was a landlocked country and there was infantry on every side awaiting the opportunity to besiege her. But she'd do it. She'd try. She'd drink the millennial Kool-Aid. Writing an out-of-office message had felt like the most boundaried thing Sarah had ever done in her entire life. It was two lines long and had taken hours of construction.

Hello,

I am away until 10th March. I'll get back to you after that.

Thanks,

Sarah

WOAH. HOLD UP. WHO WAS THIS ICE-COOL BITCH?

Sarah, that's who.

Sarah going on holiday.

Yeah.

Holiday.

The last time Sarah had gone on holiday, she'd gone to Crete for five days with the one man who had ever counted as a boyfriend, Eric. It was a delicious time — sex on tap. All of their randy detonations. The sauce of his scalp. The salt of his legs. But watching people around the pool, Sarah had felt irked by their indolence. Why are they all just lying around, doing nothing? she found herself constantly thinking. Then she'd had to have a word with herself. They're on holiday, Sarah. And, newsflash: so are you. But she wasn't. Whenever she was on holiday, Sarah presumed — unfairly, she knew, but so be it — that everyone else on holiday was less intelligent than her. After all, they were on holiday. They were clearly stupid enough to be wasting days, if not weeks, of precious time. Also, being around other people in non-work situations gave Sarah anxiety. Outside of the professional realm, she wasn't sure what she was entitled to. She was one of those people who needed to make sure she got a sun lounger. A seat. A strawberry from the fruit cocktail on the breakfast buffet. She hated trains — the anxiety of the platform — knowing it was important to be adult and wait, but also wanting to elbow everyone else out of the way to get a seat. Was anxiety an extension of the ego? Had to be. Anxiety was, more often than not, Sarah had deduced, a panic that you would not get the thing you deserved. In Crete, Eric had said: 'Why not consider, Sarah, the worst that would happen if you didn't get down to the pool early?' Really, he should have been her therapist. Really, he sort of *had* been her therapist. Sarah had looked at the pool, towel in hand. 'That's a horrible visualisation, Eric. Obviously, I wouldn't get a sun lounger.'

'And then what?'

'I would have nowhere to sit. Or lounge.'

'You could sit on a chair. Or a wall. Or the grass.'

'I want a lounger.'

'Why?'

'To relax.'

'But you're not relaxed, are you? You're stressed – about getting a lounger.'

Eric had a point. He was one to extend a point, though; some might say wring it out. 'All I'm saying is,' he went on (he did like to go on), 'it might shave more years off your life to worry about getting a lounger, to get up at 6 a.m. and run down with a towel, than it would to just sit on the ground and have no mental stress. Just go with the flow of the holiday, so it's an actual . . . holiday? Rather than . . . chillaxing in the panic room?'

Bah. The voice of reason. It was such a turn-on and a turn-off at the same time. But Eric hadn't had sciatica like Sarah so really he had no idea what he was talking about. He did, however, have a hypermobile thumb and very big, warm arms which Sarah missed, sometimes, on certain nights in December. It had ended when he'd wanted more intimacy and she had told him that she didn't need his opinion on anything. 'I just can't consume any more opinion. How do people have room in their heads for all these OPINIONS?' she'd ranted. He had been hurt by that. He had just been trying to make her feel better about a work thing. But he didn't get it. The world was so full of opinions; everyone had an opinion on everything, all the time. She couldn't take any more input, and certainly not in the bedroom. Why couldn't she and Eric just fuck and leave it at that? *Talk more with your lover*, everyone said. No, Sarah thought, with your lover you should really focus on talking *less*.

On the Cretan holiday, by the pool, a woman's legs had broken Sarah's heart. They were muscular, shaded in the lines and creases behind the knee, along the hamstring. Sarah had stared at those legs for many minutes. God, they were good legs. They reminded Sarah of that technique at school with a 2B pencil to create depth: cross-hatching. Strong, sturdy, perfectly shaded legs. They were legs that parked an estate car in a tidy garage, legs that folded themselves neatly, effortlessly, under crisp white tablecloths. Legs that walked around supermarkets buying ingredients that made actual meals. They were legs that went on biannual, fortnight-long holidays. They were legs from a life that Sarah would never know.

Speaking of which . . .

Sarah turned the motorhome into Juliette's tiny street — a cul-de-sac in a leafy part of South Manchester. She drove to the end of the road — they'd trick-or-treated here with the kids last October, summer-partied here last July — and parked up next to Johnnie's Alfa Romeo (a fuckboy car if ever she saw one; Sarah was on to him — had been for ten years, mate) and checked her face in the mirror. You didn't want to see your younger, prettier sister without checking you looked at least halfway hot.

Her harsh self-appraisal was loosening, but it was still a daily bind. Mostly she felt lost and hypocritical. Ginny had made her do an exercise months ago, on a sunny afternoon at Ginny's bougie little flat on Kemptown seafront. They were wrapped up in scarves and beanies, drinking languorously amongst the seed-heads of alliums. Half-shells of coconuts filled with seeds and waxy fat bobbed on the branches of the balconette's one small magnolia tree. Ginny was not what you'd call a keen gardener, although she did love the birds. On Sarah's previous sobriety jaunts, Ginny had pointed out that getting wrecked a few times a month and being sober-ish the rest of the time *was*, in fact, a form of moderation. But Ginny had more restraint in general. More class, you could say. For her own kicks, Ginny had obsessions with porn stars she DM'd and occasionally met up with for brunch. It didn't appeal to Sarah —

it was too much of a mash-up. It was tasting Keely and moving offices. Maybe this was why Sarah wasn't cut out for the modern world. Sarah thought all parts of you evolved as you grew older, except your sexual deviancies. Those were the same they always were. Hardwired. Ingrained in your reptile parts. Your politics could shift, but your tastes were set. She could never be turned on by certain combinations, in the same way that she could never put black pepper on a strawberry.

'I had an idea for an activity today.' Ginny was a great facilitator, and on the day amongst the alliums, she was on a feminist tip. 'We're going to make a list of older women we admire,' she said. She tore off two A4 sheets from a refill pad and put one in front of Sarah with a chewed, lidless biro. The other she placed in front of herself. Then they made their lists: Oprah, Iris Apfel, Olivia Colman, Joni Mitchell, Sandra Oh, Janis Joplin, Fran Lebowitz . . . Sarah sat back and regarded her list in the sunshine.

'Now,' said Ginny, like the magician she was, 'what do we notice about these lists?'

'Our handwriting's appalling. We should have written them before the six glasses of wine.'

Ginny shook her head. Ginny was luscious. Sarah didn't use that word often, but she was. 'None of these women are traditionally pretty and thin,' Ginny said. 'They are characterful, complex, wise, accomplished and compelling. They are engaged and deep.'

Sarah had immediately felt guilty for reducing Ginny to 'luscious'.

'So if they are our aspirational model of an older woman,' Ginny continued, 'why do we force the metrics of "pretty" and "thin" upon ourselves? I constantly do things to make myself thinner and prettier. But the women I admire from afar possess different qualities. So why do I not cherish those things in myself, and seek to nurture them, and make choices based on that nurture? Why do I spend time and energy facilitating the shallow things?'

Ginny consoled herself with a Camel Blue and a freshened glass of Whispering Angel.

Sarah thought hard. She loved hanging out with Ginny, and she wanted to answer well. She always wanted to impress Ginny, who was two years older and twenty years wiser. 'Because . . . we're socially conditioned to want to be pretty and thin?'

Ginny sucked hard on her cigarette. 'That doesn't give us the whole answer, I don't think. Or we would judge these women we admire by those things, too.'

Sarah knew Ginny had been thinking on this for some time.

'Leave it with me,' said Sarah. 'I'll circle back.'

'Circle back,' repeated Ginny, who was a manager too.

They finished the wine, and some more wine. As the sun was setting, Ginny said suddenly, as though plucking it from the inner sanctum of her most precious brain: 'I think it has something to do with saying goodbye to the girl.'

Sarah jolted in her seat. 'Which girl?'

'*The* girl,' said Ginny. 'There's only ever one. For all of us.'

Sarah presumed Ginny was thinking of a lost lover from her college days. She *had* gone to boarding school and Cambridge. Besides, it was almost Christmas. Show a person some fairy lights and booze and they were instantly at the mercy of nostalgia. But Ginny's words had haunted her since. Who was the girl? And why did she have to say goodbye?

* * *

Sarah pulled onto Juliette's gravel drive. She turned off the ignition and hopped down from the cab, her boots crunching as she landed. She walked towards the house. Well, that's disappointing, Sarah thought as she saw the new sign in Juliette's porch window. *No junk mail, no religious groups, no cold callers.* Not only that — there was an extra sign on the actual letterbox, done on a strip by a Dymo label-maker, saying: *Did you see the sign about junk mail?*

Fuck me, Sarah thought. Or fuck Juliette. Because clearly no one was. (Besides, two Christmases ago, Sarah had seen Juliette use a 'Rare Pearls' rollerball. By Avon. The sign in the porch was a ruse.)

Reassured in her life choices, Sarah rang the bell.

Juliette answered. She'd styled her hair – blonde locks plaited up either side of her head and pinned on top, like a stern German governess crossed with a Coppola-lit Kirsten Dunst. There she was. Juliette. Infinitely more boundaried. Surer, seriouser, sexier.

Juliette's youngest, Harpo, appeared in the hall behind her. He was wearing one of those kids' T-shirts saying 'THE FUTURE' that irked Sarah instantly. These were T-shirts bought by parents who wanted to feel more important than they feared they were. Harpo let out a solemn miaow.

'He's being a cat,' said Juliette.

'Okay. Thanks for the intel.' A sarcastic look that was appreciated by Juliette.

Sarah stooped to cuddle Harpo.

'It's been three days now,' said Juliette. There's bowls all over the kitchen floor. I'm praying this isn't a self-identification thing I have to deal with at the pre-school.'

Sarah pulled back and regarded her nephew. 'I'm sure we pretended to be various things, didn't we, back in the day?'

Harpo miaowed an angry sentence which had the intonation of I'M NOT PRETENDING.

'Only characters from films, I think?' said Juliette. 'He's gone quite method, really. I've had to consider getting a litter tray.'

Sarah looked at Juliette with alarm. Harpo looked sad again.

'He's in a mood because he can't come with us,' explained Juliette.

'Oh, puss.' Sarah crouched and tickled Harpo's chin. He blew his lips, purring. 'It's going to be so dull. Your mum and I are going to be stuck in a van with each other for a week, talking about how ancient we are.'

Harpo stared at Sarah, then looked towards the van. He did a moue worthy of a Parisian dame. He was the tougher half of the crowd. Sarah had a better relationship with Juliette's older and savvier child, Molly – a sharp-faced girl of nine, queen of withering looks and hyperactive dances. When Molly was a baby, Sarah had felt as though she could have put her whole body in her mouth and eaten up the fruity little solidity of her. Watching Molly learn and grow was the purest delight Sarah had ever known – she surrendered to another female's glory, maybe even for the first time in her life. But when Juliette had told Sarah she was pregnant again, with a boy of all things, Sarah had felt ransacked. A boy? Why the need for that? It was excessive in every way. What about Molly? Sarah had joked to Juliette: 'Congrats, dude, you have a penis inside you ALL THE TIME.' Juliette hadn't laughed. No one at the family barbecue had laughed. Johnnie, Juliette's husband (imagine marrying someone with the same first initial as you, the daily cringe, the monogrammed bathrobe and handkerchief confusion . . .) had a look in his eyes that said, *Mmmmmmmmmm cheers for sexualising my unborn child*. Johnnie had a lot of special looks for Sarah. Then, in a strange emotional bypass, Harpo hadn't taken to Sarah like Molly had. Fine. Let him . . . do whatever boys did. Bounce off walls. Wank in shoeboxes. Whatever. She could toss him some gems. Sarah had thought of advice already for when he was a teenager and asked her how to get girls. 'Let them come to you.' But primarily, Sarah was an Aunt Of Women. She was committed to being there for Molly to guide her through the vipers' nest. She'd be a sagacious presence in her niece's life. She could even invest in a muumuu when the time was right. The raiment of maturity.

'Where's Molly?'

'Ballet. She sends her love.'

'Sends her love? Is she suddenly thirty?'

Harpo scampered off up the stairs. 'IT'S ONLY A WEEK, I LOVE YOU!' Juliette yelled, in the panicked descant she used with her kids. Juliette started lugging out her bags and Sarah stepped in to assist. The smell of Juliette's house affronted Sarah, like always. Onions and damp. She and Juliette used to have a house that they couldn't smell. As children they walked through the same front door and smelled . . . nothing. As John Cooper Clarke said: 'The smell of one's house cannot be known.' The smell of one's house was for others only. Now, Juliette's house smelled alien to Sarah. *Unheimlich*. Did that mean the fragrance of their childhood home was a combination – a cocktail – of the four of them that they all acclimatised to? Did Sarah's flat in London smell weird to Juliette, when she occasionally pit-stopped there en route to conference days, or France?

Sarah remembered one time Juliette had brought Molly with her to stay because they'd come down to see *Frozen: The Musical*. She had woken to hear them in the bathroom together – it was a small flat – like sisters or women at a club, Juliette whispering loudly, or loudly enough for Sarah to hear in her bedroom: 'Just wipe your hands on that [the dressing gown hanging on the back of the door, had to be] – there's NO TOWEL.'

Sarah had put a towel in there as soon as she'd got up.

What had really hurt was that she had given Juliette and Molly the best towels she had – and Juliette hadn't noticed. They'd been on the dresser in their room when they arrived, and they were there, pristine and folded, when they left. They had gone to the bathroom without their special guest towels, like commoners. What had made it better, though, was that in Juliette's open case the next day Sarah had spied the same fragrance body lotion – the beauty range of a mid-price high-street clothes shop – that Sarah had got her for her birthday two years previously. It couldn't be the same bottle, it was brand new. Which meant Juliette had bought it again, after using it up. That Sarah had chosen that body lotion for Juliette had meant something. And on they went. There was an act of affection to neutralise every act of betrayal — and vice versa. The eternal book balancing of siblingdom.

In Juliette's hall, Sarah's eyes followed the wall — rows of hooks filled with rucksacks and duffel coats. Puddlesuits hung like carcasses. A sliver of lounge revealed two cats dozing on the back of the sofa. Beyond that, out through the bifolds, a vegetable patch in the garden, overgrown in early spring. The house was small and simple, and Juliette was content. It was a word you hardly ever heard in the modern world, much less applied to a living, breathing person, but so it was. That was how Sarah described Juliette when people asked her how her sister was. *Content.* But Sarah didn't buy it, not fully. In her eyes, Juliette had stepped into the drag show of the nuclear family and never stepped out. Meanwhile, Sarah felt that Juliette still saw Sarah's lifestyle as a deliberate act of delinquency. *Found anyone yet found anyone yet found anyone yet?* was the constant line of enquiry from all angles, her sister included. It implied that, rather than intentionally curating her wild and precious life, Sarah was always searching for some kind of pairing, an inner radar on, bleating out a lonely pulse. All of which made her feel not so much a person as a pair of Bluetooth headphones, endlessly seeking to be twinned. She and Juliette were vastly different, and Sarah had always put that down to the age difference: almost three years. Somehow that meant they were opposed, rather than close. There had been no social media in the 90s and people raved about the freedom of that, but Sarah had never known freedom, not with Juliette around. Juliette held Sarah to account, she scrutinised her and demanded to know her reasons, her location, her status. Juliette was the ultimate follower. She liked things Sarah said and did to get attention. The illusion was that Juliette was hooked to Sarah, but Sarah was just as hooked to Juliette. It was as though the things she said and did only had meaning when Juliette bore witness to them. Maybe Sarah's use of social media these days was about trying to get back the level of scrutiny she'd once felt, growing up with a sister. Sarah was older. She'd absorbed more of the madness, shielded Juliette from more. At least in the beginning. At least at home. Sarah went for bigger men, arty men – she wasn't averse to someone a bit beastly, clever and funny and nimble of wit, ideally smarter than her before she had the chance to get bored or turned off.

* * *

They pulled the holdalls out into the porch.

'Where's Johnnie?' Sarah asked. 'Foraging for wild edibles? Taking his lumberjack exams?'

'You are hilarious,' said Juliette.

But Johnnie was more hilarious. Always in a hat worthy of sub-zero Canada. Always bragging about his sourdough. Always an hour away from an ice plunge. Always considering how to increase longevity. For what? To be deeply boring for a bit longer? It was an odd goal in Sarah's eyes. Longevity seemed pointless when you were as tedious as Johnnie. Worse still: it was *rude*. If you're going to live longer, make an effort to be at least halfway fucking interesting, mate.

He was always listening to American bro health podcasts and walking around with a wireless bone-conducting headphone constantly on, like a David Lynch character. Like he was being controlled by some higher power, such as Andrew Huberman. He was always wanging on about zone-two fat-burning exercise and the evils of alcohol and sugar in general. Paleo? You bet-eo. The man made his own nut mixes. He was part of the anti-party movement in Sarah's eyes. One of the ones who had started to kill it for everyone. A leading global force in destroying the cultural climate. He'd found his path and now constantly had to justify it by razing to the ground anyone who thought differently. He was loud, he was opinionated, SURE. He was rich, came from a good family. Initially, she had enjoyed his natural melancholy and extreme good fortune and enormous talent. Now, she just thought he was a dick. Sarah could imagine him down the gym, educating everyone ruthlessly on the correct dumbbells for maximum muscle rip. He had a very square head, like Buzz Lightyear.

'Let's go!!' Juliette yelled. 'BYE, JOHNNIE!'

Juliette closed the door and stepped out onto the gravel drive. She peered at the van. 'Woah. Antique. It's not going to leak, is it?'

'This is the most stylish motorhome ever manufactured. It's a Hymer B500. Built in the 80s. Like all the best things.'

'Yes, but is it . . . roadworthy?'

'Should hope so. Cost me a grand for the week.'

'No pressure. Is it petrol?'

'Diesel.'

'Not very green.'

'Says the woman with two kids.'

'One of them might grow up to be the next Greta Thunberg.'

Sarah batted the bonnet. 'Well, this van might run over the next Elon Musk. Or the current Elon Musk, even.'

Juliette smiled and put her suitcase in the back.

'Slot it in the big step near the kitchen door next to mine,' Sarah instructed. 'Then they won't slide around.'

As she did so, Johnnie popped his head out of the front door. He looked like he always did: martyred and over-caffeinated. Sarah almost felt sorry for him. He genuinely thought it was Sarah's mission to lead Juliette astray. But she wasn't about to take criticism from a man who had the same name as a slang term for contraception.

'Blimey! How did you park that?'

'With my woman's hands and my woman's feet. Is your mind blown?'

Johnnie made a face like an emoji Sarah refused to use. Her sister had had sex with this man. More than once. Maybe even sober. It was too depressing.

The family's twelve-year-old gundog, Chloe, flopped out of the porch and lay on her belly, looking up at the Hymer like she didn't know where she was any more.

'Oh god, they're all coming out,' said Juliette. 'Let's leg it.'

Sarah looked down at the gearstick, which was looking more leg-like than ever.

'It's not a fast process,' she said, worrying about operating the gearbox in front of Johnnie.

Woof! said the dog, seeing Juliette in the strange vehicle.

Juliette had bought the dog, old, from a rescue centre, to 'teach the kids about death'. Chloe, however, hadn't got the memo, and was refusing to die. Just like she refused to chase sticks, or do any other gundoggy activities, or do anything other than bark and stink, which – Sarah presumed – was why she'd ended up in the rescue centre in the first place. *You had one job . . . !* 'She's retired!' Juliette always said, in her defence. She'd *been* retired, that's what Juliette couldn't see. Sarah could see the benefit of pets, in the same way she could see the benefit of husbands. She just didn't really want one. Generally, she preferred being alone. What no one knew was that, late at night, after video calls with the East Coast of America, she often stayed on as host, alone, in those abandoned Zoom rooms, her own face staring back at her, the glow of the ring-light as *hygge* as any wood-burning stove, sipping a glass of something moderately alcoholic, feeling a dystopian peace that was at odds with the rest of her life. She kept people at arm's length. She dated in the truest sense of the word. She was honest about it, and she never made anyone any promises. 'Are you autistic or something?' one man had said to her, when she refused to break her routine and let him stay spontaneously, or ramp things up to . . . *spending Christmas together.* 'Maybe,' Sarah had replied, 'but I still don't want to fuck you during repeats of *The Royle Family.'*

Juliette climbed into the passenger seat and clunked in her seatbelt. 'So retro.' The dash was grey plastic with a moleskin sort of effect, like the packaging for electrical equipment. Johnnie waved them off from the step.

'So you definitely want to go there first?' said Juliette.

'If that's okay?' said Sarah. Although if Juliette had said no, that's not okay, there would have been an atmosphere weighty enough to ruin at least twenty-four hours (if not all) of the holiday. 'It's on the way. So no biggie?'

Juliette shrugged. 'Yeah, I guess you'll want to say hi. I'm just maxed out with them.' Sarah nodded. 'The other day she FaceTimed me because her friend wanted to get off a FaceTime on their own iPad and wasn't sure how.'

Sarah could smell something punchy coming off Juliette's wrists – had she changed her perfume? Coco Chanel. The fragrance of bitches. Sarah and Juliette had worn the same perfume for years. Calvin Klein. Sarah had started wearing it first, but when she'd raised this with Juliette, one Christmas when they'd bought the perfume for each other, Juliette had said: 'So interesting that you remember it that way.'

Sarah looked at her sister. Her only sister. Her only sibling. There she was, so close. In profile. The most classic cameo of her life. Juliette's silhouette was Sarah's most familiar ghost. It was insolent, the curve of Juliette's forehead. It defied physics and all proper proportions. They had grown in the same temperature, the same womb, and something in that meant their souls were the same temperature and would be forever. Now, in person, after time away from her, Juliette took Sarah's breath away. When she wasn't near her, Sarah remembered Juliette in several ways, each overwhelming, each delicious. Hair. Song. A certain slant of golden light. Her teeth and the shape of her lips around her smile. Sarah thought she could see something on Juliette's cheek – a patch of darkness. A purple band . . . a bruise? Juliette looked at her and Sarah looked away instinctively. She turned the key in the ignition; the engine roared into life. There was a squelch as the CD drive started up again. Sarah fought the gearstick into first. Juliette sat at a tense tilt, holding her KeepCup, staring out at South Manchester's unfiltered morning sun.

When Sarah had texted her yesterday saying how excited she was about the trip, Juliette had replied, 'Me too me too!' – over-enthusiastic, a brief moment of gawkiness, like when Patrick Swayze briefly loses his cool in the car in *Dirty Dancing*. Nobody puts an appreciation of problematic movies in the corner.

'How's Ginny?' asked Juliette.

'Fine. Obsessed with porn stars.'

Sarah was aware she was slightly throwing Ginny under the bus. The sex bus.

'On feminist porn sites. The performers do Q&As.'

'Q&As? About what?'

'About their lives.'

'That's weird.'

'Women love it. Hey, Juliette, the next car that overtakes us symbolises your sex life.'

Juliette looked as the car overtook them. It was a Ford Mondeo estate.

'You saw that in the wing mirror and set me up.'

'So paranoid.'

'Anyway, the next road sign symbolises your sex life.'

Sarah looked. *HGV DRIVERS ONLY*.

'They spelled it wrong though,' Juliette continued, 'it should be HPV not HGV.'

*   *   *

A few miles later, they pulled off the motorway and onto the slip road that led down the street they'd grown up on. It seemed smaller every year, like everything. So much of her life she still saw through the trellis of her childhood. Suburbia: so much to answer for. Bin wars, magnolia tree one-upmanship, brick drives, chest freezers, double garages, weedkiller, Chicken Tonight in Le Creuset, Laura Ashley in perpetuity.

The unassuming semi squatted with its back to the motorway. Sarah thought about that house at least once a day. The contour lines of her psycho-geography. More often than not, the house came to Sarah in colours: the brown hall, the beige kitchen, the pink lounge, the black stairs, the blue bedroom, the gold bedroom, the green bedroom, the chequered box room.

It was a house with madness in it. A place of latent chaos. Ley lines of passive-aggression flowed beneath it, miles below the motorway. A house where things were still mysteriously fridged (peanut butter) and unfridged (cooked meats). Woodlice lived in her rotten windowsill. The carpets were bitty. The washing-up water was brothy. That unsterile house where she was forced to grow her dreams. No wonder some went bad.

The mid-morning rush of the M66 made Sarah feel sleepy. Juliette had once stood naked on the windowsill, pointing her twelve-year-old breast-buds like ray guns at passing lorries. Peeyow, peeyow! Peeyow peeyow! Sarah had dragged her down. 'Think about what you're doing,' she'd said. 'Think about it.' She'd said the same thing when Juliette had told her she was going to marry Johnnie. At least it had worked the first time.

Their parents came out of the house. Their mum, Deanna, first — with her arms full of kitchen goods. 'Thought you could use these for your trip!' She turned and rolled her eyes at their father, who was hobbling behind. 'Samuel. SAMUEL. Will you get the thing I asked you to get, for god's sake?'

Sarah instantly felt herself detach a little. Move backwards in her head, to where it was softer; quieter; insulated.

'Listen, Marie Kondo,' said Juliette, jumping down from the van and holding her arms up at Deanna, 'I know your game. Don't think you're palming a load of old crap off on us. Is that a chicken brick? We're in a van, Mum. There's no Aga.'

'Your father's gone to get the other box now. If you don't want them just leave them on the drive. I'm not pressuring you!'

Sarah hugged her mum, which was easy. Then continued to listen to her, which was not. Her mother's hands, like Sarah's, were raw and picked around the nails. Unlike Sarah's, they were liver-spotted and lilac-veined. It was hard to remember ever holding them.

Sarah kept her distance now, she knew she did. Sarah had often said to Juliette: 'We had different mothers.' They'd had different versions of the same woman, it was true. Sarah got her first: harried, territorial, phobia-laden. Juliette got her through the buffer of Sarah. But Juliette couldn't see that, and that was all right. It had been Sarah's job to protect Juliette from seeing that. Sarah was the human shield who went out first into the world; more sensitive as a result. Juliette was more robust: a solid unit dressed in hand-me-downs. Juliette didn't need to chew or pick at her own hands in order to sit still. She didn't remember the sofa, the doorbell, the people peeking through lounge windows while their mum shouted, 'GET DOWN!'.

Remembering everything wasn't a choice. Sarah's brain did it because her adrenaline was so high it made her constantly sharp and constantly exhausted from her own sharpness. She had the psychic keenness of a vampire and could hear the grass grow. Her mother had turned up to Sarah's thirtieth birthday so drunk that she'd fallen down a staircase and a wine bag (the bag from inside the box) had shot out from under her coat, drained, like an astronaut's naked lunch, causing everyone in the Victoria Park Bistro to look over. Deanna had left without even saying goodbye to Sarah, her father trailing behind, powerless. The next day, Sarah had gone to her hotel to have it out with her mother about her behaviour, only to find Juliette there already, emerging from the room grim-faced. Her mother was on the bed, eyes red from crying, make-up everywhere. Before Sarah could speak, her mother said, 'Juliette has made me feel so much better – she said, "Been there, done that, got the T-shirt".' 'Right,' said Sarah, her blood boiling, 'glad you've forgiven yourself.' And that was that. Except that wasn't that. Sarah had been furious for years. Never once was her mother held accountable. Never once did she have to face the consequences of her actions. Her mother wouldn't be honest, wouldn't have therapy, and as a result, her daily denials resulted in near-constant self-delusion. You'd think that Sarah might be standoffish with her mother now, or even spiteful. But she wasn't. It was in fact Juliette, who'd stayed in the same county as their parents, who was the more critical of the two. Sarah simply smiled and said all the right things. She breezed in and out of interactions with her mother like a fish skimming the surface of a pond. She smiled and said yes, then disappeared for three months at a time. It really was easier that way. She felt numb around her mother. What she did know was that it was far too late now to try to fix her; the best thing she could do was limit the energy she gave her. Sarah dipped in and out, and did it – rightly or wrongly – with a sense of royal grace. It was duty, sheer duty. Which is what brought her here now. It was different with Juliette. She could see her any time – not that either of them had any time. Juliette was Sarah's touchstone in the family. Her litmus of sanity. 'They're either the best of friends or the worst of enemies,' Deanna used to say, when she introduced the sisters to other people. That was it: having a sister was both a strength and a weak spot.

There was a photograph. In a frame, on the wall, halfway up the stairs in their parents' house, of Sarah and Juliette, aged three and one respectively. Sarah was in little brown shorts and a tight pink T-shirt with a monkey on it, her hair in a stubby, skew-whiff ponytail. She was standing at one end of the sofa, with her head tilted and a twisted smile; a smile that looked like it was fighting itself. Juliette was behind Sarah, in a yellow babygro, propped up on the sofa between two cushions, looking quite the infanta, her cheeks perfect as plums. Sarah felt like the photo captured both of their absolute forms. The absolute *them-ness* of them. She would never be more Sarah than in that photo, and Juliette would never be more Juliette. It was the essence of this photo that she knew bound her to her sister forever, to her bones. They had often spoken of a golden thread attached to one of Sarah's ribs at one end, and one of Juliette's ribs at the other, just below the heart, so that wherever they were in the world, when either of them was in trouble, the other felt a sharp tug of sisterly need at the ripcord. The Heart Alarm. Sarah felt it when Juliette almost died in labour. She felt it when Juliette got lost backpacking in Europe. Juliette felt it when Sarah took too much GHB in 2014. When she was being bullied at work. The Heart Alarm was never wrong. It was an SOS from one sister to another. The call was undeniable. You had to move for it. You had to just get to them and . . . be there.

The next-door neighbour came out to put something in the bin. He started at the sight of Sarah, like someone seeing a celebrity. Sarah waved. 'Hey, Ricardo!'

'Hello!' he said. 'Hello!' Then disappeared.

Sarah looked at Juliette. Then at her mother. 'He's got a new bowl haircut,' she said.

'He's got a new bowl,' said Deanna. Samuel put a box down on the path. 'No, NOT THERE, SAMUEL. It's wet. Put it on the wall. Blood and sand! Are you thick?' Sarah flinched. Her father didn't. When questioning who in her mind was the more powerful parent, Sarah had been around the houses. Her mother seemed to be the bossiest, to call the shots and rule the roost. But her father was more powerful because he went away. He stayed out all day and night sometimes, not having to answer to anyone. But her mother's moods were an emotional departure that seemed more final than a physical departure. Not that Deanna hadn't been guilty of both. Hadn't she and Juliette learned from the best when it came to tenacity? She and Juliette had sat out several seasons of competitive starvation when they were around twelve and fourteen – seeing who could eat the least and get the thinnest. Deanna hadn't known what to do, putting out calorific snacks on the footstool in the lounge, thickly buttering bread, but Sarah and Juliette had been staunch in their self-denial (when in fact they weren't denying themselves at all, but each other). A hunger strike was nothing when your sister was watching. It was a cinch. Sarah had survived on glucose tablets for an entire week. And when she finally succumbed – after Juliette had succumbed first – Sarah had wolfed a corned-beef and Branston pickle sandwich so quickly that she had instantly puked, her shrivelled stomach unable to process solids. But she'd out-starved Juliette. That was the key point. *She'd out-starved Juliette.* Victory was hers, and it allowed her to continue loving and pitying her sister. Teenage girls had wills of iron and hearts of glass.

Their parents' arguments these days were generally about the same things as they had been years ago: principally, their father's inability to say no to people who asked him for things. Today, it was an elderly female neighbour, who often asked him to pick up shopping, stop by for a cup of tea, fix her TV. Deanna was jealous and threatened by other women, even elderly ones. 'He's been summoned today as usual,' Deanna said, 'so he hasn't got long.'

'It's just a cup of tea,' Samuel said.

'And these are your daughters, one of them who you haven't seen for months.'

'Don't weaponise us,' said Juliette.

'I did FaceTime three weeks ago,' said Sarah.

But Deanna was on a roll. 'Suppose you've got to get her some milk on the way. Suppose you'll want some money for that, since you seem incapable of using a bank card?'

Sarah felt a deep urge to get in the van and drive away, fast.

Samuel said: 'Why are you giving me shit about this?' (Extra relish on the *shit*.) They loved to swear in their dotage. They'd become violent, aggressive, like old chimps at a tea party. They'd be together forever, no doubt. But their arguments were like awful cover records. It was as though they'd become a tribute act to themselves. And not a good one. This was not the Australian Pink Floyd. This was Elton Jeff. It was Amy Housewine. It was the Antarctic Monkeys. 'It's like the "Greatest Hits", with them,' Sarah had once remarked to Juliette. 'They have the same arguments about the same thing, over and over and over, without anyone actually listening any more.'

Their father put some birthday cards and presents for Juliette in the back of the van, then came and stood by Sarah. 'I want to have a word with you, Sarah, about selling some things . . . on eBay . . .'

Juliette snapped: 'Can we go? They do courses at the library, I've told him.'

Sarah looked apologetically at her dad. 'Sorry, Dad.' Absent as he had been, Sarah still preferred him – the one who she knew the least. It made sense. There was still a part of her always waiting for him to leave and take the pressure off. In life, you just reached a point where you . . . couldn't be arsed any more with the fight of it. Sarah was definitely at the not-being-arsed point where her mother was concerned, and she suspected the same was true of her mother's feelings towards her. Only occasionally did big feelings break through – like a few years ago when Deanna had described drinking her morning coffee in a little corner of her garden, and Sarah had been ambushed by the image of her mother innocently enjoying something. She had felt an overwhelming rush, a blast of light and birdsong; something had dawned briefly, and then the sky had darkened again.

Juliette got into the van and tooted the horn, which sounded like the horn on a clown car. 'I thought you said the campsite closed at dusk? We'll never make it!'

Sarah hugged and kissed her dad, then her mum. Juliette blew them kisses from the cab.

'Take the M67 to the M6,' Samuel said.

'No, Dad – just – do – not . . .' Juliette's exasperation was reaching a crescendo.

'Just advising—'

'Stop.'

'Glasgow should only take four hours if you hit—'

'I haven't listened. I will not remember this.'

Just before they left, their mother shoved two rape alarms through the partly open window.

'Mum?'

'It's remote up there.'

'Exactly. It would take a really dedicated psychopath to stalk us up there.' Sarah paused.

Juliette said: 'If anyone's dedicated, it's psychopaths.' Whispered: 'They should know.'

'But will there be anyone around to hear the alarms?' Sarah

pointed out, only half joking. She hoicked herself up into the cab next to Juliette. Their dad was still speaking, motioning with his arms.

'Shame he wasn't quite so involved in our movements when we were growing up.'

'Oh, come on. He had to earn money.'

'And it had to be in the middle of the North Sea, I suppose.'

Sarah looked at Juliette. 'You could have been nicer.'

'Listen, prodigal daughter, I spent a hot five hours talking him through e-commerce last week. He needs to go on a course. He can't do it himself. But he's so stubborn. And just because I tell him the truth, he goes over my head and asks you your opinion behind my back. It's insulting.'

'Maybe he just wants a different take on the situation?'

'He wants a different answer.'

'Are you saying I wouldn't give him the truth?'

Juliette was affronted. Sarah could feel her sister's old allergy to anything resembling a critique. Sarah looked at the road, but she could feel Juliette's eyes, and the sun, burning into the side of her head, like a magnifying glass angled at paper.

'Honestly, the time I spend on them. You have no idea. They're getting worse. Mum constantly asks questions she knows the answer to. I got in the habit of doing their online shop during the pandemic and now I can't get out of it. I sort their bloody mobile phones every time they can't use an app, which is every day. It's like their common sense has gone. I have to sort out every bill, every email. And they're so moody with me! And they clearly don't respect a word I say. It's like I've got four kids, not two.'

Sarah thought about the free childcare Juliette got three days a week. Plus, Juliette was still the password child and the lock-screen child. Well, Juliette's kids were the lock-screen kids now, but that was essentially the same thing. Sarah had lost her line to the throne of her parents' home screens by not having kids.

It was tense. The gearbox, the favouritism, it was almost too much. As they stopped at traffic lights, Sarah spotted some industrial waste bins.

'AWHHH NO, MY RETAINURRRRRRRR,' she howled.

A quote from *Parenthood*, where Kevin loses his retainer at a bowling alley and Steve Martin has to rummage through a dumpster to get it back.

Juliette came back instantly: 'That thing cost two hundred dollars – if you lost two hundred dollars in the garbage I THINK YOU WOULD GO LOOK FOR IT.'

It was fine. The trip was going to be fine.

Still, Sarah battled with the gears all the way to the ring road.

'Should we not swap this for something a bit easier to——'

'I'm just getting my bearings!'

'Are you all right?'

'Yes, I'm all right. Are you all right?'

Sarah shifted in her seat.

Juliette pulled down the sun shade and looked at herself in the mirror. 'Either my crown chakras are opening or I've been doing my updo too tight.'

'Maybe both.'

'Maybe both.'

'Never deny the possibility of both.'

They drove in silence to the motorway junction. Then once they hit the middle lane, Sarah felt she could breathe.

'Shag anyone good lately?' said Juliette.

Sarah made a face. 'Yeah, yeah.'

'Pub randos?'

'Yeah. I did meet one on an app. Oh, sorry, three.'

Juliette laughed. 'You must be so good at sex now, after having so much of it.'

'Ermmm.'

'Or does it even work like that? You know how they say people who are good at dancing are good in bed? Is that only true if they were *born* good at dancing? Or, if you have dance lessons, can it also make you better in bed?'

'Asking for a friend.'

'What I'm saying is, can we reverse-engineer this shit?'

'I have no idea. Never had any complaints.'

Sarah realised she was talking like a man defending a modestly proportioned penis.

Juliette sighed. 'I wouldn't have the bandwidth for the misfits on the online dating scene.'

Sarah nodded. Her bandwidth was maxing out, she had to agree. She was glitching. Her days comprised of data mining, emotional buffering and downloading. It was too much to take.

In the past few weeks there had been Ronnie Hotdogs, Paulo from behind the bar – you could call him, ironically, a 'regular' – and Thomas, who was a jaded twenty-five-year-old and, as a result, had never heard of Quentin Tarantino. In her own twenties and thirties, Sarah would have considered that uncultured; now it was exotic. She was fucking outside of the box. It felt deliciously radical. The sex itself had been basically squats. Was that what Gen Z were into? Hydraulics? But Sarah couldn't deny it had benefits. They were a healthy bunch. You had to see the positive side in everything, the older you got. After they'd fucked, she lay on the bed while Thomas went to the toilet, and she could hear him tip-tapping about on the tiling, like a Boston terrier.

'You want a bath? A breakfast roll?'

Sarah avoided the obvious gag. It was a nana gag. 'Nah, thanks. I'd best get home.'

He nodded. She could tell he was relieved. Thomas worked in PR. He had a lot of big clients – mostly food companies, one high-street budget bakery. The kind of fella Sarah's mother probably wished she'd ended up with. The kind Juliette *had* ended up with. The kind who, when he went on a trip anywhere, sorted all of his own chargers out as soon as he got into the room. All of his USBs and USB-Cs. Then he could relax and think about other people.

She spotted her knickers on the floor, twisted into a figure of eight. Or maybe it was infinity, on its side.

'What are you smiling at?'

'State of my knickers.'

She could tell Thomas wasn't sure what to say about her knickers. He looked anxious. Like every possibility was incriminating. She could feel sorry for men, she really could, if they hadn't had it so fucking easy for so fucking long. Part of the joy of modern feminism was watching them squirm.

She savoured the moment, then she stood up. Thomas lived in Hastings, in an apartment with the whole top floor as his bedroom. He had one of those leather high-backed chairs like a 1990s businessman or a Bond villain. She couldn't look at it, during. She'd seen better bedrooms when she was a teenager. But oh, that view through the window. Rolling down to the sea and dancing pylons and miles of cloudy blue. She could go a long way for a view like that. And she had. Ten miles and fourth base, on a Tuesday.

Is there a fifth base? Juliette had asked her, decades ago.

You bet your ass, Sarah replied.

A sixth?

Oh, a seventh, eighth, ninth and tenth.

What's tenth?

Your little sister.

Sarah rooted around for her jeans and top. Had she taken them off downstairs? Sometimes that was the way it went. Fast. Faster in the aftermath. No cuddling. No pillow talk. She used to worry they'd think she was using them. Now she knew that was part of the appeal. No one wanted a needy older woman. Everyone wanted a selfish one. Fully dressed, she'd tidied her hair in his hallway mirror – an incongruous gold thing with angels around the edges. So 90s it hurt.

*   *   *

In the retelling, it was the mirror that Juliette enjoyed the most.

'That detail says it all.'

'Doesn't it?'

'The 90s were beautiful, though. The freedom. We memorised phone numbers. We memorised directions. No one knew what we looked like. No one knew our reasons. No one could reach us. We were gods – and we didn't know it.'

'Aye, sister.'

'Anyway, it beats what I did last night.'

'Johnnie?'

Juliette ignored the dig. 'Here's a mad statistic. At any given time, 40 per cent of under-tens in the UK have threadworms.'

Sarah made a face.

'I don't understand what the point of a threadworm's life is,' Juliette continued. 'Live in an arse. Lay an egg. Die.'

'Threadworms probably think that about us,' Sarah countered. 'What's the point in human life? Host threadworms. Become alcoholic. Die.'

'I suppose so.'

'At least threadworms have the dignity to keep it brief.'

'That's a new perspective. Thanks. When I was shining a torch into Molly's arse at midnight I should have considered it from their point of view.'

'I like to think I'm opening minds, one parasite at a time.'

'I would come to your TED talk.'

They hit traffic on the M6. Every time they stopped and started,

Sarah prayed to the god of gears. She found she was getting used to the vehicle's temperamental ways. Like they were becoming family. The traffic itself stressed her out, though, there was no denying it. Starting a journey then coming to a near-standstill was nothing short of torturous. Juliette was weathering it better, her natural stoicism coming to the fore. She stared trance-like at the road ahead. Sarah fidgeted and twitched. Her legs cramped. Sensing her discomfort, Juliette said: 'Do you know what a mantra is?'

'Of course.'

'I use mine in traffic.'

Sarah was annoyed at having to demote her adventure to meditation.

'Do you want to know what I have planned for your birthday?'

'Yes, please. You know I hate surprises.'

Juliette hated birthdays. Her own and other people's. She wasn't a joiner. She liked a few people and a few things and she was strict about expending her energy on anything else. It was one of the many things Sarah admired about her. Sarah also knew Juliette's hatred of occasion had its background in self-protection. Juliette had been let down in the past. There had been too many empty seats in pubs; too many leftover slices of cake; too many unclaimed party bags. Sarah made a point of always going to someone's birthday when she was invited because the alternative was potentially leaving them with no one, if everyone flaked. She'd seen Juliette upset too many times. Last time she was up north, Sarah had taken Molly swimming, only for them to see several of Molly's classmates in the changing room and discover there was a child's party there that day – to which Molly hadn't been invited. Sarah had felt that old protectiveness, hairs springing on her palms, canines lengthening . . . How dare they exclude her niece? HER NIECE? *Her sister's child?* A hex on all their souls. She had taken Molly shopping afterwards, and bowling, and for ice cream. 'Tell them all about it at school on Monday,' she'd instructed. 'Tell them all what a great Saturday you had.' When she told Juliette, Juliette said: 'Yeah – I never understood people who stabbed other people until Molly didn't get invited to one of her classmates' birthday parties. Then, I understood.'

Sarah had plotted a route up the west coast of Scotland, along the top to the middle, and then down again. Their mother's father was Scottish – a Mackey, anglicised to Mackie. It explained Sarah's red hair. Back in the day, the Mackey clan held the most northerly and westerly coastlines. The most weathered and the most beautiful. Sarah thought they might feel something up there – something elemental, key into an old family power. A heritage of toughness and salt.

Sarah said: 'I was thinking a few distillery tours, a whirlpool and a mountain.'

'What are we going to do on the way back down – wrestle a griffin?'

Sarah accelerated into the outside lane. Pots and pans banged around in the back. 'Are they going to do that the whole way?' Juliette asked.

'Is that going to bother you?'

'There's no *going to* about it.'

'Well, we're in too much of a rush to sort it now, but I'll sort it when we stop. Just try and be intrepid. You'll enjoy this more.'

Juliette pulled out a vape and opened the window a crack.

'Is that a vape?'

'I just have a little toot sometimes when I'm excited.'

Sarah grinned.

Adventure wasn't always the answer. Peace was the answer. Sanctuary. Calm.

But in the meantime, here they were. Two people occupying the same small space and making it dense with meaning. Two creatures with such a strong mutual understanding that they could at any given moment cancel each other out – like strong words in a short sentence, heightening each other's meaning while at the same time threatening its existence. Two ideas at once complementary and clashing. A paradox. This was her happy place. This casual, intimate, vaguely dangerous roughhousing was the very definition of her comfort zone.

She looked at Juliette. 'You've got some Up Dog on your lip.'

Juliette batted her lip. 'What's Up Dog?'

'WHASSUP DAAAAAWWWG.'

'Oh, man. You are fifteen. Eternally.'

Fucking Mr Keaveney

Is something I think about a lot. I bet he's got a dead smooth chest like a Ken doll but also – crucially – a penis. Nessa says she reckons he's got a hairy back but she's in a mood because Matt from the band 4Princes got a nipple ring she doesn't approve of. When Mr Keaveney and I are together, I mean like properly together – when we're married, when I'm twenty, which is in five years – people will look at us and know instantly that we are in love and that we are meant to be together. No one will be able to say otherwise.

Miss Fine is saying something to me now.

'Sarah Hudson, you're to go to Miss Lawton's room immediately.'

'What for?'

'I'm sure she'll tell you when you get there. Now go on.'

I look at Nessa and she puts two fingers to her lips and sticks the tip of her tongue between them. International Sign of the Lesbian. I leave the room and pull the door to. I'm alone in the corridor but I'm not scared, just apprehensive. I go through all the things this could mean. All the things I've done over the past twenty-four hours. I always feel guilty to be honest, so it's hard to know when it's justified. It can't be about The Thing. No way José. I mean, they'd have hauled him in, too. There'd be police, presumably.

I start walking. I have a good walk; I've been working on it. It's sort of slouchy with a little flourish of the heel every other kick. It is possible to cultivate a habit. It's like the way I relearn my own handwriting after every summer holidays. I even gave myself a twitch last year. I just sat there in front of the TV every night and twitched my eye every three seconds and within a few days it was twitching of its own accord. Mum went mad, so I had to reverse the process. Juliette just said, 'Typical.' But she was only gutted she didn't think of it first. Point is, my walk is my perfect walk because I have made it so. I hope to get there with smoking one day too but I'm not there yet. Cigs still take effort to finish and I never really want one, but you've got to look like you can handle it, haven't you? Miss Lawton's had it in for me since I put washing-up liquid in the town fountain on Founder's Day but I was only thirteen and it was a dare and you don't not do a dare unless you're some kind of stiff. I don't reckon Miss Lawton has ever even smoked a ciggie or had sex (since 28 May 1997 I have smoked fifty-two ciggies and had sex with two and a half men. The half was a hand-job that I held against my fanny for bit and then he came before we could put it in. Nessa and I agreed it would count as a half-sex).

Lawton has suspended me four times over the past five years but I don't care because I'm not here much longer and she'll have to be nice to me soon, won't she? She'll have to treat me as an equal and not someone she can talk down to.

I get to her room and the door's open, so I walk in.

'Morning, Miss Lawton.'

'Good morning, Sarah. Close the door behind you, please.'

I do that and then I stand back in front of her, to attention. There's no way I'm asking what she wants – if she wants me for something she can tell me what it is; I'm not psychic. Except I think I was that one time when I made a glass move in that caravan in the Lakes. And sometimes – I can't explain it, you don't even understand – but I feel like I have fire that can come out of the end of my fingertips if I want it to.

She starts to speak.

'Did you accuse a young man of' – she coughs – '*masturbating* on the bus this morning?'

I absolutely cannot wait to tell Nessa Miss Lawton just said 'masturbating'.

'Wasn't me, miss. Wasn't there.'

'There was nobody else matching your description travelling on the 135 at that time this morning,' she says, eyeing my red hair. 'So unless this lady is lying, and I don't think she is . . .'

I hate my hair I hate my hair I hate my hair. I'm like a walking matchstick. A constant advertisement for myself.

'What about him? Is he in trouble?'

'The police have been given a description and I'm sure they'll do their best to find him. What I won't stand for is girls from this school using words like that in public, whatever young men on the bus might be doing.'

'He wasn't young. He was about thirty.'

'The lady described him as a young man.'

'That's cos she was about a hundred.'

She was as well. Some silly old cow on the way to Europe's Most Famous Market (whatever) for her crumbly Lancashire cheese and California tan tights because she thinks they're the height of fashion. Nothing better to do with her life than grass me up for telling some wanker he's a wanker.

'Half an hour in the library after school where you can write a letter of apology to the lady in question and another one to the bus company. And if I ever hear of you using language like that around the school, or anywhere in your uniform again, I will not hesitate to suspend you, Sarah Hudson. And I must say I'm disappointed you're here with only a week of school until your exams start. Not a very good send-off, is it? Imagine if you end up unable to do your exams?'

I think, you have no idea, absolutely zero idea. Your awareness of the bigger picture is borderline zilch.

'You can go now, and tell the next two to come in.'

Anything for you, miss.

As I walk out of her office there's Amanda Tattersall and Nikki Symonds and I pull a face and squeeze my tit and they laugh and I feel strong.

Now I've got to find Nessa and tell her about the bus wanker and Miss Lawton's humdinger. I jog past the language lab and CDT and turn the corner and I hear someone shout, 'WALK IN THE CORRIDORS!' but I don't look round because it's just some suck-up prefect and she can eat my dust. Up the stairs and along past science towards the new part of the school where they've put all us fifth years. 'Keeping you lot well out of the way,' said Mrs Hamlyn. She's all right. Really I think it's our pumping tunes they want to keep out of the way more than anything, because there's nothing like contemporary music to make the older generation feel sad and the best thing about being a fifth year here is that you get to play music in your form room although it's usually just Nessa's choice which means it's nothing but 4Princes all break and lunch.

On the top corridor near the staffroom and I get a flutter in my stomach because this is always the part of the school where I might see him, other than during lessons. I'm always hoping to bump into him but also always hoping I won't bump into him because it's so intense I can hardly deal. It's like I get all shaky and the harder I try to calm down, the shakier I get. I have to really concentrate to hold my pen still in lessons and when he walks nearby I have to stop writing altogether. He's the same, you know – he gets a sort of sweat on when he's near me and he can't meet my eyes for very long when we're not alone.

I spotted him right off. First day of term. We've got to keep it secret a bit longer but that should be easy cos it's been months now and we've only got another week to go. His name is Mr Keaveney, Danny Keaveney, but I still get embarrassed saying his full name out loud or even seeing it written down or even hearing the names Danny or Keaveney or even seeing the letters D or K anywhere. He is my one true love, the only one for me, and I don't care whether you think that's impossible to know at fifteen because I know what love is and I know my own heart.

He's not around the staffroom. Maybe he's gone into town for a bit of lunch, sometimes he does that to get some fresh air; he likes a walk in the afternoon, we both do — that's why we've picked Scotland. I don't like not knowing where he is.

I keep jogging towards the form room and when I'm close, I see Nessa's outside and she's got Liz Goldstone up against the wall by her neck. From inside the form room you can hear the new 4Princes single — 'Girl, You Girl' — and a few other girls are looking out through the glass bit of the door.

'I'll cross it out,' Liz Goldstone is saying, but she can't talk properly with Nessa's hand round her neck.

'Not good enough,' says Nessa, dead calm like always. 'You'd better rip the whole page off.'

'But it's the cover!'

'I don't care. You shouldn't have written it. Rip it off.'

I can guess what this is about. 'Silly bitch wrote something she shouldn't on the cover of her rough book,' says Nessa without even looking at me. Liz Goldstone has got Nessa's back up before. Someone saw Liz with a Matt sign at the last 4Princes concert and on the Monday, Nessa said she had her eye on her and she'd better watch out.

I look down to the floor and see Liz Goldstone's rough book with the offending heart on it. Oof. That'll do it. Liz has got a nerve. She should know better, and there's three others to choose from.

Nessa's mad on Matt. She's got a Coke can on top of the TV in her room that someone sold her for a fiver because they said he'd drunk from it. She buys every magazine 4Princes are in, sometimes going without lunch for just two pages' worth. She records every TV performance. It's so hard for Nessa because Matt Daubney doesn't even know her name. Sometimes I think I have it bad, but there's so many girls in love with 4Princes, like millions, Nessa's got her work cut out. We went to the Apollo concert last year and she loved it but she got so pissed off and upset when she saw all the other girls there for him. She's got a picture of the two of them in her purse where she's cut their heads out of photos and stuck them onto a bride and groom from a magazine and it actually looks all right, like a real photo. And who's to say they won't end up together? Everyone's got to end up with someone. And if you think about something long enough and hard enough and see it as a real thing in your mind then it can happen – Nessa and I both believe that. We both have powers. Nessa's six months older than me but they held her down a year because she took Es during her mocks – although they don't know that, all they know is she went loopy and couldn't sit down for the exams. Matt Daubney says he's nineteen in the magazines but everyone knows this is a lie because someone saw his passport once and it said he was born in 1974, but they tell them to say they're younger to appeal to teenage girls like we're all idiots.

I'm bored of watching Liz squirm now.

'She said she'll rip it off, Nessa – leave it. Anyway, I've summat to tell you.'

Nessa drops her hand from Liz's neck and Liz bends down and tears off the cover of her rough book and throws it towards Nessa and then storms into the classroom. Her hair's a right mess. Another girl puts her arm around her and Liz shakes her off. Just before the door closes, one of the indie girls, Emily Owen sticks her head out and says she's going to get Mrs Ward, who is the hardest teacher with a long plait and we all think she's in some kind of Viking or medieval re-enactment society at the weekends – she does teach history, after all – and Nessa tells her to fuck off and if she's not careful she'll have her too and Emily Owen says she's a slag and puts her head back inside and slams the door so hard the glass rattles. The indie girls all look down their noses at me and Nessa because we like pop and – newsflash! – we're prettier. Whenever Nessa's out of the form room they put Shed Seven on. It drives Nessa up the wall. They wear band T-shirts on non-uniform day and one of them was wearing one that said 'Common People' once and I've heard that song and I think it's hysterical how they all sit in their big houses up in Rochdale listening to songs about how it's cool to have no money and then they go out to all the most mingingest places with the most mingingest boys and they don't see how thick that makes them. And anyway Emily Owen is a slag because someone saw her giving Paul Riley a nosh behind Pilsworth pictures. Nessa's not a slag but she sometimes pretends she is to piss off the actual slags and if she decided to be a slag she'd be better at it because she's prettier.

'Is this about the bus wanker?' Nessa says, flexing her hand. She looks me up and down. When she does that, she reminds me of an animal, but I'm not sure which animal.

'Yeah,' I say. 'Just got done by Lawton. Says she's gonna suspend me if I say wanker in my uniform again.' Nessa laughs and I feel strong. Then I can't explain how I know he's coming, whether it's the first blast of his aftershave or just a psychic thing like when a cat or a dog knows its owner's car's going to turn into the drive but I'm suddenly on high alert and the hairs on my arms stand up and he turns the corner at the bottom of the corridor oh god oh god don't shake stay cool Sarah for god's sake stay cool. He strides towards us. He looks angry but he's not fooling me, he can't fool me.

'What's going on up here?' he says. 'I heard there was a commotion. Vanessa?'

Nothing.

'Not what I heard.'

'You heard wrong, sir.'

'Sarah?' He looks at me and my whole body burns. It's so weird that it comes out of him, just like that, his voice, saying my name. Like the letters pass through him and for a few seconds I'm inside him, sort of. He's close, a metre away – that's where he stops in school to be safe. I'm a bit taller than him so our eyes meet on an almost absolute level. I'm tall for my age and he's just short. I reckon his jeans would fit me. We can share jeans. I can see where he's nicked his face when he was shaving this morning. There's a little red scab just above his jawline. I'll shave his face for him when we're living together, when we have more time. I'll do it really gently and neatly. I never nick my own legs now – they're smooth like on the adverts.

He can't look at me for long so he looks back at Nessa. She shrugs and does the thing where she opens her mouth and lets her tongue just sit there. She got it pierced last summer and they keep making her take it out and she keeps putting it back in again. He looks down and picks up the rough-book cover off the floor.

'To whom does this belong?' he says.

I bite my lip because I always want to laugh when he says 'whom' and I know he does too.

'Says on it, doesn't it, sir?' says Nessa.

'Liz Goldstone loves Matt Daubney.'

I can feel Nessa's blood boiling, hear her teeth grit. 'Just Liz Goldstone'll do.'

He opens the classroom door and girls scatter back to seats. 'Liz?' he says. 'This is yours, I think.'

She comes over to collect it. 'Everything okay?'

'Fine, sir. Must have fallen off as I came in.'

He doesn't believe that because he's not thick but there's nothing he can do – Nessa's bombproof because they're all afraid of her and everyone knows it. He watches Liz Goldstone go back to her seat and then closes the door and looks at me. My stomach does ten back-flips. I smile at him in the windswept way I always smile at him, like my lips and teeth are all out of control, and he winks, winks at me, in full view! And I look round but no one else saw, probably; not that I'd care now – it doesn't matter if anyone sees at this point. I sort of want them to see, anyway. I want them all to know. We've got this mental connection thing where we know what each other's thinking. Oh, my love, my pain is your pain. Not much longer now. So hard to say where it started – a glance through the swinging glass doors on the way to assembly, a slightly too-hard pencil stroke in the margin. But it's there and there's no denying it. It's more than love. It's everything. There isn't a word big enough for it. But whatever it is, we have it.

He turns around and walks back down the corridor. As he gets further away I feel my heart contract like it's not got enough air even though hearts don't run off air, that's lungs. Nessa rolls her eyes: *such a teacher's pet.* Nessa thinks I'm mad for carrying on with a teacher. I know I'm not mad, though. This love is real and it's about to get a lot real-er. He is in love with me too, and it doesn't matter whether anyone believes us because we're going to prove them all wrong. Even Nessa will change her tune when she's head bridesmaid at our wedding. But first we have to get through GCSEs – we've waited this long, what's another five days? Almost four and a half days now. Then I'm going to meet him at his car after the last exam and we're going to Scotland and we're going to stay there until I turn sixteen in August, and then we're going to come back and make everything official. It won't be easy for them to accept, at first – especially my mum and dad. But they'll get used to it. They'll have to.

Nessa clicks her fingers in front of my face. 'So did you see it then?'

'What?'

'His dick. The wanker on the bus.'

'What's the big deal, not like I haven't seen a dick before. Seen a few.'

In actual fact Nessa has seen seven dicks and I have seen ten.

'Did you, though?'

'Yeah, he sort of had his hand around it but I saw the end and it was bright purple and a bit shiny like it was made out of plastic.'

'Maybe it was a dildo.'

'Hahahaha yeah.'

We try to keep it so we're honest about what we've seen and done sexually. That way no one feels left behind. Although she did say she'd done a sixty-nine and I knew she hadn't, because as she started to explain it, it was clear she thought it was doing the same thing sixty-nine times and not just when you're both upside down. Also I have told her I've done a blowjob to the end but I haven't. I did definitely lick a penis though and it smelled like a hot bathroom. Now I'm lying to her again, about what happened on the bus, but I'm making out it was less than it was, instead of more. I don't want her thinking less of me, that's why. Luckily mine and Nessa's boobs are exactly the same size although mine look bigger because I put those chicken fillet things in my bra.

Nessa's a right one. I first met her outside the corner shop in lower fourths. I'd seen her before and thought she looked hard with her Naffco54 puffa jacket and her hologram eye pendant and her hair moussed back in a shiny bun. I hated going to the shop because there was always this gang of boys outside and they used to sing 'Did you have to be a ging-er did you have to did you have to did you have to be a ging-er' to that Cranberries tune, or ging-gugugingingingingug gugu-gingingagingingingingaging – that Blue Boy one. I hate that one more. Nessa turned up with a load of fourth years and tipped a whole long blue ice-pop over Eliott Cole's head. 'Got a licence for that face?' she said and he didn't know what to do and his neck went red and he ran off and I felt a sick sort of relief with everyone looking at me like I was famous.

The next time I saw her was about a week later in Blackley where she lives. I'd gone round to another girl, Michelle Ryan's, because her parents were away but really I was secretly hoping to bump into Nessa and lo and behold when we were outside having a spliff, Nessa walked past with her cousins. There was this big water butt full of water next to the front door, which Michelle's mum used for her gardening. Nessa was looking at me like she knew me or remembered me but I pretended not to remember her and we smoked more spliff and passed it round and all pretended to enjoy it and feel something off it and then someone said, 'What's that water for?' and Michelle said, 'Me mum's tomatoes,' and Nessa said to Michelle's brother, 'Give you a quid if you get in it,' and he said, 'No way, it's freezing, are you mental?' and I said, 'I'll do it and I don't even want your quid.' And I did it and Nessa kept her mouth open like she couldn't believe it and no sound was coming out and my jeans were wet and when I put my head under it was pure ice. I came up gasping but laughing and they were all laughing saying, 'She's mad her, she'll do anything.' The following Monday morning in school Nessa asked me to meet her the next day at 3.45 at the interchange. We smoked Consulate Menthols by the hot-potato man and she said, 'Know what I can't stand? Those girls who pretend they're stupid to make boys like them, know what I mean?' I said, 'Yeah.' She said, 'At least I know I'm stupid and that's why boys like me.' I said, 'You're not stupid, that was dead funny what you said about Eliott needing a licence for his face.' She said, 'You're all right, Sarah Hudson, I've always thought so.' I was so chuffed I didn't sleep that night. Being picked by Nessa was better than anything, better than being picked by any boy (apart from you know who). Although sometimes I wish I hadn't done the water-butt thing because now they're always expecting me to do something mad when I go to Blackley and I think it's hard to stop being the way you've set yourself up to be with someone, even if you change inside. In fact, sometimes you can end up being more and more that way because you've found a way to be, even though it might not feel like you any more at all.

On the way home I go through the ten mental zones I've made to make the journey quicker. The first zone is the stretch of pavement from the kebab shop to the hairdressers. I hate this town with its little streets and little minds and everywhere you look it's grey. It's always raining and there's nothing to do except dream and they don't even give you much time to do that with all the coursework. We live right next to the motorway and you can see it from my bedroom window, although not from Mum's because hers is round the back.

When I get home there's a new Argos catalogue on the mat, which is brilliant. My mum's in her chair in the front room with Juliette and they're watching Sally Jessy Raphael. I say hi but I decide not to tell them about the bus wanker because Mum'll just worry or blame me.

I didn't tell her when I took Dad's car when I was twelve when they were both out for the day and I drove it down to the sweet shop with just me and Juliette in it. We parked it right outside the shop and went in and bought loads of sweets and then I drove it all the way back up the street again. It was brilliant being in a car and driving it rather than walking along the pavement having nasty words shouted at us from cars. This time, we were the ones in the car and no one could shout anything at us. Mum never needs to know that happened either, and Juliette swore she'd never tell, and that was three years ago so I guess that now means forever. Just to be extra sure, I made her cut her hand and we did a blood pact even though we have the same blood.

In the veg rack there's a bit of random veg and in the cupboard there's a jar of curry sauce and some boil-in-the-bag rice and I think

I can probably do something with that. We learned how to make stir-fry in Home Ec last year. I start chopping an old saggy red pepper but the knife rips it more than cuts it. I peel a brown spot off and then slice along the lines of seeds. Cooking makes me feel orderly, especially chopping vegetables – although it is important to get every single seed off and sometimes they ping onto the floor, which vexes me.

I take three plates of stir-fry through to Mum and Juliette. On the mantelpiece is a photo of Ambrosius, our old cat – well, it's more of a shrine, I suppose, because there's also a little glass pot with some pins he had put into his leg after he was run over, and a chunk of fur in a clip frame. I sit on the frayed couch and everything around me is beige. I'm grateful for what we have but also sometimes I just want to run up the walls because sitting still somewhere so plain just doesn't work for me now that I'm lighting up inside.

'You've got more than me,' says Juliette, which is what she always says.

My mum laughs. 'Give your little sister some more. Not like you need it, big lanky lass. You won't get through the doorframe if you grow any taller!'

Begrudgingly, I give Juliette some more – but surely if I'm bigger than her, I need more, don't I? The woman lacks logic.

When everyone has finished we take the plates through to the kitchen and Juliette does the washing-up. I open the back door to let some air in even though it's raining. I wish I was out more, like my dad. My dad will be home later, after work and the pub, and he'll get himself something to eat on the way home. And yeah yeah before you say anything I get on fine with my dad and he's a nice man so I'm not looking for a replacement in a gross way, although I do miss the way the world was when me and Juliette were little and there was a sort of warmer light on or something. It was all a bit more orangey than it is now. But I think in all honesty, more than anything I miss that feeling you have when you're little of being purely happy and everything is easy – and I know it can never be that way again. You have to find actual things and people to make you happy from the outside, like Mr Keaveney. The thing that scares me the most is living a little life that's just going to get smaller, like how my nana lived in smaller and smaller houses and then smaller and smaller flats until eventually they put her in her coffin – the space you're in just ends up shrinking until it's basically the size and shape of your skeleton and that's it. Unless you find love – love makes you grow. And that's what's going to get us out of here and conquer all the doubters. I've sort of always had a feeling that I could be big, bigger than this town for sure, but when I say anything like that to Nessa she gets all offended, like I'm saying it about her personally, which I'm clearly not.

Juliette washes a glass really gently and carefully and I want to tell her about the bus wanker, about how it wasn't just funny and I shouted at him because he touched me and he had the most hideous yellow teeth. I want to tell her but I can't and a layer of something falls over me. Maybe it's just the silence that feels heavy. But it covers me like a soft fabric. Whatever it is, Juliette is on the other side of it. She has no idea.

I go and talk to Nessa on the upstairs extension in my mum's room but she hasn't got much to report – just how excited she is about the concert a week on Friday that she doesn't know I'm not going to yet. I look at my mum's nail polishes on the dressing table and wonder if she'll notice if I take some away with me.

I do a bit of revision but I can't really concentrate and I don't really need to – it doesn't matter any more. So I get the new Argos catalogue and choose the things for our house – the kettle and toaster and tumble dryer and all the baby stuff and maybe even an inflatable swimming pool for the garden – for the summer – even though they're £200. It's all right though, we'll have the money. I highlight all our purchases with my highlighter pens and I can see them all exactly where they'll be.

Juliette comes into my room before bedtime to show me a scrapbook she's making about otters. She really loves otters, even though she's thirteen. They're her thing. She's grown up — she's had her period since she was nine and drinks Danish vodka with her friends — but she's got a table in her room with otter things all over it. Who knew they made so many things featuring otters? Juliette's got them all, anyway. I suppose her brain isn't that different to mine now we're both teenagers, but the otter thing divides us. Juliette's smart but she's in bottom-set English. You better believe she's wily as hell if she wants something from you, like an otter up a drainpipe, but get her watching *Countdown* or playing Scrabble and she falls to pieces. It makes me sad and it also makes me happy, knowing I'm bigger than her.

Juliette takes her otters back to her room. I look out of the window and watch the sky go dark above the M66. I used to think the motorway was as beautiful as a river, but that was before I saw an actual river. The noise of it is a lot like rushing water, especially when the road is wet. The sound of it gets slower throughout the night until it's just a swoosh every ten or twenty or twenty-five seconds.

I get on my front and touch myself. Nessa does it on her back but I do it on my front. It takes a while because of what happened on the bus. It keeps popping into my mind and I have to keep sending it away. I manage to fend it off for long enough to accomplish my task. The split second before I cum I feel like I am all of myself all at once. I feel his lips and his stubble on the back of my neck when I'm on my front, and I know he's thinking about me in that exact same moment and we join up across space and time. At some point I fall asleep in his arms. This is how it will be. Every night of my life.

Not long now.

Loch Lomond

They were late. 'Shit,' said Sarah, seeing the campsite's locked gate. She could feel Juliette stiffen in the passenger seat. The campsite was tucked in a forest on the east side of Loch Lomond. It was just full dark. Sarah drove up to the gate and turned off the engine. 'We couldn't control it,' she said as though Juliette were accusing her of something. 'There was traffic and bad weather. They have to let us in.'

'We'll just have to hope the place is run by a characterful boomer,' said Juliette. 'They might be more lenient. If it's a millennial, we're fucked.'

It started to rain.

'At least we don't have to pitch a tent,' Juliette said. Sarah knew she was trying to sound optimistic but at the same time trying to guilt her, and in the same sentence, somehow, remind her that it was also her birthday and Sarah needed to be better than this. The layers of subtext siblings could manifest with minimal words was really something.

There was a deserted reception building to the left and, beyond that, a static caravan cataracted with grotty curtains. She opened the door, pulled up the hood of her raincoat and stepped down from the van. As she started to walk towards the reception, a woman appeared.

'I told you we closed at dusk.'

A hard woman of the woods. Gravel in her voice. A bulldog clip in her hair. The clip suited her face.

'Sorry,' Sarah said. 'The traffic was worse than I thought.'

The woman peered into the cab. 'Just two of you?'

'As you see,' Juliette butted in. Sarah could hear she was tired, impatient, entitled.

'Women?'

'If you want to make it about gender,' Juliette replied.

Sarah turned her face away.

'This once, then,' the woman said. She walked to the gate and lifted the barrier. 'Park where you like, apart from the hardstandings on the lochside. Unless you want a deluxe? Five pound extra.'

'Sure, we'll take a deluxe,' Sarah said quickly.

'Baller,' said Juliette, pleased.

'What exactly does deluxe mean?' Sarah clarified.

'Better view. Harder hardstanding.'

'Okay. Those sound like things we'll appreciate.'

'Fine. Pay in the morning.'

'Fantastic. Thank you so much.'

'Wi-Fi's down, by the way.'

'Super fantastic.'

Sarah had an idea. She got the whisky her dad had gifted them out of the back of the van. Handing it to the woman, she said solemnly, 'I'm a Mackay.'

The woman stared at her. At the whisky. At Sarah again. There was a deep judgement being made. Sarah felt insubstantial, plastic. The woman turned and went back to her trailer. Took the whisky though, didn't she.

Sarah got back in the van and drove through the gate. In the rear-view she saw the woman lower the barrier and lock the gate. She stood watching the van for a minute and then walked back to her caravan.

'Well, she's clearly going to kill us in our sleep tonight,' said Juliette.

'I think she'll be too busy watching Ross Kemp investigating something untoward.'

Juliette laughed, then looked at Sarah like maybe this wasn't going to be so bad.

'Lucky Mum gave us those attack alarms.'

'Yeah, nothing says bon voyage quite like a reminder of female vulnerability.'

'You gave her the whisky, though. Dad gave us that.'

'I'm off it.'

'Off whisky?'

'Sort of off everything.'

'Why not. Another one.'

'Hey! It's not like that.'

'I thought this was meant to be a celebration.'

Sarah considered it. Maybe she could drink for her sister. Maybe just a couple, to look sociable and loyal. For camaraderie's sake. Ugh. Had she just been waiting for an excuse?

The one-way track wound past two empty camping lawns and a dimly lit toilet block. The loch was dead ahead. Three or four caravans squatted on standings, equally spaced, parked straight. People who'd arrived early, chosen their spot, made a cup of tea and taken the dog for a run before peeling vegetables and rigging up their TV aerials. Lives full of planning. Lives without drama or disgrace. Screen lights flickered through the windows. A man's face appeared at one and stared at them as they passed, and Sarah had a childish urge to goggle at him. *Take a picture, grandad!* Her therapist had told her she was 'girlish'. That was why she struggled with boundaries. People didn't respect her or feel safe in her custody, because she was bolshy, immature, defensive. She let people in too easily when she first met them, was too personable, she wanted to be liked, to be friends. *Girlish*. The word stung.

They found a spot away from anyone else, under a tree, just in sight of the loch's slick black span. Sarah reversed the van onto the cement and turned off the engine, then she tried to remember what to do first. She had done some mandatory YouTube research. The electricity hook-up. That was it. She went to pull out the orange cable from the little locker at the back of the van. She was nervous, out in the dark – for that, she blamed *The Blair Witch Project*. She and Juliette had terrified themselves watching it. Mostly because it made the outside scary for the first time. Previously, if you were in a haunted house, you could run outside to escape ghosts, but after *Blair Witch* there was no such thing as alfresco solace. The scary thing WAS outside. So there was nowhere to run. Sarah comforted herself with the idea that, like most women, she had always felt an affinity to witches – even the bad ones. So if she was ever pinned to a brick wall, with a witch uttering incantations behind her, she could just say, 'I see you, I feel you, I hold your dreams with mine' and the witch would desist.

Juliette and Sarah had promised to haunt each other, after they died. More specifically, they would take all the cushions off the sofa in the other's house and scatter them all over the floor of the lounge. Then the other would know that they were okay; that they were still around.

Juliette followed Sarah out into the dark, lighting the way with her phone flashlight.

Sarah had seen the 'toilet cartridge' in a little closet parallel to the electric, and she was not looking forward to that aspect of the trip. She was going to be making a blanket rule for number twos being done in the campsite toilet blocks, or in the woods, whatever the weather. Bonding exercises were all well and good, but there was no need to turn this into a gross-out 90s sitcom where they would be frat-boying each other daily about their bodily functions, or banging each other around the head with saucepans.

Sarah hauled the heavy, plastic-coated cable out from its coil and across the wet grass to the raised socket at the back of the pitch. She pulled open the plastic rain cover and pushed the plug in with effort, then motioned for Juliette to head back to the van. Then she twiddled the Calor valve after unlocking the little gas cabinet. 'We'll fill up our fresh water in the morning,' Sarah said, diving for the open door, the rain falling in nails around her. That was it for the externals – now they could get warm.

Inside, Sarah flicked the power on and the van lit up. 'There!' Sarah had brought steaks to cook for the first night. She roasted potato wedges in the little oven and boiled a milk pan of green beans on the gas burner.

Juliette tried to call home, growing increasingly frustrated with the flaky Wi-Fi.

'Why are there no basic communication facilities?' she moaned.

'You're in the mountains,' Sarah said defensively.

'I need to speak to *my children*.'

Sarah felt the flip of that. The card turned. Her move. What did she have to put down? 'Yes,' she said, 'I have lots to check in on at work. They can barely cope without me.'

Juliette looked at her expectantly.

Sarah nodded. 'Maybe I can ask that really friendly woman if she can help us out in the morning.'

'I'll ask, it's okay,' said Juliette, relenting.

'Sure.' Sarah did a slightly wounded face, broken by a brave smile that Juliette couldn't be sure wasn't real. Flip. Snap. An old game they both played well.

Sarah began to unpack her things into the cupboards, pushing in the little silver buttons to make them shut. Juliette followed suit. Sarah rolled up her jumpers, arranged them in colours, like it was a shop. It was pleasing to make things neat and compact and minimal. Juliette had brought a few sentimental items – a weird teddy she always slept with, her wellbeing diary, AirPods (was she expecting Sarah to be boring/annoying?), a blanket from the sofa that 'smelled of the kids' (which part of them? – the question shot through Sarah's mind). Sarah had a few books, make-up, her favourite pillow, but that was about it. She was more nomadic by nature. Juliette saw Sarah looking at her things and said, 'You know what I was thinking lately about you?'

'That I'm a fabulous sister for taking you on a wonderful trip?'

'That it's really odd you never had a transitional object. You know like kids have a teddy or doll to take the place of the mother/child bond – to ease the realisation that—'

'I know what a transitional object is, Juliette.'

'Well, you never had one. Did you notice that?'

'I have been in therapy for several decades.'

Juliette nodded. 'Of course.'

Sarah thought of the train tunnel. The broken-down train. She had been six, Juliette four. The train door open and their mother, running down the track towards the light, terrified. The strangers who had comforted them and called the police. Sarah waiting, waiting, for the figure of her mother to reappear in the tunnel. And it never did. When she'd brought the incident up in therapy, Sarah felt a bit like she'd told her therapist to watch *Citizen Kane* because it 'might be quite a good film'. Her therapist had – poker-faced; she was a good therapist – nodded and said, 'Yes, Sarah, I can see why that would have been upsetting.' Mother Runs Away in Moment of Crisis. It was therapy gold: textbook abandonment. Sarah had, one evilly spirited day, made her mother watch the film *Force Majeure*. Her mother had fallen asleep.

When the food was almost ready, Sarah heaved out the table pole and slotted it into place. Juliette pulled a bottle of red out of her holdall.

'You're allowing yourself the odd glass of wine? Never pegged you as a quitter.'

Sarah looked at the wine. At Juliette. At the stars in the sky outside. There were equal reasons to drink and not to drink. 'Come on,' said Juliette. 'Don't leave me the lost millennial in the bar on the edge of the night.' Sarah didn't know what Juliette was quoting; maybe she'd got to that age where she was just quoting herself. 'You owe me,' Juliette went on. 'You *owe* me.'

Sarah smiled. She already knew she was going to do it. She'd already known for a while, in fact. The relapse moment didn't happen when you took the drink; it happened before that, when you knew there would be an occasion soon when you took the drink. The relapse moment was an act of personal prophecy. It certainly sounded less cowardly that way. She took a glass of wine from her sister. Raised it to her lips. It was good red wine but it was acidic, like all wine. When people described a wine as 'mellow', they'd just been drinking too much wine. Had she *ever* actually *liked* drinking? Or had she forced herself to? Or was it purely for the effects? At some point, someone had told Sarah that she liked going out. But she didn't, not really. And then maybe she had. For a while she'd end up in a burger joint at 11 p.m., fisting in fries, the alcohol not sating her; rather creating more need. Drugs were a different matter. But then, she never took drugs sober. She loved them when she took them, but alcohol was a gateway and an enabler where they were concerned. Ginny had called Sarah 'a woman of fantastic appetites'. She wondered how much she wanted that to be true. Regardless of drugs and alcohol (she needed more time to work out her complicated relationship with those, evidently), she knew she loved food and she liked sex. Those evidences of life. Those footholds on the cliff-face of humanity.

They ate at the dining booth, tucked in opposite each other on hard-backed plasticky chairs, drinking red wine, laughing about the woman on the gate and Ronnie Hotdogs. The flimsy blinds were drawn. Sarah wondered if people outside could see them moving, like shadow puppets. As she started to clear up, Juliette began fruitlessly trying to connect to the Wi-Fi again, growing increasingly frustrated. Sarah, too, felt the constant itch to look at her phone. She knew, from her relationship with her own work, the way you felt as if your identity had been stolen every time you went away. How you worried they wouldn't cope without you – and then realised that the real worry was that they *would*. Because where did that leave you? Sarah could feel Juliette's anguish – and Juliette blamed Sarah for the Wi-Fi situation, Sarah could feel that, too. There was tension. Sarah did what she always did to dispel tension: she started to sing – to hum and let the odd word break through. It was a coping mechanism and a tactic, forged in the childhood home (where else?). Her singing was a cat's purr – saying 'I am non-threatening'. She did it to chase ghosts away, to not be frightened, but mostly she did it to let female family members know she wasn't in a mood.

'So how's work?' Juliette asked.

'Okay. I went to a conference last week and they put me up in a hotel. I had a starter, a lamb rack and three glasses of Shiraz. Then I overheard a waiter talking about the dessert chef who was a finalist on *MasterChef* and I thought there's no way I'm not having a dessert, so I ordered a selection. Then I was so full, I lay in bed and wept.'

'Oh god.' Sarah could hear the wine in her sister's laugh.

'The worst thing was, they'd put me in the bridal suite. They're overcompensating because they've promoted this younger woman underneath me and I know she's already on more money than me.'

'Oh. I wondered why you were desperate to get away from work. It's not like you to take a holiday. Now I understand: it's revenge on a younger woman!'

'What? No, it's not that at all! It's your birthday!'

Juliette stood up and put her glass down. 'I can have a number one in the toilet here, can't I?' Juliette asked.

'Yeah. Although the toilets are just by reception . . . you could take a torch; we could go together, even, in about half an hour – just let me get another glass in.'

'Oh god, you're going to be weird about the toilet.'

'Just go in here, it's fine.'

'It probably won't be much wee anyway, I'm dehydrated after the journey.'

'Don't flush and I'll wee on top of your wee. Save the fresh water.'

Sarah wanted to pee second, what with the current situation – the mystery that had been plaguing her. A brackish water emerging at the end of every pee. A discomfort in her abdomen. It was making her self-conscious pre-sex. She had googled – always perilous – and found of course that the most likely explanation for red-brown discharge was womb cancer. Maybe it was time for her womb to do something. Seriously, though, was it the menopause? The peri-menopause? The peri-peri-menopause? She did like Nando's . . .

Sarah told herself to relax. She could tell Juliette about it and they could laugh, like they did when they were growing up and their mum had referred to her period as 'Horace'. Like it was an aristocratic Victorian man who visited every month. 'I've got Horace,' she'd say, when she had to go to the toilet to change her pad, and the girls would look at each other, amused and revolted.

Juliette went into the tiny bathroom. Sarah poured out two more big glasses. She topped each glass up in turn, wondering whether she'd take the slightly bigger or the slightly smaller glass, which was the more powerful choice, until they were up to the rim and she was out of options.

Juliette took a hot minute in the toilet. This could be a big problem. In every sense of the word. When they were growing up, Juliette was renowned for the size of her stools. Sarah wondered at one point whether she might be like Paul Slack in the year above, who'd apparently had to start taking tablets to reduce the size of his, after he'd cracked the U-bend. Juliette had left one in a chalet once on a skiing holiday. The toilet had refused to budge. Convinced the flush was broken, Juliette, incensed, had called for the maid. '*Regardez!*' she'd said, pointing in the toilet. The maid had edged in, nervously. Juliette had pressed the toilet lever with another '*Regardez!*' At which the toilet had . . . flushed. The maid nodded, confused. And Juliette became known forever after as the girl who liked to show people the size of her turds.

Juliette emerged from the bathroom.

'Did you send some logs downstream?' Sarah said.

'I don't do those any more. They've got smaller . . . with age.'

'Like everything. No need to be touchy.'

'I'm not being touchy.'

'You are being a bit touchy.'

'Well, you're being a bit annoying.'

Well – Sarah had to stop here and grow up and remind herself she was the elder one. Juliette sprayed her pillow with lavender spray, pressed a clear plastic retainer onto her bottom teeth, applied an elasticated eye mask that looked like a strapless bra for monkeys, and then got into bed, pulling the covers up to just under her armpits. She exhaled once and lay there, rigid, awaiting sleep like a stone carving of a knight errant on top of a tomb.

'Remind me again why you're not having sex?' said Sarah.

Juliette tried not to laugh. Failed. 'Here we are,' she said. 'Living together. Always a pleasure.'

This cut Sarah, although as she hugged Juliette goodnight, she wasn't sure Juliette had meant it how she'd taken it; but by then it was too late to say.

Sarah stayed up an hour or so later, idly drinking wine, listening to Juliette snoring and burbling. She wondered whether her decision to finish the bottle had really been because driving with an open bottle of wine might mean they'd lose their deposit. Or whether it was something else.

*   *   *

The next morning, Sarah woke first and watched Juliette sleeping. This felt normal and natural, the two of them alone together like this as the sun rose and the dew dropped. It took Sarah back to all those early-morning dates. Just the two of them up at dawn, holding hands down the stairs, stepping into the darkness as their parents slept. Ripping open curtains, snapping on lights. The only people alive in a brave new world. Two children on the brink of infinity. Taking it in turn to make the sandwiches – ham and butter, corned beef and Branston – and put them on the plastic trays with scampi and lemon Nik Naks, Club biscuits, cherryade. The sweet comfort of the late 1980s and early 90s, and all the movies they could drink. The greatest cinema in history. Everything on VHS tapes and later DVDs, lovingly lined up and labelled, with hearts drawn over the 'i's. A catalogue of all their hopes and feelings. Even when Sarah had been to the revered Nitehawk in Brooklyn, which she'd adored – the cocktails themed around the movies, the waiting staff, the mid-century side tables with pencil pots – she'd felt it was all well and good, but it could never compare to the Cinema Paradiso she shared on that crappy old sofa with her sister in Manchester on Saturday and Sunday mornings.

*   *   *

By Loch Lomond, Sarah took a walk over to the bathrooms with her toiletry bag and the previous night's pots and glasses in a bowl. The bulldog was standing outside the shop, watching Sarah as she made her way back from the shower block, hair wet, washing-up done. Sarah detoured and walked over to the shop. She put her washing-up bowl down. She noticed in the reflection of the window that the cardigan she'd slept in was buttoned up wrong. Camping was so liberating. She left her cardie as it was and went in.

'Good morning!' said Sarah, risking brightness.

'Morning,' the site owner said, looking behind Sarah. Was she refusing to make eye contact?

'Ten fifty,' the woman said, still looking towards the corner.

Sarah tapped her card to the machine and followed her gaze. In the corner of the shop there was a bird on the floor. A robin.

'It keeps bashing its head against the window,' the woman said, punching at the till. 'I've opened the door wide as I can but it's a stupid thing.'

Sarah walked over, knelt, and caught the robin in her hands. It didn't struggle. She carried it to the door and threw it into the air. It flew away towards the trees. When Sarah got back to the till, the woman gave her a five-pound note.

'You've only been here a few hours.'

Sarah almost cried. A flake of kindness from a stranger was all it took sometimes and she was open like an archway. She felt awkward then, so she bought several things she didn't need: bleach, a tin of ravioli and a very tired-looking cauliflower. The woman rang it through. Almost six quid. That felt better. She wasn't a charity. 'Oh!' she said, almost forgetting. 'Do you know when the Wi-Fi might be back up?'

'Mast has gone down,' said the woman, as though it was the fiftieth time she'd been asked this morning.

'I'll take some tin foil too,' said Sarah. 'Two rolls.'

She got back to the van to find Juliette waving her phone around.
'I need my phone to work!'

Juliette looked pale in the morning, her freckles showing through.

Sarah put her bags down and sighed. 'There is something we can do, apparently, but it's a bit risky.'

'I don't care. Tell me. It's an emergency!'

Sarah pulled the tin foil from the bag. 'We have to make our own mast. The woman in the shop said it's worked for a few people this morning . . . She couldn't guarantee it, but . . .'

'Make our own mast? What with?'

Sarah looked at Juliette solemnly and beckoned her inside the van.

*   *   *

Juliette stripped down to her thermals and Sarah began to wrap the foil around her arms and legs. She coated Juliette's limbs in three layers of tin foil, and then made a special hat for her to put on her head – a long cone with a sharp point 'like a lightning conductor'. She told Juliette to get on top of the van and move her arms in certain directions, until her phone picked up a few bars of signal.

Juliette climbed onto the bonnet with difficulty, then stood on the van, wrapped in foil, waving her arms. A few people walked past and looked at them curiously. Sarah smiled like it was a normal morning. 'Hello! Glad to see the rain has stopped! Have a good day!'

Juliette focused on her task.

'Any luck?' Sarah asked.

'Nothing!'

'Stick your leg up a bit more! No, the other one.'

Sarah got out her phone and snapped a photo. 'I'm just going to show the kids how hard you worked trying to contact them, when we finally get reception back.'

Juliette stopped and put her leg down. She looked at Sarah.

'You fucking bitch.'

Sarah started to run. Juliette was after her, layers of tin foil falling off her as she hared around the campsite in pursuit of her elder sister, eventually catching Sarah – who was nearly puking with laughter at this stage – by the loch. Juliette seemed like she might push Sarah in. 'DON'T!' Sarah screamed.

Juliette was laughing too now, hard. 'You're SUCH A MASSIVE TOOL!'

'From the woman dressed like a takeaway.'

*   *   *

They had bacon muffins for breakfast, eating in camp chairs, watching the other campers go about their mornings. A little girl skipped along the edge of the hardstandings in a slogan T-shirt.

'If I see one more five-year-old in a "BE KIND" top, I'll go postal at a pre-school,' said Juliette. 'All that chat about becoming more right-wing as you get older, I think it's balls. I think we're all born right-wing. Fascism isn't something people grow into; it's something they grow *out of*. Fascism is the factory setting for humans.'

'Maybe a better sweater for a five-year-old would say something like "Be Less Fascist". We should make them.' Sarah thought of the other business ideas they'd had, in their twenties: a beach sauna; a vegan cocktail company; a crêpe shack.

'Tell me Johnnie got Harpo the "The Future" T-shirt.'

'He did.'

Sarah shook her head. 'Yep. There he goes, congratulating himself again.'

She half expected a rise out of Juliette, but Juliette just

sniggered in agreement. Ooh. Sarah logged this one. Excellent, excellent. Maybe by the end of the trip they could make a plan to hire a hitman.

They packed up the van, unplugged the mains, turned off the gas. The question of the oven being left on was a far more pressing matter when you were travelling at 50mph on a B road. As they were putting the table pole back, Juliette hunched suddenly. Sarah lunged to support her. 'Jeez – what—? Are you okay?'

'Yes,' Juliette wheezed. 'My body just hasn't quite forgiven me yet for having babies.'

Sarah nodded in what she hoped looked like solidarity. 'Mine feels the same about crystal meth.'

'I have a Picasso vagina. You know they stitched me up wrong?'

'I remember.' What Sarah meant was, Juliette had told her years after it happened, when she was drunk at their dad's seventieth. 'You should have sued.'

'Isn't it funny it never even occurred to me. If they'd done that to my hand, or my foot – botched it – I'd have complained so much. But my vagina didn't feel half as important at the time.'

Sarah looked again at the faint marks on Juliette's face and didn't know how to ask about them.

She set the next location: Glen Nevis, along the A82.

The woman from the shop came out and stared at them, perplexed, as they went past. 'She probably thinks we're a hen do,' said Sarah.

'Misery loves company,' said Juliette. 'You two depressives bonded, I can tell.'

'I'm not a depressive! Where has this come from? I'm optimistic!'

She turned out onto the road.

'It is very possible to be depressive and optimistic,' said Juliette, helping herself to Sarah's new pack of cigarettes. So Juliette was a smoker now. A smoker who didn't buy cigarettes. 'In fact,' she continued, 'you might argue that optimism leads regularly to depression. You just go round and round on a great big wheel. Hoping for something better. Realising there isn't anything. Hoping for something better. Realising there isn't anything.'

'Thank you for that deft insight into my psychology,' said Sarah. 'Anyway, you know what misery loves more than company? Whisky and sex.'

'Sounds great,' said Juliette.

'You're a married woman. Can't imagine you have much cause for sex these days.'

Juliette gave Sarah a slit-eyed look. She traced her finger on the van window, looping round the raindrops on the outside.

'Look, it's not a surprise party, is it?' Juliette said.

'What?'

'Just tell me you've not got everyone arriving by train to Inverness to jump out on me in a crap pub somewhere.'

'I swear I haven't! You'd hate that!'

'I would.'

'How offensive that you'd even think that.' Sarah's turn to take the high ground.

'Sorry,' said Juliette. 'That would just be my worst nightmare.'

'Give me some credit.'

'I don't even have any friends any more.'

'Who does?'

'Hey, do you ever speak to that girl from school, what was her name, Nessa?'

Sarah shook her head. 'Nope.'

'Word innit.'

'Life.'

All the friendships changed in the run-up to forty. After the mid-thirties cull. Sarah had contacted Nessa once, five or so years ago, high on coke, at around 4 a.m. An email after getting her address via Google and her website — she ran a childcare company and wasn't on social media. Vanessa (as she now called herself) hadn't replied. It was okay, Sarah was relieved the next day — and more than a little embarrassed. Nessa was from a previous life. The shift of that year had been absolute. They'd started to drift and never got each other back. Sometimes things happened that were so bad they made your life stop and start again. They dragged you kicking and screaming from the past to the present, and vice versa. Sarah had quickly made new friends, who she felt were more sophisticated, but she also wasn't always sure about that.

Sarah effortfully tried to waggle the dog-leg gearstick into third. 'Fucking thing.'

'So what do you have planned?'

'Just give me a— This fucking— There.'

'You do have something special planned?'

'Is this not special?'

'Um . . . you mean the van?'

Sarah made herself look like a person trying not to look too hurt, which she knew was more effective than just straight-up looking hurt.

'I'm sorry!' said Juliette. 'I do appreciate you doing this. I'm just in a weird spot. We can . . . talk about it. Just . . . not now. Ignore me for now.' She looked out of the window. 'I'm being a baby.'

'I have plenty planned,' said Sarah. 'You're never going to forget this trip. And if that sounds ominous, that's because it is.'

'Are you going to drive us off a cliff, Thelma and Louise-style?'

'You guessed it.'

'Just let me fuck Brad Pitt first.'

'Sounds like Johnnie isn't cutting it.'

Juliette didn't answer.

Too much, too soon. Later, Sarah told herself. Later.

* * *

They parked up at the distillery, next to a larger motorhome, silver and slick with bright raindrops. It had the word 'AVENTURA' stuck clumsily along the top spoiler in big black cursive.

They made their way into the distillery and booked onto the next tour.

'This is fun,' said Juliette, peering into the dark, twinkling distillery, which was all wood, copper and fairy lights. 'Obviously neither of us drink as much as we used to, being grown-ups now.'

'I definitely can't. And I'm not being a pussy.'

A speaking look from Juliette.

'I'm not *just* being a pussy,' corrected Sarah. 'The limit in Scotland is tougher than in the rest of the UK. I can only have one. Legally.'

There was something lovely in this. In Juliette's face. The competitive starvation lived on, in different ways, forever. She would always have to beat her to love her.

Juliette wagged her finger at Sarah. 'You're doing this to control me. So I get pissed and you get to win, somehow.'

Sarah replied, 'It's a cultural activity and a birthday gift. You're being suspicious.'

Juliette was smashed by the third shot. Sarah delighted in her sister's demise and started looking for chippies on Google Maps.

The whisky master passed them an aged cherry-wood single malt. 'Cowabunga,' Juliette said.

'What do you get from that?' the master asked.

'This one tastes like the time my sister stole my boyfriend in Year 8,' said Juliette.

'Funny you should say that,' said Sarah. 'It tastes to me of your lifelong smug moral superiority.'

Juliette smacked her lips and looked at the whisky master. 'Do you have a wedge of lemon?'

The response from the master was snooty. 'We're past lemon season in our garden.'

Sarah leapt to Juliette's defence. 'Don't lemon-shame her!'

'Huge apologies for any offence caused,' the whisky master replied. 'Is there anything else you'd like with your shot?'

Juliette asked for another shot to go with her shot.

Sarah bit her lip to not laugh. Juliette looked at her — cock of the distillery. Boss-eyed cock. Sarah recalled the empty vodka bottles lined up on both of their windowsills at university, hundreds of miles apart. Empty bottles as proof of . . . something. Some kind of erstwhile pissing competition. She was at her limit, alcoholically and emotionally. Should she leave the van in the car park overnight? They could sleep here? Get drunk together? Had she already decided they would do that together, too? The second stage of her relapse?

Sarah made eyes at a man across the room who appeared to be in his late fifties. He looked sparkly. Drinking alone. Drinking whisky and a pint, like them. Maybe it meant something. Juliette followed Sarah's gaze.

'Oh my gash, what are you doing? Are you flirting with that pensioner?'

'There's something twinkly about him.'

'There's something *wrong* about you.'

'He's only about fifty!'

'He's seventy if he's a day.'

'He's dynamite in the sack, that cat, mark my words.'

'Looks a bit geeky.'

'I love a geek.'

'I know you do, you grub.'

'I'm going for computer programmer. Vegetarian computer programmer. Moneyed but with an eye on the future.'

'Very specific read.'

'Yeah. It's only myself I don't understand. Everyone else makes perfect sense to me.'

'He looks like he's halfway through having his prosthetics applied for his role in the *Rats of NIMH*. He's a beast.'

'Well, we both said by the end of *Beauty and the Beast* we'd rather he'd stayed as the Beast, soooo . . .'

'And I cannot forgive a bootcut jean.'

'I quite like a rat-beast in bootcut jeans. That is very much my jam. My sex jam.'

'You're a pervert.'

Maybe Sarah was. She did like the older ones. She had only fancied a younger man for the very first time recently. She had puzzled over that shift in taste. Suddenly she got it. Their energy. Their puppyish ricocheting. Their connection to all things that seemed like life and awareness. What had caused her to switch to younger men? Was the reason something as banal as social *power*? Had she fancied older men until the tipping point – when men become less powerful, around the age of fifty-five – and now her tastes were veering younger, back to the thirties, where men peaked? Ugh, so basic. Was she really that basic?

Her relationship with her own age was another thing. Sarah was genuinely shocked when people she met were younger than her. To her, they all seemed to look how she felt: mid-twenties. She wondered whether she had age dysmorphia. She looked in the mirror and still saw twenty-five. Part of her didn't want that to stop. There was a hopefulness to delusion. She was still holding out for something more – still clinging to the notion that, somewhere out there, there was a better life for her. That she could change it, if she tried hard enough. If she was *good* enough. If she was better.

'Prince William has a bald spot. And *he's* a *millennial*. Millennials are old now, Juliette, get used to it.'

'Wouldn't shag him. Or a Gen Z-er. It isn't an age thing.'

'What's wrong with Gen Z-ers? Apart from the fact they're too young to shag. Generally.'

'Gen Z-ers will respect your pronouns but not you as a person. Stay in your generational lane.'

Sarah was wondering whether desire was the same thing as looking. Sometimes a person was just looking. We should be allowed to look and not desire.

'Do you not want to meet someone — like properly meet someone?'

Juliette had changed tack.

'Oh, here we go.'

'Are you not scared of dying alone?'

'No. It'd be my preference. I don't even like being sick in front of another person, you know that. He looks fun.'

'He's probably on Viagra.'

'None of us are spring chickens any more, Juliette . . .'

'That's the second time you've brought up my age in the past minute, and it's meant to be my feelgood birthday trip. That's what you said. *Let's spend some quality time together.* That was the sell. Anyway, I still pass for thirty-five. And when I get my teeth done with my birthday money I'll go for thirty-two.'

'What are you doing to your teeth?'

'Veneers. They don't look after themselves. Pam Ayres was right.'

'I think you'll find her correct name now is Pam *Uluru*.'

The older man came over.

'Hey,' said Sarah.

'She's too old to use "Hey" like that but she persists,' said Juliette, and then by way of explanation: 'She's an X-er.'

The man frowned.

'Generation X,' said Juliette.

Sarah looked at her. 'Since when was that relevant?'

'I think I'm just about an X-er too,' he said.

'No you're not,' said both sisters in unison. 'Just no way,' said Sarah, suddenly territorial over something she barely owned.

'Anyway, it's Steve.'

'Hello, Steve, hello. Sarah. Juliette. Sisters.'

'That's nice. So what's the occasion?'

'Sex tour,' said Sarah. These words hung in the air.

'Just kidding,' Sarah said. 'It's her birthday next week.'

'Congrat—'

'Guess how old I am. Guess.'

The man looked uncertain. Like there were multiple wrong answers. He looked from Juliette to Sarah.

'There's no right or wrong answer,' said Sarah. Which was the biggest lie she'd ever told.

'Ballpark,' said Juliette, gnashing her teeth ever so slightly.

'Oh, er, thirty.'

'Bullshit,' said Juliette. 'Let's get drunk.'

'I don't think . . . they like you doing that here,' said Steve.

The staff's faces confirmed it.

Juliette told the carpet this was 'bullshit'.

There was a long pause.

'I customised my van,' Steve said. 'It has "Aventura" on the side. That's Italian for "adventure".'

Oh yes, thought Sarah. To *not* fuck him would be the less exotic thing.

'How about you?' asked Sarah. 'Just a holiday?'

'Actually, I'm a musician.'

Juliette sipped her drink.

'Really?' Sarah was all ears.

'Yeah, I play bass with a few small bands. Got a gig this week at Aviemore. You know, the ski resort?'

This was good. Sarah was invested. She could go for a musician all day long.

'What do you girls do?'

'I own my own tablescaping business,' said Juliette. 'And she works in travel even though she hates holidays.'

'I'm head of sales.'

'She's SO good at sales. Like, she *is* sales. It's a constant thing.'

Sarah looked at Juliette.

'Classic love-bomber,' Juliette explained. 'Not with me. But with everyone else. It's a transferable skill! You're amazing at your job because you ARE your job.'

Sarah assessed the situation and decided Juliette must be very drunk indeed.

Juliette said: 'But we're honest with each other. I know that. We tell each other exactly what we think, always. Sometimes we don't even need to say it – we're telepathic, like twins.'

Now Sarah really knew she was drunk.

Juliette took a step backwards and almost fell over. Sarah made an executive decision. She looked apologetically at Aventura Man. Then she put her arm around her sister. 'Come on, hun.' *Hun!* The word was out before she'd even thought about it. Juliette flinched.

'I'll see you around,' said Steve.

Sarah nodded. *Yeah. The psychic wankbank. See you there, silver fox.*

She strong-armed Juliette out of the distillery.

Juliette stopped Sarah in the car park. 'TAKE MY PHOTO!' she shouted. She posed in front of a huge bottle of whisky, trying to look sexy. She moved her tongue towards the bottle.

'Don't lick it,' said Sarah. 'You'll regret that.'

Sarah moved away to get the best picture. She moved closer and Juliette's features became blurred. She moved away and they were clearer again. The frame was more meaningful.

After the photo was taken, Juliette took the phone and got a selfie of both of them.

'You could at least try and look happy,' Juliette said, regarding the result with dismay.

Sarah *was* happy. I am inscrutable, she thought. I really am. Even to my sister.

Her therapist had told Sarah that whenever she talked about something that had been difficult for her, she simultaneously provided the solution. She talked about how she'd overcome the problem like you might in a job interview or an application. It was a pitch. She presented a shiny, complete story. *Look what I made!* She left no space for anyone to help her. This was why she couldn't be vulnerable. Her patriarchal view of strength and success meant no one got a look-in. Even now, on the path to enlightenment, the thought of sitting with someone in her own emotional mess made Sarah cringe. There was one word for it. Urrrrgh. She had been trained to complete the narrative. It was a performance, a pitch. In that way, Juliette was right: Sarah was an excellent saleswoman. But she had promised herself she would try to start presenting things to people that were half finished. Human. Real. She would try to let people into her broken little house of horrors.

Sarah took back her phone and looked at her own face on the picture. She saw the opposite of what Juliette saw. Sarah was smiling, Juliette was not.

I put my little blue TV on

While I get dressed so I can watch the war coverage. I set my alarm for 5 a.m. especially. Now it's 7 a.m. and the Gulf War is still happening. I'm a bit worried Mr Keaveney's going to have to go away and fight and that could spoil everything. I don't think he'd make much of a soldier, though, what with being short, plus he's got quite scrawny arms and he looked away during the bloody bits when we watched the film adaptation of *Macbeth* in March, so what does that tell you.

I turn over to the entertainment news. A young American girl called Britney Spears is being interviewed walking through a mall in London. She's sixteen. They show a clip of her video. It looks hilarious — schoolgirls dancing in the corridor of an American high school. It's not 4Princes but it's good and I think I do want to be like her. She's wearing a lot of make-up and a crop top and she sounds like she's been alive a long time.

We're not allowed to wear make-up for school but I have to put some mascara on my eyes. I found some in Mum's make-up bag three years ago and it was like suddenly EYES! POP! WOW! I love it. I have a short haircut and not everyone likes it, but the important people do. I think it's striking, especially with me being so tall. And anyway I like standing out, tall and broad, with super-short hair. I like looking too modern and too big for this town. It's the truth. Plus, you've got to do something dramatic when your school uniform is pale blue and grey: the colours of depression. I've got a mole on my chin so I make it darker with kohl pencil. If you can see something, make a feature out of it, as they say.

I make my way through the zones to the bus stop – out the front door and into Zone One. It's thirty steps to the tree and Zone Two, then another twenty to Natalie Semp's driveway where her dad parks his furniture van from the markets, then thirty-three to the smooth sloping-down bit that used to be good for skateboarding, which is Zone Three, then Zone Four is the bus stop where there's no one else because it's so early; sometimes there's a woman who I think is a cleaner, but not today. Zone Five is the bus journey, which takes thirty minutes. Zone Six is the stop I get off at with the little shop where sometimes I buy an egg mayonnaise bap for my breakfast and the filling is still warm because they just made it. Zone Seven is the section along the back of the town hall to the playing field, then onto Zone Eight which runs along the back of the playing field where we run for cross country. Zone Nine is out on the road of the school and along the other side of the playing field, and finally Zone Ten is the thirty steps up the path and stairs and in through the front door of the school. Sometimes I think anyone could get in here if they had a school uniform on, but then let's face it who would want to. Okay – me, when I've got double English.

I'd always noticed him cos there aren't many male teachers at the school. There's like Mr Blackburn who teaches chemistry but he is properly old and has teeth like a sheep. Then Mr Service who teaches CDT but he has a wife and I think she is actually called Carol. No joke. None of them are as young and fit and single as Mr

Keaveney. I know he noticed me too and when he started teaching us last September, that's when things really got going. It was the second lesson together, 10 September, and he read us a Shakespeare sonnet, number 73. He had on his red checked shirt and his black jeans and it went:

That time of year thou mayst in me behold,
When yellow leaves, or none, or few, do hang
Upon these boughs which shake against the cold,
Bare ruin'd choirs, where late the sweet birds sang.
                    In me thou see'st the twilight of such day
                    As after sunset fadeth in the west,
                    Which by and by black night doth take away,
                    Death's second self, that seals all up in rest.
In me thou see'st the glowing of such fire
That on the ashes of his youth doth lie,
As the death-bed whereon it must expire,
Consum'd with that which it was nourish'd by.
                    This thou perceiv'st, which makes thy love more strong,
                    To love that well which thou must leave ere long.

Yes, I memorised it! Ta-da!

Anyway, after he'd finished reading it he said what do you think that's about? No one answered. He was new and I think we were all a bit bowled over. I looked around to see who else was looking at him. Everyone – course they were. He smiled in a cheeky way and waggled his eyebrows which made me smile too.

'Ah, you're all too young,' he said. 'Tell you what, do me a favour and make a mental note to read that in twenty years, and I promise you it'll feel very different. It's about mortality – something that becomes more of a pressing concern when you're ancient like me.'

'How old are you, sir?' said Nessa. 'Fifty?'

'Ah,' he said, 'a comedian. You must be Nessa.'

'That's my name, sir – don't waste it, got to last me the rest of my life.'

I rolled my eyes at him and then I thought, did I just side with a new teacher over my best mate? I think I did.

'It's a terrible thing, age,' he said. 'It frightens poets, just like everyone else. Shakespeare wrote a lot about it. It gets all of us in the end, guaranteed. I think death is more of a truly universal theme than love.'

I said, 'Well, you're only getting older, sir, while you're crapping on about it.'

Nessa laughed and a few others gasped. He looked at me and narrowed his eyes and we held each other's gaze just that bit too long and Nessa kicked me under the table and I guess it was inevitable from that point on. The next week he marked an essay with a heart next to something I'd written and I knew then we were on the same wavelength and what is love apart from a wavelength – a radio station tuned in for only two listeners? After all, if everyone was tuned in to the same station, you wouldn't be able to make out a thing over the din.

The next day I woke up and I couldn't wait to see him and going into school was easy for once rather than hard. Even though I had double maths. The thing I don't get about maths is that anything multiplied by zero is zero. How? How can that be? No one can give me a satisfactory answer.

All you need to know for now is that it's real and there's no denying it. It's everything and it's only just begun, even though I feel like I've loved him forever. I want to consume him I want to eat him I want to be inside him I want him all to myself. I want to take over his body and grow all over him, like the ivy on our next-door neighbour's garage. I am defined by my desire. That's how I feel. Strong and weak at the same time. I almost don't care if other people start to find out. I sort of want them to. It won't be easy for them to accept at first. Mr Keaveney is pretty old. He's twenty-five. I know! That's almost thirty. He remembers when computers didn't exist, if you can believe that. He's the youngest teacher in the school but that's not saying much. He's been here for a year and before that he was at a school in Yorkshire teaching slightly younger ones, but he said it was boring not having an adult conversation with anyone all day and I know what he means. I can't stand boys my age. They go all mumbly when they talk and they move in to kiss you with their arms straight out like robots and they stink of Lynx Tempest and the word that describes them best is 'sad'. Mr Keaveney wears Obsession by Calvin Klein and I know this because I asked him once because it's important I know things like this for the future for Christmas and birthdays. It's a proper smell. Classic. I wear the women's version now but I'm not sure whether he's noticed because men aren't so good at noticing such things.

Now we look for each other in assembly, and in his classes he alternates between barely looking at me and not stopping looking at me – he's either ignoring me or staring and I know I'm doing the same and it scares me half to death. Love gets you like that – it makes you unsure of yourself – and that's not a bad thing. When he marks my essays and writes longer and longer comments on them, he presses so hard with his pencil it's like I can see him doing it, late at night, in his chair all alone with a lamp on. We have developed our own special code – a secret language. He writes things in the margins of my essays and I put things in my essays for him, and we have to be clever about it in case anyone finds them. Really they're the best kind of love letters because no one will ever be able to understand them apart from us. I've kept them all in a shoebox under my bed.

It makes me sad, my bedroom. My bed also makes me sad. Under it is even sadder. Okay then, so I will tell you the thing that happened, because it cheers me up thinking about it, and then you'll know. We'll be on the same page. He brought me his copy of *Shakespeare's Sonnets* – it's dead nice with a hard cover and italic curly font on the front and thick paper inside – and he'd written his address and phone number in the front for me. Why else would someone give you their phone number? They just wouldn't, would they? I haven't phoned it, but I'm going to, although in a way there's not much point now because we're leaving this weekend. That's what all the messages and clues in his comments on my essays have amounted to: The Plan. My last essay used the word 'ready' over 100 times so he can be in no doubt from my end. But just in case, I got into a classroom early the other day before anyone else and I wrote YES in capitals on the blackboard, and I sat there nodding slowly when I saw him read it and for a few minutes afterwards.

At our wedding I think we should read a sonnet. Not the one about ageing though, the one about not being shaken by tempests. I've still got his book – I'll pack it to bring with us next week along with a few clothes and bits and bobs and that's about it. It'll all have to fit in a car. Certainly not my old diaries and notebooks, I'm going to burn those – cringe! That's how it'll be – that face a few centimetres from my face, looking at the road ahead.

There's no feeling in the world as good as waiting for the person you love – it's better than sex, better than shopping, better than watching your favourite film on a Saturday morning with a bowl of microwave popcorn. The thing is, when you fall for someone, you lose a bit of yourself and then as you're scrabbling back, if they're stronger than you – which they will be, if you've fallen for them like that – you're literally putty, moulded by their moves. And the worst thing is: I want that fall. I don't think it's love or passion or romance otherwise. So I'm doomed, I tell thee. DOOMED!

Nessa is next to me doing the white bit of a French manicure with some Tipp-Ex. I think it looks shit but I've told her and she keeps doing it. She's a law unto herself.

I know he's here before the door even opens – I feel it on my scalp like a buzz. He comes into the room and I lose my breath. He's wearing a black shirt and black trousers and he says GOOD MORNING LADIES like always and we all say GOOD MORNING SIR like we're kids, but you have to go through this rigmarole and it's not for much longer, not for me anyway. He looks my way super quick and away again because that's what we have to do when we're in a room of other people and then he puts down his briefcase (I hate that briefcase; that briefcase is not staying) on the big front desk and holds up the book. We're doing *Twelfth Night*. Out of all the Shakespeare ones I've read it's my favourite because it's absolutely ridiculous, and when I say ridiculous I mean ridiculous. He looks tired, like he hasn't slept so well, and I wonder whether it's his dad again, I know he's desperate to move out of his dad's place just like I'm desperate to move out of my parents'. He puts on a brave face but he can't fool me. I know every inch of him, every last millimetre. I can spot any tiny change. I know him like I know something I've looked at a lot – like my bedroom ceiling.

'Okay, ladies,' he says, 'today I want to talk about symbolism.' He starts to walk down the row next to me, like always. He says, 'Say I give Sarah here a box of chocolates. Is that just a simple, delicious gift? Or is there more to it? What do you think?'

Nessa boots me under the table and I burn.

'Sarah?'

'I don't know.' I know it's rude not to say his name but I cannot say his name.

'Do you like chocolate, Sarah?'

'Yeah, I love chocolate.'

Nessa laughs. 'You love chocolate – why don't you marry it then?'

He laughs and the whole class laughs and my face is hot-hot.

He says, 'What I'm talking about here is subtext, whether there's more to something than what's on the surface. It's about an underlying theme.'

Kindness.

Love.

Chocolate.

'Now,' he says, and he goes back behind the desk. 'Act two scene three.' As everyone's finding the page I look at him and smile in that way where I make myself have dimples and I think I will never get bored of this man looking at me, never, not even if I live to be 103.

'Any takers for the cast today? Vanessa, do you want to take Viola?'

She's not happy with that – she likes being Sir Toby Belch but he's not in this scene.

'Sarah, Orsino?'

He makes a point of giving me and Nessa a part as often as he can without being obvious.

I open my copy of *Twelfth Night* and start to read.

'Give me some music now good morrow friends.'

Morrow!

Then I see some words coming up and I know why he gave me this part and I think oh god Sarah don't shake don't shake hold your book hard and tight.

Nessa – who's a girl pretending to be a bloke – says, 'About your years, my lord.'

And I say, 'Too old by heaven let still the woman take an elder than herself so wears she to him so sways she level in her husband's heart for boy however we do praise ourselves our fancies are more giddy and unfirm more longing wavering sooner lost and worn than women's are.'

I can't look at him. I look down at the page but I burn with fire inside.

When we've finished the scene I keep my eyes on my pencil case and my pens and pencils and the pencil sharpener and the bits of sharpenings and the rubber (not that kind – you've got a filthy mind!) and the compass and the protractor and the set square. I look up eventually and he looks at me for another lifetime.

After class Nessa says, 'God it's painful watching you mooning over him all lesson.'

Mooning – I like that a lot. 'But it's two-way,' I tell her, 'it's mutual mooning.'

She makes a face. So what. I love him and he loves me and people are just going to have to deal with it. It's absolutely love. Why else would I think of him always and do everything I can to see him? I know he's for me. It's strange because I've never felt this way before, not properly. I usually say, 'Oh he's fit,' but I never really mean it. I think about what it will be like when we are married and have children and sometimes I sit for hours imagining our home, walking from room to room, making it as I go. I'm not obsessed, just lovelorn. But there's not long to wait now – especially not when you consider how long we've already waited.

'What you doing after school?' Nessa says. 'I'm going to Matt's – wanna come?'

She does this at least once a week – catches the 96 to Oldham and sits outside his house with a load of other girls, picking at the wall. I used to go with her but now I find it a bit boring, though I'd never tell her that. One time we even met Matt up there, I have a photo to prove it, and we got him to sign a few things we had loose in our pockets. We'd helped his mum carry her shopping in out of a taxi, which was great because we got to see some of what he eats.

'The classy way round,' Nessa whispered, 'rather than rooting in his bins like some of those sad bitches do.' His mum, Mary – which Nessa says is right because she is the Mother of God – well, she told us his brother Leo was at the local cricket ground so we went to find him, thinking he'd do that day. But when we got there, Matt was there. He was wearing a Heinz Baked Beans hat. I thought it was pretty stupid but Nessa loved it. We were buzzing. He was . . . Well, it was hard to understand his face exactly. He just kept saying, how did you find me how did you find me, and we said, it was your mum! But we were actually looking for your brother. He posed for some pictures and Nessa said she could feel their closeness even from just that. We asked if we could stay and watch them play cricket but he said we couldn't because of insurance reasons or something, but to be honest we'd had enough for the day and we smoked cigarettes and went over and over it on the bus all the way home.

Anyway I've got to start packing tonight, got to start going through all my old stuff and throw a load of silly babyish things away. Pack a bag and keep it under my bed next to the shoebox. I can't tell Nessa about it though, not until the beginning of next week. It's too risky and anyway I've promised.

'I'm revising,' I say. 'I'm behind.'

She rolls her eyes. 'Don't bother revising for English – he'll give you an A* whatever.'

'Shut up.'

'We've got next Friday out together anyway. Gonna be big.'

'Yeah,' I say, 'about that . . .'

She looks angry then and I hate making Nessa angry. 'What?'

'I can't come any more.'

'But we've got tickets. I got up at five to queue for them.'

'You'll have to sell mine to a tout and I need you to say I'm with you if my mum rings in the morning.'

'What? Where you going?'

'I can't tell you yet. I'll tell you next week.'

'This is about him, isn't it?' She nods in the direction of the door.

I look around. I don't want anyone else to have heard but people are just packing up and chatting. She's smart, Nessa. She only needs a few clues and she's off, like Jessica Fletcher.

'I can't tell you until next week but I'll tell you then and—'

'Forget it.' She gets up, grabs her bag and storms out the door.

'Nessa!'

She'll come round. She'll have to, or she won't get to be a bridesmaid.

I look down. Everything in my pencil case is having sex.

I stand up. 'Wait up, Nessa,' I say. 'Wait a sec, I'm coming after all.'

Might as well – Mr Keaveney has band practice on a Tuesday and I don't want to go home.

*   *   *

We smoke Consulate Menthols on the top deck. When we get close to Matt's, Nessa gets antsy and smokes faster and says she wishes she had a cider or a Hooch or something to take the edge off. Matt lives in a terraced house – well obviously he doesn't any more because he's always away on tour or in the recording studio – but his mum still lives there. Outside his house there's a load of girls hanging around the wall as usual. They just like to be close to some part of him, I suppose, even if that part is a brick wall. Nessa has a piece of mortar from the wall about half an inch long in her purse that she had to chip out discreetly over about two hours because his mum kept coming out and telling people off. They took soil from the front garden for a while too and she doesn't bother planting flowers any more because they'd have no chance. His mum recognises Nessa now and lets onto her and Nessa sees this as progress. I can't know

Mr Keaveney's mum now because she's dead, but I've seen his dad a few times and it's only a matter of time before that particular introduction.

At Matt's house Nessa stares up at the small front bedroom window that she has deduced is his room. She whispers to me, 'None of the others know that's his. They all think his room's round the back because that's what Mary's told them to stop them shouting up.'

But Nessa threw a pebble up once and he peeked out fast then ducked back again. Nessa says it looked like he was lying down, which means his bed must be along the radiator under the window just like hers is in her room, but it's all academic at the moment because we know for a fact he's in Japan. We stand around for half an hour or so smoking our Consulate Menthols and scoping out the scene. Nessa's main concern is that none of the other girls are as pretty as her, which they aren't although one girl has got a good pair of real purple Docs and I hear Nessa hiss when she sees them because that's what he said his favourite shoes were in an interview except they're really expensive. I'm bored now so I say to Nessa, 'I'm going home for my tea,' and she says, 'Ring you later – I won't be long after you,' but I know she'll try to be the last here after all the others have gone, because somehow that means something.

I get back on the bus but I don't go for my tea. Course I don't! I go to Mr Keaveney's house for a bit even though it's not really on the way. His dad's campervan is such an eyesore and the neighbours have complained. I stand eating crisps behind the hedge and I peek up at the windows. A cat comes along the wall. I always greet cats because they are actually people.

Then it starts to get dark and I've got no money to buy anything else, so I decide to go home. I make little deals with myself along the way to make the time pass even faster – I've been doing the zones so long now I'm even bored of those, I suppose. I tell myself if I get to a certain lamppost in a certain number of breaths then we'll definitely have sex next Friday, for definite.

I get to the lamppost and rejoice.

When I get in, Mum's asleep on the sofa – must have had a good session – so I go straight up to my room with another bag of crisps.

God, I can't wait to get away from this wallpaper most of all. It's snide Laura Ashley, little white flowers on a blue background, and I've covered as much as I can with posters of topless men but stupid little flowers still poke through in between and all over. I hate this whole room in fact. That rock-hard bedding box full of Mum's shoes. All these Body Shop baskets covered in dusty cellophane. I don't know what to tell you except people keep buying me them! The only things I like are the things I've got from the Corn Exchange like the buddhas and some of my jewellery and clothes and the Shakespeare book because that's our thing and that's how he gave me his phone number.

My mum shouts up the stairs, 'Saaaaaarah! How was your daaay?'

My heart sinks because now I have to leave my room and go and say goodnight or she'll come in here and won't leave. I remind myself again and again that it's not for much longer and soon it'll be just me and Mr Keaveney round the table in the evening, eating a dinner of pasta with homemade sauce and talking about our days. There will be two cats, one dog, a baby on the way and cans of Coke in the fridge not bottles in the cupboard. I can endure a few more times of sitting down there and her asking me how my revision is going and telling me Nessa is a bad influence and why don't I make other friends. I can endure all this because Mr Keaveney and I have an actual real-life plan, which is to run away together – and I know that sounds mad but hear me out.

This is it, what we're doing: I'm going to meet him at a pub in town next Friday and we're going to run away to Scotland and stay away until August and then we're going to come back and make it official.

'Shall we order a pizza?' my mum shouts. 'Let's order a pizza – how about a deep-pan Hawaiian with some pots of that garlic and herb sauce you like?'

I say okay because that actually sounds quite good. I love pizza. I either love things or I hate things – it's purer that way.

I take some paper and a pen and a magazine down with me and I do the name test again, this time with our middle names, while we're waiting for the pizza to arrive. The name test works out your compatibility based on the letters in your names – ours comes back as 60 per cent, which can't be right. It my name's fault, has to be. I mean, it starts out all right: Sarah. Like the girl in *Labyrinth*. Then . . . Hudson. Splat! Travel from fairy tale to Lancashire in two seconds flat. I'll take Mr Keaveney's name when we're married, not because of all that honour and obey shit but just because it's a better name.

Then fifty years later I'll have white hair because that's how gingers go and I'll be dressed like one of those women you see admiring their own reflection in the fancy shop windows on Deansgate. I'll know everything about the world and I will be formidable in the extreme. I'll have taken our six grandchildren, and Juliette's grandchildren too – the more the merrier! – out for lunch somewhere posh like Debenhams and they'll have chosen what they want from the counters, including pudding. Their trays will be laden. One of the children, the youngest – the one I love the most because she's naughty and clever – will pipe up, 'Tell us how you met Grandad, Grandma!' And I'll roll my eyes like I mind when I don't really and I'll put my cutlery down and say, 'You can't possibly want to hear this story again,' and they will all shout, 'WE DO, WE DO!' And so I will say, 'Oh all right all right, settle down then. This is how it happened, my dears. This is how love breaks in and blows your world apart.'

'Will you put that away and watch the TV,' says my mum because she's obviously in the mood for having a go.

'Okay.' I say, but I keep sneaking a doodle.

'PUT THE CLUCKING PEN AND PAPER AWAY,' she says and grabs the pad of paper and throws it across the room. She's drunk as a skunk. I want to laugh but then I want to laugh at most things.

'Constant aggravation,' she says. 'You are constant aggravation.'

I look at the cover of the magazine.

The morning after: what to do when you've gone too far.

Twenty golden party looks.

'I think my mum's boyfriend fancies me.'

The pizza arrives and we get the kitchen roll and black pepper. Mum is so grateful to the pizza delivery boy that it makes me cringe and I look at him with an *I'm sorry* look in my eyes. He laughs. She's basically falling over herself to tell him how good the pizza is and having an orgasm every time he hands her something.

'We love your pizzas,' she says, 'they're *so tasty*. And a free garlic bread! A free garlic bread, Sarah! Would you look at that.'

I'm looking at it and I'm like yeeeeah it's just a garlic bread, don't cream your pants. You should see her open a present. You'd think she'd never opened a present before. Christmas is exhausting. She says I've got a dangerous imagination and sometimes she can tell I'm just not there. I suppose half the time I'm pretending to be somewhere I'm not but this makes me happier the other half of the time and closer to the person I want to be, so what's the problem with that? I only think there's a problem if you end up pretending to be someone you don't want to be. Otherwise it's just self-improvement and that's healthy and human.

I wolf down my pizza then go up to my room again. I just like being up there with my imagination. It feels so real. Oh, Mr Keaveney. Teacher of English, lover of poetry, devourer of Werther's Originals, driver of a silver Peugeot that he parks near the exit of the car park so he can get out quickly to get home to his dad who's sick and who he looks after. The Peugeot is his dad's, he just drives it. I was relieved when I found that out. He sleeps in the spare room, in a single bed, like a child – or so the rumours say. When he and I have a bedroom together we'll curl round each other like two pieces that fit perfectly, like otters in the nest, like the yin–yang sign Juliette did on my army surplus rucksack in Tipp-Ex and black marker. I'm a bit taller than him but that doesn't mean that it won't work in bed. When you're lying down you can just budge down, can't you? Juliette comes and gets in my bed at 9 p.m. and she says she has a secret she needs to tell me, but I say I don't want to know it. She is really hurt at that.

I wonder whether she knows about my secrets, the good one and the bad one? The bad one being the bus wanker. And whether this is her way of trying to wheedle the information out of me. I want to tell her, I do, but I can't find the words. I just need more time to pass, to focus on the future, not the past. It wasn't like I was hurt. I wasn't at all. He was quite fit when his mouth was closed. He had okay hair. No one saw. I will stop thinking about it. I can make myself do things and think things when I want to. I have that power.

THE QUIZ!

IS IT JUST A FLING, OR MORE?

1. What did he do after your first kiss?
    a) Was sort of awkward and lingered for a while
        before leaving ✓
    b) Said he had remembered a dentist's appointment
        and had to leave
    c) Stuck around and asked you to watch another movie

2. What happens when you see each other in school?
    a) He will say hi in passing, but he won't stop to talk ✓
    b) He gives you the head nod
    c) He says hi and chats with you by your locker ✓

3. What did he do for your birthday?
    a) Asked if you wanted to 'celebrate' later
    b) Made you an awful, but cute, card
    c) He forgot ✗

4. When he kisses you, he
    a) Pulls away, smiles, then kisses you again ✓
    b) Pulls away to kiss you on your forehead
    c) Has his hands all over you

5. When you two aren't kissing, what are you doing?
    a) You're on the phone to each other
    b) Going bowling with friends or watching a movie
    c) Not speaking ✗

Tyndrum

The A82 was open and long, the stretches of land on either side swatched with brown gorse and washed-out heather. Clouds with wispy edges hurtled across the sky, like the ghosts of buffaloes. Just before the turn-off for Oban, Sarah pulled the Hymer into the forecourt of the Green Welly Stop – a small service station with a sign that had a laughing green wellington boot on it.

'Look at that dick,' said Juliette, about the boot.

Truckers and bikers in jeans and leathers congregated round the petrol pumps. Sarah braced herself. There was still the old fear. Sarah had been bullied at school for being a redhead and she still got nervous walking past groups of teenagers, or builders, or walking down the top deck of a bus towards the back. Juliette, blonde, hadn't grown up like that, was unaffected by all the gingerism of the 80s and 90s. Any time Sarah stripped naked she used ferocity as a coping mechanism. It was fine, although men sometimes didn't know how to respond when she instantly got on top; they flipped her around, she flipped them back – sometimes sex was like a ludicrous roly-poly, rather than a pleasure. But it was her nature. To win. To fight. To be extremely loyal. To bear a grudge for a million years. Sarah was the first in her family to go to university, and she would not fail. She got out of the van confidently — *Look at me, just your regular lady trucker* — but she couldn't find the petrol cap (mortification) and when she did find it (why had she not committed this to memory, done a practice run, even) she could not figure out how to remove it. Was this the green welly's revenge, for Juliette's comment? *Yuh-huh, now who's the dick, babe?* She tried various ways, wiggling the key around, becoming gradually more embarrassed and flustered, feeling the amused looks gusting around her, feeling Juliette peering over the lip of the window, ashamed, until a Forestry Commission truck pulled up and she had to capitulate and ask the ranger to assist. He was moderately attractive, which made it worse. 'Thanks,' Sarah said, blushing. This was as bad as when the IT guy at work had helped her connect her headphones. He was literally two years younger than her, and he'd patted her arm when he'd done it like she was a fucking granny.

'My pleasure,' said this hero. 'Easily done. When I first got this thing I parked on the wrong side in petrol stations for months and had to stretch the hose over the roof.' 'Oh, you're just trying to make me feel better.'

'Is it working?'

Was he . . . ? Was he *flirting*? Sarah swallowed cold saliva. What was it with her and the fifty-plus-ers? She smiled, lips pulled in, little nod at the end. Brisk. She was a masochist, but she wasn't a fucking masochist, as George Clooney had almost said in *From Dusk till Dawn*. The ranger removed the cap in one magic twist — FUCK THE PATRIARCHY! — and Sarah sheepishly filled the tank. A flashback to being stopped by the police when Samuel was driving too slowly, towing the caravan along a mountain pass somewhere in Wales. The shame of being pulled over and sitting on the roadside as people passed, peering at them. Samuel and Deanna out front, giving the officers both barrels; Juliette sobbing hotly in the back; Sarah staring at the empty sky, fucking fuming. Boomers, millennials and X-ers captured in one single tragic tableau.

When the tank was full, Sarah glanced at Juliette – who had saucer eyes now, *morto* – and hurried inside the shop to pay. She bought some new sunglasses – red plastic, the frames shaped like love hearts.

The shop had a little collection of single malts behind the counter. Sarah was captivated. The woman working there noticed. 'You know there's a whole whisky shop back there? All the names. Just next to the café.'

Sarah nodded thanks and went back to the van. 'Fancy getting a few bits from the Green Welly?'

Juliette nodded. 'Is there food? I could do a soup. Nice sunglasses.'

There was food, and there was soup: 'Cullen skink' – made of cream, potatoes and smoked haddock. Sarah didn't like the look of it, but Juliette gobbled it up. Sarah took a run at a colossal jacket potato with a mountain of coleslaw and cheese. As she ate, she watched a couple in the queue arguing about the size of the jacket potatoes they'd been given. One server was giving out bigger portions than the other. She had served Sarah but had since gone on her break. The new woman was stingy, giving small plates, and they were all shouting at each other.

Two pensioners on mobility scooters looked on, brazenly, mere feet away.

'What's going on?' Juliette asked.

'There's a new server giving out smaller portions than her predecessor,' Sarah explained.

'Yours is obscene.'

'You need it in the mountains. But they saw mine and I think they have an issue with fairness. Really it's about justice. Potato justice.'

'No one I know eats potatoes any more.'

'Oh, fuck them.'

'Carbs are a personal choice.'

Ignoring her, Sarah said: 'They shouldn't be shouting at the new woman. The disruptor is the one giving the huge portions. She's disrupting the system whilst making herself popular with the customers. She's a genius!'

Juliette laughed, soup spraying from her nostrils.

'Look, I can't eat any more of this giant potato.'

When they'd finished eating, Juliette and Sarah went over to the shop. So much jam, so much tartan, so much shortbread — were they in the Highlands, were they? In the far back corner, caged off seductively, was a whisky shop, featuring hundreds of whiskies. They glinted at Sarah. She approached like a child at Christmas.

'Put them in your purse.' Juliette was behind her. *Home Alone*. Uncle Frank to his wife about the crystal cruet set on the plane. 'PUT THEM IN YOUR PURSE.' Sarah and Juliette had communicated via film quotes since they could talk. During their childhood, sometimes it had seemed like there were months when they communicated no other way but through quotes from *Home Alone*, *Beaches*, *Jaws*, *The Craft*, *Clueless* and all the corny classics of the 80s and 90s. *Pretty Woman*. *Forrest Gump*. *The Addams Family*.

Sarah's relationship with alcohol was in flux. Yesterday's bottle of wine had reminded her of that fact. Maybe it always had been, but now she felt the push-pull of its involvement in her everyday life almost hourly. Too often it left her damaged for days. Too often it was the gateway to drugs: a cheeky bag of coke — that was all right, wasn't it? Wasn't it? But it was happening more and more often. It was the longest, most romantic relationship of her life: her and alcohol. But it was going stale. She was terrified of what that might mean. Her therapist had told her to experiment with not drinking at parties. To let other things rush in to fill her clamouring brain: other people's opinions, the simple need to go home; silence, even. (Sarah was so afraid of silence when she was around other people.) Sometimes Sarah thought she just had to simply 'relearn' how to drink alcohol. Like she was back at school. Surely she could educate herself to savour and enjoy just two to three glasses. The two-drink high was the best thing anyway; it never got any better than that. But then Sarah would have a night where she drank two bottles, smashed a gram and was merrily chatting to celebrities on social media and she'd think, there is literally nowhere I'd rather be. And that's the danger of living in a world of constant comparisons, of gauges and references. The grass is always greener. And if it isn't, change the filter. Ah, that's better. Feeling worried and inadequate again? *Bon. Bon.*

Sarah bought a bottle of Highland Park while Juliette was in the loo. As they got in the van, Sarah stashed it under her seat. This was her thrill, doing things in secret. It had worried her, sometimes. The way she preferred taking drugs when no one else knew – better yet, when they disapproved. The forbidden aspect was as exciting as the intoxicating aspect. Did this make her a bog-standard rebel?

Continuing on the A82 north, they listened to Yusuf – Cat Stevens as was: 'Can't Keep It In'. Their dad always played Cat Stevens on road trips. Suzanne Vega. Bob Dylan. Billie Holiday. The road ribboned around a forest and there were bridges and youth hostels, bushes and bunkhouses. Thin red and silver poles, snow-markers, spiked the embankments. Warning signs depicting running stags. Roadkill reared up: pheasants, foxes and one time, horribly, a badger. Every one of them was full of raw mince. Sarah hoped nothing ran out in front of the van. She'd run over a squirrel once, driving past Southern Cemetery. The wet thud of bones on the undercarriage was a too-tactile memory, still.

The landscape became harder, paler. Sarah became briefly obsessed with a woman cycling next to the cab. She could have a future with a woman, if a future with anyone was an option.

As they saw the first sign for Glen Nevis, a car going in the opposite direction flashed its lights at them.

'Why did they do that?' asked Juliette.

'I don't know,' Sarah replied, her adrenaline up. Were they going to come back and chase them, catch them? (God that film, *Duel*. God. Why did people make films like that?) Did men ever have that immediate thought when another driver flashed them? (When they got in a taxi? Walked across a park?) Probably not. 'Maybe there's a police speed trap,' she said, optimistically. She worried then that there might be something wrong with the van (more horrors, this time mixed with urban myths: a man poised behind her seat holding cheese wire . . .) Should she pull over? Then a little further ahead, she saw a tree had fallen and was lying halfway across the road. She slowed down, drove carefully around the tree and onwards, picking up speed again, willing someone else to come along in the opposite direction so she could flash them and let them know about the fallen tree. After a minute, result: A CAR. 'Flash them, flash them!' said Juliette, sharing the social responsibility joy. Sarah flashed the lights several times and the other driver raised a palm to acknowledge the warning. 'Tree!' shouted Juliette, doing strange charades. 'TREE!' It felt good, and important, and right, like the right thing. They looked at each other, breathless. Like they'd saved the fucking world.

Juliette checked her face in the mirror. Applied foundation.

'What's the occasion?' Sarah quipped, glad Juliette was making an effort – it held promise for the night. There was a bar at Glen Nevis – she'd googled it, part of her planning. Maybe they could just get wasted together and talk freely. The years would disappear. The healing would begin. She could get to the bottom of those bruises. The bottom of everything.

'How many years have you and Johnnie been married now?' Sarah asked. Groundwork, that's what this was.

'Nine,' said Juliette.

'Impressive.'

Juliette looked at Sarah, wary. 'I'm in a soul contract with him,' she said. 'It's not even love any more.'

Sarah heard the tough talk but she saw it in her sister's eyes. The fear. Sarah had seen it happen with several friends recently. They'd almost split up, they were at the door, there was no sex, no love, no point any more, and then something scary would happen – a parent got ill, a person got made redundant, a pandemic hit – and they'd fly back together. Sarah had always believed it: love does not advance by weddings; love advances by funerals. Fear and death. Those were the things that kept people together. Fuck love. Love was for teenagers.

'You'll never marry, will you?' Juliette said. 'You disapprove, don't you?'

'What? I have six marriages already.' Juliette waited for the punchline. 'Eden, Katie, Alison, Sally, Ginny . . . You . . .'

Juliette sniffed. 'Right on.'

'It's true. My closest friends are my partners in life. I share a deep, complex love and commitment with each of them. Long-term friendship is a marriage. They all drive me mad in different ways. And we don't have the same conflict because we let each other grow – it's not a land grab like it is in marriage.'

'SARAH!!!'

Sarah looked ahead, screeched the Hymer to a halt.

It was roadkill, in the middle of the road. Except this was big. Proximity revealed hooves, haunches; a pied, tufted backside. It was a deer, its back end half torn off. It was still moving, just slightly, its head lifting and dropping, its chest heaving. Sarah couldn't believe no one else had stopped. But the roads were quiet and the light was fading.

The light was fading.

She looked ahead, saw a caravan swing around a corner and disappear. She looked back at the deer. She looked at the steering wheel. I'll just drive on, she thought, I must.

'It's alive!' said Juliette.

That was it. They were stuck now.

Sarah pulled up the handbrake and shifted the gears into neutral. They both gingerly got out of the van and walked along the road, their legs jelly, towards the animal.

The deer was in a bad way. One of its back legs moved in a confused spasm. The other leg was almost fully detached. There was a lot of blood on the road, gathering in thick, sticky pools. It was strange being so close to a wild animal. Sarah sensed something wrong in the grand scheme of things. The deer's glassy black eyes flickered. Pain, she felt it.

'Shall we call a vet?' said Juliette. 'The RSPCA?'

Sarah shook her head. 'I don't think so.'

'What then?' Juliette looked desperate.

The deer moved its front legs – it felt an instinct to get away from them, still.

'I don't know!'

'Run over it! You have to!'

'NO! I can't do that. That's . . . horrific.'

Juliette looked at Sarah and, without another word, walked round to the side door of the Hymer, opened it, and climbed inside. Sarah, transfixed by the deer, said, 'I'll deal with it,' without really knowing how.

Juliette emerged from the van holding the table pole in both hands. Sarah watched her, confused at first, then—

'What are— Juliette . . . ? Juliette, what are you doing?'

Juliette didn't reply or look at Sarah. She walked straight up to the deer, gripping the long metal pole, and struck it on the head, one time, two times, very firmly. Its skull cracked open and its tongue rolled out. It twitched violently for a few seconds. Juliette stood back so that its blood didn't spray on her boots. Then its front legs stretched out to full length, its chest stopped moving, and it was still.

Sarah couldn't speak. Ontological vertigo – she was suddenly alone, watching this stranger masquerading as her sister coolly wipe blood from a metal pole on the grass by the side of the road. What was happening?

Who was the person standing in front of her? Juliette had a look in her eye – the thousand-yard stare of a war veteran, doing a job that needed to be done. Sarah felt freaked to her very core. This wasn't the way it should be. Sarah should be the one with the pole. She should be the one defending them. Doing the life and death stuff.

Juliette tried to move the deer, not ungently, with the table pole, into the ditch by the side of the road. She struggled. She didn't look at Sarah for help, but Sarah felt her unspoken cry. The Heart Alarm going off. She went and took the deer's back end. She was the back-end girl. She thought, compulsively, of the back half of the donkey in the Christmas nativity, 1994.

When it was done, Juliette took the pole back into the van and emerged with a simple: 'Shall we go?'

Sarah got back into the driver's seat. She turned the key in the ignition. The music started up again. Yusuf/Cat Stevens: 'Oh Very Young'.

Sarah looked over at Juliette. Her eyes were closed.

Sarah said: 'You didn't even used to be able to watch *Watership Down*. You had a shrine to otters in your bedroom. You were the first vegetarian I knew. You fast-forwarded the start of *The Lion King* every time until after Mufasa died . . .'

Sarah could have gone on.

Juliette took out her vape and put it between her lips. When she spoke, it was in her most wry and sardonic voice, Sarah's secret favourite of Juliette's voices. 'Happy birthday to meeee.'

Sarah found herself doing her breathing.

'What are you doing?' Juliette asked.

'Wim Hof?'

'Sounds like labour breaths.'

'He's a Danish guy. It's good for stress.'

'Is he hot?'

Who ARE you? 'Another good way to calm down is to move saliva around your mouth.'

'Does it have to be your own saliva or does any saliva work?'

'I think it has to be your own, Juliette.'

* * *

They arrived at the next campsite, higher, colder, in the shadow of mountains. Sarah parked the van over the grid and emptied out the grey water, the used water from the sinks and shower. The chalky river flowed into the grate. She hadn't told Juliette but she'd forgotten to empty it at the last place before they left – a rookie error – and then she'd remembered as they were driving, feeling the water sloshing in its deep murky tank in the bowels of the vehicle. Sarah felt closer to the van, physically. There was nothing worse than needing the toilet on a long journey.

Sarah had always wanted to be Louise, because Susan Sarandon was cooler, but she feared she was definitely Thelma. Juliette was Louise. Telling Thelma that *she'd always been crazy, this was just the first time she'd had to express herself*.

Because Sarah made jokes when she should have made scenes. After anything awful, Sarah completed the circle in her head, instantly making it fine. Pitching her fineness to herself – how twisted was that? She said it over and over to herself: I will stop thinking about this. I will stop thinking about this. It was like the way she'd trained herself to change her handwriting every September. Or cultivated a twitch, just to annoy her mother. In time, it faded. Things, other experiences, overtook it.

But sometimes you couldn't complete the circle. Sometimes it was better not to.

That man from the bus when she was fifteen, the worst year of her life. She had seen a man who looked like him, on TV, when she was in her mid-thirties. He was the right age, same teeth and hair. He was the head of a new garden in Manchester and he was telling the interviewer on the gardening programme about landscape design. Juliette had been to the garden with their parents. Sarah thought of the Smog song, 'Cold-Blooded Old Times'. We were all lizards before we were apes. Maybe they met him, not knowing how he had changed Sarah. Maybe they shook his hand.

I take in

A Findus Crispy Pancake, like half a frisbee. Mum's asleep again after her Mateus. Juliette's at the desk by the window that looks out to the motorway, same as mine. She's doing her homework. I put the plate down and then I turn around and I'm glad I've put the plate down because if I hadn't I'd have definitely dropped it. You'll never guess what the little wassock's gone and done. Only turned her otter table into a table of 4Princes — and more specifically, Matt Daubney.

'Juliette! What you playing at?'

She doesn't turn around, doesn't have to. Knows exactly what I'm talking about. Which tells me she knows how bad this is, too.

'Thought it was time for an update,' she says.

'Fine, otters are pretty babyish, agreed, but you didn't have to go in this direction. There's so many options. Think again. Pick a band that's for kids like you. Hanson.'

'Loads of people in my class like 4Princes.'

'They're being precocious.'

'You used to like The Beatles.'

'Look, Juliette, you are absolute dead meat if Nessa sees this. I can't even admit I've seen it. She'll go nuclear. She's due round in fifteen minutes so this needs to be gone.'

'I like him. Nessa doesn't own him. She's only met him once. You and Nessa don't own the world. It's a free country.'

'I'm just so confused. Where has this come from? *You* don't even know him. It's all so sudden. You haven't put any of the work in and you've jumped straight to a . . . table. An entire table of him.'

'Are you a lesbian?'

'What?'

'Why don't you like anyone from a band. I find it weird.'

'Stop changing the subject.'

'It's fine if you're a lesbian. I won't tell Mum.'

'Destroy this. You've got fifteen minutes.'

She doesn't answer. The doorbell rings. Both our eyes go wide. Nessa is early.

'Oh my god. I'll get her away from here.'

I run down the stairs and open the door. Nessa's there with a bag of my clothes she borrowed. She's got a small packet in her hand.

'Wotcha.'

'All right.'

'What's up with you?'

'Nothing. Let's go to the shop.'

'Wait, I'll just run this up to your sister.'

'No, I'll take it for her.'

'I have to put it in her hand.'

Nessa won't be stopped: she dives into the house and goes right up the stairs.

'JULIETTE!' I scream. 'NESSA'S GOT SOMETHING FOR YOU.'

Shit shit shit shit shit.

I run after Nessa as fast as I can, which is easy with my long legs, and I get to Juliette's door at the same time.

'She just got out the shower,' I say, grabbing a towel off the bannister. 'Hang back.' I'm so good at lying sometimes I amaze myself. I could be a spy.

I open the door a crack and throw the towel over the table. 'JULIETTE,' I say, 'NESSA IS HERE.'

Juliette hasn't moved from her desk. She looks at me, the table, the towel. She nods.

Nessa goes in. 'Is the coast clear? I've seen tits before. Got some even. Oh, you're dressed.'

Nessa hands Juliette a baggie.

'What?' I intercept.

'It's just weed.'

'She's too young!'

'She's not! We had it way before that.'

'It's for a house party,' says Juliette. 'I'll give most of it away, but I think it'll make me seem like I know what's what. You know.'

'I do know,' says Nessa. 'Smart cookie, this one.'

I'm not sure how I feel about Juliette having drugs. What a day. It's one bomb after another. At least I have a constant in my life. Him.

*   *   *

Later that night, I'm hanging out the window of my room, smoking. I don't normally smoke in my room but I'm stressed out with all this stuff all over the floor. I can't believe I have all this after only nearly sixteen years on planet Earth. I was planning on taking one bag but I suppose now it'll have to be two. As for the rest of the stuff, it'll have to stay here until August. It's mostly diaries and journals and silly quizzes, god knows why I've kept it! I'm going to have to fill some bin bags and put them in next door's bin or something. I'm pretty sure Mum will want to have a part in the wedding, so we're going to have to find a way of sorting that even though we'll be up in Scotland. I suppose she can get on a train and Mr Keaveney – Danny! I need to start calling him Danny – can get her from the station in his silver Peugeot 206. I held his hand in that Peugeot 206 last December.

It was the first time we properly touched, after all the looks and words and signs. It was the anniversary of his mum's death. She had cancer, ten years ago. I'd known he wasn't right all morning and something was up so at lunch I followed him out to his car. He got in and started crying in the driver's seat. I rapped on the passenger window and he let me in. His car was warm and smelled like Christmas with some apple cinnamon air-freshener thing hanging from the mirror. I asked him what was wrong and he told me and I reached over the handbrake and took hold of his hand and squeezed and he squeezed mine back. The windows misted up and we sat there, we were holding hands for ages, like eight minutes, until Miss Kendall rapped on the window and asked what was going on. She's all right – she's a geography teacher who looks like a fitness instructor; I can see her in top-to-toe Lycra, if you know what I mean. Someone tried to tell me she and Mr Keaveney were going out but I know it's just a vicious rumour. Sophie, Mr Keaveney said – because that's Miss Kendall's first name – and he took his hand out of mine and got out of the car and walked round to her side and told her about his mum. She said how sorry she was and hugged him but she was staring at me over his shoulder as I walked away and it was like at the end of an episode of a soap where you know the character isn't really feeling what they're doing.

I wonder whether to get in bed and have a think-wank. Sometimes I think about Mr Keaveney and I make it so that I am him, fucking me, and I'm the one on top, thrusting.

There was one before Mr Keaveney – Hartley Boon. He was a car mechanic with dumbbells in his room. Sixteen years old. I was so in love with him that I used to save the labels off Hartley's jam jars and stick them up inside my locker. I was a kid and I can see that now. We went out for three weeks and when he rang up to end it with me it was a Friday night and I was halfway through a Chinese takeaway and I couldn't finish it. He said it was because we didn't gel but I knew it was really because he was scared of getting in trouble. Jailbait was what his friends probably said. Also I think I'm not so great at tests and I felt like we were still in the testing period and I wasn't at my best. It'll be like my driving test – I know I will be able to drive but I might bottle it during the test and that won't be fair. It doesn't seem fair to be judged when you're not relaxed because that's not the normal you. After Hartley finished with me, my mum asked what was wrong and I couldn't tell her out of a weird kind of shame. I felt like she'd lose respect for me or something. My own mother! Weird but true. I hung around his parents' pub for a few months after, wanting to make him see me and regret it. When I saw him kissing someone else in a fur coat I went and put a brick through a bus shelter. I had no idea he would go for a girl in a fur coat. It was horrific.

I put my ciggie out in the sweet tin I use as an ashtray. I don't inhale properly Nessa says and you can tell I'm not a proper smoker by the way I hold my cigarette. Apparently you should hold it between your first two fingers and let your fingers curl slightly so you look casual. I hold mine with my finger and my thumb and she reckons it looks too stiff so I guess that's something to work on. I hate this bedroom now, it feels so small and silly. Eight days to go. Just over a week. That's all. We're meeting in Danny's (oh it sounds too weird! I'm blushing here!) favourite pub. He first told me about it after a lesson on Sir Walter Scott, in January. We'd been looking at an extract from his novel *Peveril of the Peak*. After the lesson I asked him why he'd picked it.

I said, 'I didn't think it was all that good, sir.'

He looked at me, stopped putting his papers into his case. 'You've read the whole thing?'

'Yes, I found the book and read it.'

I looked at his hands, the hands I knew so well by that point, that had been close to me, been on me, but I still stopped the safe distance away. There were a few others in there, packing up.

'You're not the first to think that,' he said. 'It's generally acknowledged as one of his weaker works. I think there's something fun about it, though. I thought it'd make you laugh. And Scott brings together Romanticism and the Enlightenment like no one else.'

It was one of those things people said to impress other people and it didn't mean much.

I said, 'Yeah, it was all right. It just felt a bit repressed.'

He smirked. Grinned. Looked to the others in the room, taking their time to leave. I saw his neck go red. Two can play at that game. He went back to his papers.

'It's also the name of my favourite pub in Manchester city centre,' he said, 'so maybe that's why I like it. Simple word association. But then what are books for except to create overwhelming subjective reactions? That's why people fall in love with things. Because they speak to something unspoken, inside.'

He looked away quickly again, and I stared at him, and as I stared at him I thought, every single night, every single night I'm going to kiss you for the simple reason that you say things like that. Every Friday he goes to the Peveril and plays a little gig in the pub with a few mates – they're in a band. He plays the bass. Then he gets a kebab on the way back home. I can understand why he'd rather go and drink in the big city because there's so much more chance of something interesting happening there and you don't have people watching you like hawks and feeling like they know you.

Nessa can't keep her mouth shut ever though, so she was all, 'Pub, who wants to go to a pub, they smell like old men and dogs and they're full of pervs, you know that much from walking past 'em.'

He looked at the girls leaving the room. One of them looked at me, then him, then me. I said, 'Take a picture, it'll last longer.'

He straightened up. 'You shouldn't know what pubs are like at your age.'

Nessa said, 'We go to pubs, sir, and we go clubbing too.'

'Do you now?'

'Yeah, has she not told you?'

I glared at Nessa. I didn't want him thinking I go round town looking for other men. I really hope he doesn't——

'Yeah one time last year Sarah got naked and streaked across Piccadilly Gardens!'

I glared at her but it was too late. She was on a fucking roll.

'Yeah, we couldn't find her inside the club and then my cousin said she'd seen her outside, getting naked under Queen Victoria!'

I burn, wholeheartedly.

'I don't think you should really be——'

'But it's true! Hahahahaha! She was running round screaming, "I'M HERE, BRIGHT LIGHTS, TAKE ME!"'

'I only did it because I was bored and drunk,' I said.

He's laughing but he's also trying to picture it, then not picture it, then picture it, then not picture it, I can tell. It makes me burn less. I feel my face cool.

'Come on, Sarah, we're gonna miss the bus.' Nessa walks to the door. 'Matt's off to Oz tomorrow so it's the last time I'll see him for a while and I want to pick up some freesias for his mum.

'My future mother-in-law,' she explains.

He looks confused then shakes his head. His eyes are the brightest.

'Well, have fun, ladies. Don't let her lead you astray, Sarah.'

I say to Nessa when we're on the bus, 'What do you think he meant by that?'

Nessa says, 'I think he wants to put his P in your V.'

'And he called us ladies, not girls,' I said, 'did you notice? What do you think that means?'

'Mate,' Nessa says, 'not everything has to mean something.'
But she's wrong.

*　　*　　*

Later when I'm doing my homework on the bed I hear a car engine do a big gurgle and then Nessa's brother Lee's red SEAT Ibiza turns the corner. It stops outside our house and Nessa looks out from the back window and waves up. There's a boy in the passenger seat and another boy in the back by the look of it. I wave back. I put on a bit of Impulse and more mascara and some mango lip balm and I'm ready – except Mum's on my case.

'Sarah, it's quarter to nine!'

'I'll be back by ten. It's just a quick spin to the park and back.'

'What about your revision?'

'I'm on top of it. All rest and no play, Mother . . .'

'Just because Nessa doesn't care about her future.'

'Miss Lawton says it doesn't matter if we end up running a fish and chip shop as long as it's the best fish and chip shop in the North.'

Listen to me, quoting Miss Lawton. Nessa will spew!

Juliette comes out and looks at me like I'm going to war. She has no idea about cars and boys. 'Go back in your room, Juliette,' Mum tells her.

Then to me, Mum says, 'I give up.'

'I'm nearly sixteen.'

'Whatever.'

Mum and Dad used to go out, once a year or so. One time the babysitter let me watch *Poltergeist* and Mum and Dad came in so we pressed pause and it paused on the bit with the man in the hat in the cave doing a big grotesque skullish smile. I stared at it while Mum and Dad staggered to the settee and sat down, wide-eyed.

'She smoked a funny cigarette,' Dad said, pointing to Mum. The babysitter laughed and started putting her Reeboks on. I never did get to see the end of that film.

*   *   *

I get in the back of Lee's car. They're playing 'I Wanna Sex You Up' by Color Me Badd.

'I love this song,' I say, even though I don't, but that's manners.

'We're having 4Princes in a minute,' says Nessa. 'This one's just to keep El Chief Saddo happy in the front.'

'Fucking *Driving Miss Daisy*, this,' says Lee. 'Constant mouth like a bird pecking my swede.'

His two friends laugh. Lee's just turned seventeen and this is his first car, his pride and joy, and he stretches his index fingers to the middle of the steering wheel as he drives. The press-studs under my body are poking into my fanny but I try to sit still. I'm glad Nessa's in the middle. I wonder whether anyone will make a ginger joke or whether they can see the colour of my hair in this light. Nessa's got some prawn cocktail crisps and she passes them round.

'They're not real prawn,' she says, 'in case you've gone vegetarian.'

I say, 'My sister's one but I'm not. She doesn't eat anything with a face.'

'Just cut its face off, then you can eat whatever you want,' says Macken, the boy in the passenger seat. They all laugh. Someone always has to be the boss in a situation and sometimes it's me and sometimes it isn't, and when it isn't I go quieter in all ways. I look out of the window. A sad song by 4Princes comes on, 'Why Can't You Be My Wife Tonight' from the new album, and I pretend to be in the video for it and make my face go all soft.

When we get to the park, Nessa says, 'I'm going over to the

putting green with Jonno — will you be all right with Lee and Macken?'

That's when I realise this has all been worked out. 'Course,' I say.

'We'll take her golf balling,' says Lee. 'And we're going to smoke some weed.'

None of this sounds like much fun. I hate sports and every time I have weed it makes me want to vom, but it's sort of exciting to be in the dark with boys, and I've got a reputation to uphold as the girl who'll do anything, remember.

Macken is staring at me and I think I remember him from a Friday night at Nessa's months ago, something about him being in the training squad for United and having his own new little house on a main road in Blackley.

'Don't worry,' Nessa whispers in my ear before she gets out, 'he's going with Lisa Bird.'

I walk to the golf course and I stay on the Lee side of Macken. It takes eighteen minutes and I start to worry about time. When we get to the golf course, Lee says, 'Let's go into the woods — that's where the yuppies don't bother to look.'

I climb through branches and over roots because I'm not scared of undergrowth. Lee is in front of me and Macken is behind me. I can see Lee's bum muscles moving in his jeans.

Then he shouts, 'Got one!' and turns and holds up a golf ball. He hands it to me. 'There you go, Sarah Bear. Present for you.'

'Thanks.'

'I like your hair.'

'Thanks, it's . . . short.'

'S'nice. Bit different. Here's another,' he adds. 'We're doing all right tonight, Sarah, you must be a lucky charm.'

'Not bad,' says Macken, leaning round me to inspect Lee's find. 'Titleist. Mint.'

We come to an open spot at the edge of the woods. 'Let's have a smoke,' says Lee.

We all sit down. Lee lights up. Macken gets it next. I take a toke and hope they don't notice I don't inhale. It tastes sickly sweet and the roach is soggy but there's no way I'm telling them that. Macken lies down on his back and lets his hand flop to one side. His fingertips land on the very very edge of my thigh. I wonder about what time it is and where Nessa is and where Macken's fingers are and what my thigh feels like to his fingers.

Macken says, 'Not as many stars as there used to be, are there?'

'You what?' I say. I talk more common round boys, especially lying down and I don't know why. Also his fingertips are. They are.

'Not as many stars as there used to be.'

'Maybe you just forgot how to count.'

Lee laughs. 'Aw, Sarah, that's well shady. It's not his fault he got no GCSEs. Don't be snidey. Be not a purveyor of snide.'

Macken takes his fingertips away and says, 'Anyway I'm gonna play for United.'

I stroke my chin. 'Reck-on.'

'I am.'

'He is.'

'Definitely more of 'em when I was a kid.' Macken sounds huffy. I feel a bit bad then.

'I'll leave you two to argue this one out. I'm going to look for more balls. Save us the end on that, Macken.'

Almost as soon as Lee is out of sound and sight, Macken puts his full hand on my waist. I stiffen. There's only a T-shirt between me and him, my Little Miss Trouble T-shirt I got from London. That was a nice day with Mum. Two go wild in Camden.

'Got a boyfriend?' Macken says.

'No, but aren't you going with Lisa Bird?'

He reaches for my hand and I wonder whether we are going to

hold hands and then he puts my hand inside his flies and I feel his penis. He tries to move my hand up and down but I think of the wanker on the bus and pull my hand out and he says, 'What's wrong?' and I say, for some mad reason — and you'll die at this — 'I want to wait.' Want to wait! Like I'm a virgin. And like I'd wait for Macken! Imagine the children. I want children like in the catalogues with Mr Keaveney and they're going to be called Nicholas and Liesl. I flex my hands slowly and I'm ready then just in case, ready to blaze and rage and burn him right down to his bones, he has no idea. But he zips up his flies and I can tell he's in even more of a huff and I try to make conversation about the constellations but he's not interested. I feel like he's gone off me without even knowing properly what he's gone off. I am a mix of feelings when Lee comes back.

'Where's Nessa?' I say quickly.

Lee raises his eyebrows at Macken and motions for him to spark up the joint, then says, 'Let's go back to the car — nothing much doing in there anyway, think we've had the best of them.' He passes me the joint and I take it and take a big puff, just because.

'Proper little weedhead, aren't you now?' says Lee, laughing.

I nod.

'She wishes,' says Macken.

Nessa is back at the car with her boy. When we're all in, I whisper, 'How could you leave me like that?'

'I had something to do. Anyway you're leaving me next Friday to go to a concert on my own and you won't tell me why when we've had this plan for ages.'

'I will tell you. Next week, I promise. I'm just scared something will go wrong if I tell you before that.'

'You should be scared something will go wrong with me if you don't.'

The boy next to her laughs.

'You should be scared I won't tell you at all.'

'Shaking in me boots, Sarah. Shaking in me boots.'

I stare out of the window and there's no way I can pretend I'm in a video now or anything.

'You're going off with him. You have been for months,' Nessa says. She's back on my case.

'Who?' says Macken.

'No one,' I say quickly. I want to tell Nessa what's happening, I really do, but the thing with plans is they're like dreams and you can't let them out too soon or they die or get lost like butterflies in winter or something else thin and not ready. Also, the plan me and Mr Keaveney have is going to shake the whole school. No one's going to get over it.

'Let's go out together this weekend,' I say. 'Royales. I'll do your hair in little knots that way you like.'

'What about your precious revision?'

She doesn't know my revision is pointless, absolutely pointless.

'I don't need to do it,' I whisper in her ear. 'Like you say, I get good marks for sexual favours. I get a B for every blowjob.'

She laughs.

Louder, I add, 'Yeah and A for anal.'

'WOAH,' say the boys and I don't know what to say and no one does for ages.

They drop me off and I wonder how to explain to the parents that I'll be going to Royales a week before my last week at school. It's all right, Royales. You get the odd sleazy old fella in his thirties but more often than not it's teenagers and people in their twenties just having a drink and a dance. It's better than the bowling alley and the pictures where all the saddos go.

Mum and Dad are still up in the lounge. 'Night,' I shout as I go up the stairs but Mum comes out into the hall so I stop halfway up the stairs. She's been drinking, I can tell. Has she found something in my room? I feel guilty, but then I always feel guilty.

'You know not to shout rape, don't you? No one comes for rape. You have to shout fire. Shout FIRE at the top of your lungs, Sarah. FIRE.'

'All right, Mum, shh you'll wake the neighbours.'

'It's just gone eleven.'

'Something happened tonight, Mum.' I know she'll let me off if there's gossip.

'What?'

'I think I've got a boyfriend.'

'Not that Nessa's brother?'

'No, his friend. He's in the United training squad. I'll tell you about it properly tomorrow. Hey, in the meantime' – I lower my voice – 'don't mention it to Dad, will you?'

'You know what he's like.'

'Our little secret.'

Hook, line and sinker.

She nods, pouts, widens her eyes. I know she has one too – a hyper-lightspeed brain, considering everything she says as she says it and considering all the possible ways it might be interpreted, all the things it might do. It doesn't half tire you out, thinking like that. Joining up dots that aren't there. Making new pictures. It's fun for a bit and then it's not fun. She's taking tablets. I've seen them in her knicker drawer. The thing about your mum, my dad says, is she feels everything. If that's true then I think he fell in love with the mad bit of her actually, but I said this one Christmas and that was a frosty meal. My dad pretends to be really tough and emotion-free but he's not. Few men really are. It's just they consider it 'girly' to show their feelings. Dad can watch *Ghost* and not even sniffle but if anything happened to me or Mum or Juliette I know he'd be a nervous wreck. That's just Dad. He's tough and 'macho' until he realises he can't pretend any more.

I lie awake with my eyes shut and listen to the motorway and I think about the night that has passed and the night on the horizon next week, hanging there like something bright, and how I can't ever tell Mr Keaveney about Macken, or the two and a half shags, or the bus wanker. Then I'm angry all of a sudden and I don't know why. I'm so angry I could set fire to something. I used to set fire to McDonald's bags whenever I got one because they're paper and go up really well.

The next day Nessa comes in just before registration and Mrs Hamlyn gives her the evils. Mrs Hamlyn wears a lot of eyeliner and dyes her hair a bit purple and someone said she used to be a punk. Nessa looks different. I look at her as she makes her way to the back row and sits down next to me and says, 'Yes, miss,' to Mrs Hamlyn and Mrs Hamlyn looks at her and shakes her head and winks. She's got all of them right round her finger, has Nessa. Apart from you know who – he's round mine. Nessa's looking good, like she's got some new make-up on or something – she's all glittery and shiny and I can't stop staring.

'Nessa?'

She bites her bottom lip, shrugs her blazer off.

'What's up, mate?'

Karen Partington in front of us turns round and smirks; she loves it when me and Nessa argue, they all do, the saddos. Whenever anyone is funny with me I get worried and think they must've found out something bad about me. I can't help it. Now I've actually got this massive secret this is especially hard.

'Well, look who it is,' I say. 'Over-Achiever of the Year.'

Karen Partington turns round again.

'So did you or didn't you with Macken?' says Nessa.

'No, I just put my hand in his pants.'

'You whore! Did he have a stiffy?'

'I think so.'

'You *think* so? Was it that small? Hahahaha.'

'Listen mate, don't say anything to Lee or anything.'

'I just hope Lisa Bird doesn't find out. She's really hard. Lives on the Croft Estate.'

I feel very sick, like maximum sick for a person to feel without actually vomming.

'Anyway,' says Nessa, 'you'll see your other boyfriend in a minute, won't you? It's English first.'

*   *   *

He walks in and I feel better, like him just being there a few metres away makes everything okay, the left-hand side of his shirt always so reliably untucked and wrinkled from cleaning his glasses in the same spot. He seems flustered, like he's not quite with it, and I strain and strain to try to work it out but it's like he's blocking me; he doesn't glance at me, not even once, and the lesson goes by slowly. At the end of the lesson though – hallelujah – he lets me back in. He's trying to put his things away and his book falls to the floor and I bend down to pick it up and hand it to him and he says, 'Oh, Sarah. What would I do without you?' And I say, '*Your life would be sour grapes and ashes,*' and he laughs because it's one of our favourite quotes and Nessa can keep her scally shag on the putting green. I wouldn't want that in a million years. I want SO much more. And I'm going to get it.

He says, 'You should write.'

'Write about what, sir? I've nothing to write about.'

'Write about being young.'

'That's boring.'

He smiles, then looks away, and I feel like I sort of lost him. I should have said something more interesting, like 'young is a relative term'.

Anyway, here I am, Mr Keaveney, this is all for you. And when we're married and old and grey we can take this diary down off the shelf and laugh about it.

At lunchtime, as we're walking into town to get a sausage roll, Nessa says, 'So are we still on for tomorrow? You can come to mine to get ready if you want.'

'Great,' I say.

'Come for seven and we can watch *Blind Date* while we do our make-up. Anyway,' she adds, 'turns out you're not the only saddo in school.'

'What?'

'You must have heard?'

'What?'

I'm dreading the answer, dreading it because my brain instantly goes to the worst thing and the worst thing is that something's happened between another girl and Mr Keaveney.

'Candice made him a mixtape and put it in his pigeonhole.'

'I'm off home.'

'Oh, don't be like that. Come on, I was just jestin'.'

I feel myself cooling down and with the coolness comes a sort of sadness, like a comfy hole that wants me in it, in my mind. I put my sunglasses on to shut everything out.

'I can see myself in your sunglasses,' Nessa says, and she starts doing her hair. I know she's getting bored of me and then that'll be that, but I don't need friends any more now I've got Danny. Danny is my future.

'Seven at mine tomorrow, then?' says Nessa.

I want to say no. I want to say no. I say yes. I can always change my mind if I have to and say I'm not feeling well or my mum's bad. I am always reacting to things too quickly and answering questions too quickly and it's the story of my life and it makes me tired.

We skive off school in the afternoon. We play four games of pool in The Knowsley and drink two pints each of cider and black.

There's a few blokes cracking on to us and one of them calls Nessa a 'fridge' so she puts her fag end in his pint. I beat Nessa at both games. Miss Kendall catches us at the interchange afterwards.

'Why should I have to go into school if you don't?' she says.

'You get paid to be there,' I say, and Nessa puts her hand over her mouth.

'You've been drinking,' Miss Kendall says. 'Tell me where. It's not your fault.'

'Yes it IS my fault,' I say. 'Don't you dare try and take that away from me.'

'God, it's backwards up here,' says Miss Kendall. 'I miss the South.'

I say, 'I miss everywhere other than here, and frankly some days there's nothing else to do but drink through the pure shitness of it.'

I light up a Consulate Menthol and she snatches it out of my hand. 'You won't be able to do that in a few months,' I say. My eyes are on the same level as hers and both of us feel that. I could hit her in the face if I wanted to. Nessa's agog.

'Maybe not,' she says, 'but I can do it now – and two months is a long time, madam.'

'Yeah,' I say, 'must feel like even longer when you teach geography.'

'You do know if I report this to Miss Lawton you'll get suspended, Sarah? You're on probation. Do you even care about your exams?'

'Do it, miss,' I say, 'because it won't make any difference to my life.'

She softens a bit then because she thinks I'm feeling sorry for myself when in fact I'm feeling quite the opposite. Nessa cannot speak for not laughing.

'You know,' she says, 'I think Mr Keaveney is far too soft on you. He thinks you're really talented and in danger of going to waste but I can't see it. Anyway, I won't tell him about this. Ruin his good opinion of you.'

I can't speak, I can't. I stare at her so hard I hope she bursts into flames.

When Miss Kendall is gone Nessa says, 'I was gonna tell you, someone saw them last week in the Curry Cottage having a meal. And then I saw them.' She swallows. This is hard for her, I can tell. 'I walked past the fountain the other evening after netball club and I saw him sitting on a bench. Guess who came and joined him: Miss fucking Kendall! I hid behind the hot-potato man. She gave him a sandwich. She had one too. They ate sandwiches. Together.'

I want to be sick. I might be sick. I crouch down on my knees and let my mouth just hang open and fill with saliva.

'Look, there'll be other people for you – I know loads of lads who fancy you.'

'Stop, Nessa. Stop.' I stand up. 'I'm fine. Go get your bus. I'll see you tomorrow.'

I have to escape the crisis then I can process it. If this is all true, including the sandwich, then he has lost the most perfect person the universe ever created for him. The questions spin in my head. Why was she giving him a sandwich? What does this mean? Had she made him the sandwich? Does she know what he likes in his sandwiches? Does she owe him a sandwich? What the fuck is going on. I swallow hard cold gozz. I wonder whether they have fucked and I think about Macken and whether this is some sort of payback or whether I have any right to feel jealous at all after what I did. Maybe this is even-stevens. But I think them sharing sandwiches might actually be worse than them fucking, somehow. If they were egg mayo, I really am going to commit suicide.

Glen Nevis

Sarah boiled water for coffee and put a cup next to the hob. Juliette climbed gracefully down from her bunk. Sarah sensed her every muscular movement, like a predator.

'Want a brew?' said Juliette as though the kettle wasn't boiling.

'Yes,' said Sarah, 'I've got a cup there waiting.'

Sarah watched territorially to see if Juliette would acknowledge her waiting cup with waiting coffee granules inside.

'I'm not going to steal your hot water,' Juliette said, without turning around.

'I wouldn't for a second think you would.'

'Although technically I am the guest, haha! But no, seriously, I'll make sure your cup's filled too.'

'Yes, I didn't realise you were awake, or I'd have filled it more.'

A beat of horrible tension. An atmospheric failure.

'It should be enough for two small cups.'

'Mm.'

Sarah didn't want a small cup. It was early in the morning. She needed a big cup.

Juliette yanked off the lid of a water bottle and filled the kettle to the max line.

'I'm sure it would have been enough,' said Sarah, relieved, but annoyed that Juliette had made such a fuss of it.

After she'd emptied the grey water, Sarah filled up with the blue pipe. The pipe of hope. The pipe of freshness. An altogether more psychically pleasant affair. Juliette inspected her hands, stealing a look at Sarah now and then to see how she was progressing. Sarah thought her sister seemed edgy, tense. Not surprising, really, now she was a murderer. She'd polished off an entire vape on the way. 600 puffs. Each one the shape of a deer.

The holiday park at Glen Nevis had been built in the 1960s. There were shower blocks, a scullery. Plastic ivy in the planters in reception. As they waited by the desk, Sarah stared at the list of 'rules', which seemed to be from the 1960s, too.

Our clients, many of whom return year after year, are mainly families, couples, walkers and a few well-supervised groups who enjoy the natural beauty of the area. Persons seeking nightlife, clubs or discos are discouraged, and indeed would not find Glen Nevis suited to their needs.

She nudged Juliette. 'Tempting to go back to Glasgow for some crack.' Juliette smiled, looked relieved. Sarah could picture them both in canvas chairs outside the Hymer, naked, smoking it. Caravanners passing and clutching their pearls.

'Do you want to talk about—'

'Nope,' said Juliette.

They paid for two nights and drove round the almost-empty site, choosing a pitch with the best view of the mountains, settling after much debate for a spot under a tree.

After they'd set up – chocks in place, electric hooked up, gas and fridge turned on – Sarah walked to the toilet block. A couple of hikers walked out of the shop one after the other and Sarah knew they were together because they were both eating bananas. Which then felt like an odd deduction but, as they held hands, turned out to be true. A man with a big ginger beard sat on the open side of a navy VW eating something from the lid of a flask. He nodded at her as she passed. She nodded back.

In the toilet block, they were playing 'Danny Boy'. It was hard work pulling down her pants, in the unheated climate. The toilet seat was so cold it made her wince. As she peed, she thought she heard a tap come on, a pipe. Was someone else in there? Sarah looked around, listening to the lilting music, creeped out. Could toilet blocks be haunted? A parallel thought that had occurred to her last night: could *campervans* be haunted? The stillness inside the tiny space had felt oddly pressurised – like an aircraft cabin, or an airlock on a space station. Like her old bedroom.

That smell – there it was again. Sarah stood up and surveyed the bowl. A dribble of reddish egg white yo-yoed from her vulva. What was it? She should book a test. She should book several tests. She would. When she got back.

Sarah thought, not for the first time, that she was probably guilty of not talking to *herself* in an honest way. Was that the root of vulnerability? It was exhausting, trying to liberate yourself. Who could teach her to do it? At this age?

Back at the van, Juliette had got changed and was putting on more make-up. Sarah wondered whether she'd drink tonight. Every night, every day she asked the question. Will I drink? Should I drink? She had tried to do it, go without alcohol, but she never managed longer than a few weeks. In some ways, alcohol was the longest and most passionate relationship of her life. She had to have time apart from it sometimes. She needed that space. But she always came back to it. Trying to get to sleep without a drink felt like she was missing a weight on her. She felt exposed and vulnerable, like there was a layer absent from the night, or too many layers in the air. She'd been drinking heavily for twenty years – the equivalent of a bottle of wine per night at least. She liked being drunk, it suited her, it worked for her – but it was also necessary, to subdue the dreaming.

Outside the van, light spilled onto the gravel pitch in a bright crescent.

The bar was a five-minute walk across the campsite. One or two brave souls had pitched tents under the trees. Caravans were dotted across the standings, like the helmets of discarded robots. Silhouettes, awnings, gravel. On all sides, the sleeping mounds of the mountains; themselves each a story of things sliding, shrinking slowly, back to being buried. Ben Nevis with its torn-paper edge, grizzling skyward.

There was a millstone marking the doorway to the campsite bar. A disused payphone hooded in orange Perspex. Next to the bar: a shut restaurant. The restaurant interior was low-lit, everything laid out for tomorrow's breakfast: a perfect dead scene, begging for zombies. Sarah realised that campervans and caravans had always struck her as post-apocalyptic. That compact survival space. That fugitive feeling. Everything you need in three square metres, on wheels. Everyone on the run from something.

Inside the bar, it was rowdy and warm. Sarah couldn't deny it: it felt like home. She was a pub lover. There were polished brass kettles in eight or nine glass display cases all around the room. Collected things. Treasured things. The song playing was 'Cherish' – gaudy 80s glorious. Sarah felt like she might crack when she heard it. The carpet was covered in green and orange Celtic knots and there were empty plant trellises in dried-out pots. In the corner, near the entrance to the darkened restaurant, there was an empty cake fridge and a chalkboard announcing 'Soup of the Moment: Traditional Scotch Broth' – 'The Moment' being 1968. The crisps were only 50p – and they only had cheese and onion. 'Perfect,' said Juliette, because it was. Sarah noticed that Juliette had a small gold pendant around her neck that was the symbol for infinity. She smelled of rain.

Sarah looked up at the pine planks around the bar and ceiling, like the wood on the bunkbeds they'd had when they were kids. And somehow, this year, her little sister was about to turn forty. How did life do this, suddenly start shifting in decades? It was like making plans these days – she and her friends made them months away. 'See you in spring!' they said, in autumn. 'Let's make a date for summer!' they said, in January. Time. Just like that. Gone. Boom.

They ordered pints of beer – seemed safest – and whisky chasers. When in Rome . . . Sarah raised her glass and claimed her metamorphosis.

Juliette was drinking hard again, on her phone intermittently. 'Kids,' she said whenever Sarah looked at her enquiringly.

'They all good?'

'Fine. Fine.'

Sarah got a proper look at Juliette's screen. 'Are you actually on Instagram?'

Juliette turned her phone so Sarah could see. 'A bit.'

She was adjusting the photo Sarah had taken of her at the distillery.

'Do you think I look older?' Juliette asked. 'A lot older?'

'Than what?'

'Than I am in your mind?'

'No.'

'My face is fucking collapsing!'

'Your face is not collapsing. It's just having a more meaningful conversation with gravity.'

Juliette posted the picture and went to the loo. After she'd gone, Sarah went onto Instagram on her own phone and commented:

Happy 45th, sis!!! Love you xxxxx

Sarah stared at the message, drinking. Suddenly it vanished. It had been deleted.

Sarah wrote it again.

It was deleted.

Juliette called her. Sarah dropped the call. She copied the text and pasted it ten times.

Juliette came running out of the toilet. 'Are you trying to ruin my life?'

Sarah smiled. 'Why are you so bothered about your Instagram all of a sudden? You have like forty followers.'

'Four hundred,' Juliette said. 'Growing every day thanks to the business. We can't all have 4,000 because we've been on there since 2012.'

They both took a deep breath and then sat drinking in silence.

Sarah decided to say it. 'Have you ever done that before?'

Juliette knew what she meant. She swallowed. 'Killed something? No.'

They were silent again for a moment.

'It was weirdly impressive.'

'I know. I impressed myself.'

Sarah raised a glass to her sister and gave her an eye-flash that she hoped was alluring and made Juliette feel lucky.

Get drunk they did. Teenage drunk. On the way back to the van, Juliette dared Sarah to stick her finger up a horse's butthole. Sarah dared Juliette to buy a sporran codpiece. Neither of them made good on the dare. 'Juliette,' Sarah said, 'I fear we're losing our touch.'

They sat in the camp chairs, working their way through a bottle of whisky. Something in the Hymer ticked and then stopped ticking. Around midnight, Juliette put her head on Sarah's shoulder. Sarah stiffened. Juliette felt it. Sarah felt her feel it.

'Are we okay?' Sarah asked quietly.

'Course we are.' Juliette sighed heavily. 'I just worry about you, sometimes.'

'You don't need to.'

'Why didn't you ever stay with anyone?'

'None of them were good enough.'

Which was sort of true.

Sarah also thought that no men were good enough for her friends. She knew this was her problem. Stemming from jealousy, probably. Possessiveness and a healthy dash of worry. But really, the whole thing was never good enough. Not so much the idea of one man forever as the knowledge of it. Because: then what, then what? Surely not just The Rest of Time? Sarah knew how to phase out a lover. She could split the bliss, piece by piece, dry it out respectfully, coolly, preserve it while killing it. At first she thought it was just boredom, but then it struck her that it was more profound. It was a sort of sadness. (Dissociation, as her therapist put it, but that sounded too active.) This mad intimacy followed by throwing each other into the flames, followed by cold, wide silence.

Juliette went into the van. She came out with a little box filled with six apothecary-style bottles with handwritten labels on.

'What's this?' asked Sarah.

'Witchy brews,' Juliette professed. 'A witch who lives near me in Manchester made them. The set is called "Sort Your Life Out". You take a sip from each one and by the end you know what to do with your entire life. They're alcoholic.'

'I don't want to sort my life out.'

'But you feel bad.'

'Only sometimes. And what's wrong with feeling bad? Feeling bad is useful. Why do we try and stop feeling bad quickly instead of savouring it? It serves a purpose. All this talk about feeling better, it ignores the usefulness of sitting with the bad feeling sometimes.'

Juliette unscrewed the first bottle. It was called 'Into the Woods'.

Sarah sniffed and retched. 'That is foul.'

'It's not meant to be a pleasant experience,' said Juliette. 'It's transformative.'

Sarah watched Juliette swig and stared hard at her.

'Why do you need to *sort your life out*?' she asked.

'I'm so glad you asked,' said Juliette.

'You are being quite odd.'

'You're being odd.'

'You're being odder. Or maybe it's just that we don't spend so much time together any more. We have no idea of what each other's normal is.'

Juliette poured them both a lidful of the second bottle. 'This one is "Saddle a Warthog".'

'Sounds full-on.'

Sarah regarded her sister as she took the lid and sipped. It was only slightly less revolting than the first. 'Still no sorting of my life,' Sarah gasped. She looked at the next bottle. It said 'Embrace Your New Season'.

Juliette said, 'Sarah, I have to tell you something.'

Sarah nodded. 'You can tell me anything.'

Juliette nodded, opened her mouth, but Sarah spoke again first, fast, gripping her sister, slurring almost with drink and panic: 'He's hitting you, isn't he? That's why you've become immune to violence. Listen, I'm going to help you get away . . .'

'What? Who's hitting me? Not Johnnie!'

'Don't think I haven't noticed your bruises, Jules. I know your face. I know every crease of it. Every freckle. We don't have to involve the police – we can if you want – but I can just get you away from him. I know some scary people. Or people who know scary people. We can fuck him up once we've got you clear.'

'These?' Juliette touched her face where the bruises were, the purplish bands around her eyes. She started roaring laughing. 'You

133

thought— Oh no! No, Sar, it's not from anything like that. It's Botox!'

'What? You're too young for Botox!'

'You know how I bruise! Like a peach.'

'I thought it was Johnnie.'

'Johnnie wouldn't know how to hit a woman.'

'Weird thing to say.'

Juliette sighed. 'Yeah, I probably shouldn't be so down on him. It makes it easier—' She stopped. Took a breath.

'You're bored,' said Sarah.

Juliette shook her head. 'Boredom would at least be peaceful. Most days I want to rip his head off and pour lighter fluid in the hole.'

'I see.'

'I hated him for a long time.'

'Sounds like you've really come round.'

'It flares up now and then. It started after we had Molly – I went to war and he didn't. And he'll never know where I've been. He just got to live in the free country and say he hates soldiers. He gets to play the pacifist, play possum, while I know the real score. What a luxury. Anyway, I hated him for ages. And now I don't.'

'Why?'

Juliette paused and looked at Sarah, assessing something. Then she said: 'The kids.'

'Of course. Protecting them.'

'Respecting them,' corrected Juliette.

'Protecting them more,' corrected Sarah. 'Because they are just kids.'

Juliette was freely drinking the potions now. The ritual had gone. This was unobserved.

Sarah said: 'I took those collagen sachets for a while. Drank one every morning. Tastes like fish vomit. Probably because it is fish vomit. Anyway, I stopped because I realised that these little moments of disgustingness can add up to more than the life you gain on the other end. The maths. It's fucked. That's what you often find with a lot of things, as life goes on. The maths is fucked. It just isn't worth it any more.'

Juliette continued, as if Sarah hadn't spoken, '. . . but I think he'd work me to death in order to live the life he thinks he deserves. The coldest part of me thinks that of the coldest part of him.' Juliette swigged. 'Maybe I'm just perpetually self-shafting. With the great Dildo of Doubt. Maybe that's my lot. The modern girl's way. Still, you reach a point when it's just you, naked in the shower, and your whole body is threatening to slide down the plughole and you don't even *own* the plughole.'

'But you do own the plughole.'

Juliette shook her head. 'The house is in Johnnie's name.'

'So change it! Good lord, Juliette. Marriage 101. Get property.'

* * *

Sarah put Juliette to bed and then stayed up alone, drinking. She cracked open the Highland Park she'd bought. What had Juliette wanted to tell her? She couldn't stop thinking about the sound the deer's head had made as Juliette cracked it. It reminded her of all the dreams she'd had of dropping Juliette as a baby. A recurring bad dream that had plagued her life. In the dream she always dropped Juliette on her head, onto the pavement. Was it Jung who said you can't solve the biggest problems in life? All you can do is outgrow them – something like that. It was true. There was no such thing as closure; only assimilation. Maybe you just grew so big you swallowed and absorbed the problems around you.

Nevertheless, Sarah had an apology for Juliette. One she'd been working on, with her therapist, and on her own. Part of her ongoing mission to achieve vulnerability. To be open to people. To walk the walk as well as talk the talk. The apology centred around something that had happened fifteen years earlier, when they'd lived together briefly in Manchester, after Juliette had finished uni and Sarah had finished her master's. Just before Sarah moved to London and started working in travel. They'd got a kitten – a rescue cat someone's auntie had been getting rid of. Sarah had thought it was agreed that living together would only be a short-term thing – and not only that, she'd agreed to pay the remainder of the twelve-month lease when she moved out after six. But Juliette had taken it hard, and things had been strained between them afterwards for a few years. During this time, Juliette had met Johnnie. Back then, Sarah had been confused about Juliette's reaction – unspoken, indirect, but keenly felt in every unkissed text and unanswered call – then she'd felt angry, then irritated. Sarah had a vision in her head of Juliette's face as Sarah had bid her farewell, just staring frozen. It was awful, now, how shocked Juliette had been. The kitten by her side, the two of them staring down the tunnel of the dark narrow hall, as Sarah closed the door. Turned into the daylight. Got in her cab to Piccadilly to catch her train. Like her mother had abandoned her, Sarah had abandoned her sister. Sarah had scared Juliette into choosing a normal life.

Sarah needed a hit of something, after the day. She tried Juliette's vape. It was fake and minty. The smokable equivalent of Johnnie. So not her type. A proper cigarette was what she needed. Something hard and honest.

She quietly – the secret thrill! – left the van and crossed the campsite in the mizzle. The bar was still open, just. A few dregs of the evening left. She went in and up to the bar, ordered her cigarettes. As she waited for the bartender to fetch them from the back, she saw two people walk in: a young woman, early twenties, dressed up for the evening in a sequin top and mohair cardigan. But it was the other person Sarah couldn't take her eyes off: a man in his late forties or early fifties. Were they father and daughter? No, they were holding hands in the interlocked way, like their hands were having sex. Sarah ignored the bartender saying her cigarettes were just there. The couple walked up to the bar, a few metres away, and he ordered their drinks (pint of Guinness and a Bacardi and Coke). As he spoke, Sarah's stomach recognised him and fell through her bowels. Her brain caught up, and she turned and ran towards the ladies', fucking ran, saliva bubbling in her mouth and bile rising from the pit of her. She turned at the door and held the doorframe to look back and check, double check, triple check, oh the terror in her, who knew there could be so much terror and so much shame in her after all this time.

It was him.

Him.

When I get to Nessa's

Her mum Cheryl lets me in. She has her beautician coat on because she's been at work today. I say, 'Hiya, Cheryl,' and she says, 'I'm going to tint Nessa's eyelashes in a minute, do you want yours doing?' and I say, 'Yeah, that'd be great please.' Nessa's mum met Nessa's dad when she was sixteen and he was twenty-one and that's not that different to me and Mr Keaveney and no one bats an eye – in fact they have a great relationship and sometimes have a bath together in the afternoon.

Nessa's in the shower so I sit on her bed and wait. There's a set of underwear laid out – pink and lacy, tags still on – and a magazine open with two pages of pictures from the new 4Princes video. It's for the song 'Girl, You Girl' and it's got an actress in it who is meant to be Matt's wife after he comes home from the war but she looks more like a model because she can't really act and she's got loads of lipstick on and she just smiles in a dead pathetic way. Anyway, then he finds out she had his baby while he was away and it's a little boy who looks a bit like him and he appears in the doorway behind the model actress and we're all meant to go nuts and wish it was our baby.

The water stops in the shower. Nessa comes in the room with a towel round her body tucked in at the side of her boobs and a towel turban on. I try not to look at her boobs but I want to and I want her towel to fall open so I can see how much hair she has and whether the bits between her fanny lips stick out too.

'All right?'

'All right.'

Her mum comes in and says, 'If you girls want your lashes doing it's now or never – there's a programme I want to watch in forty minutes.'

I lie down and close my eyes. While my eyes are closed I think about the fact I haven't called Mr Keaveney even though I've wanted to every night. I must be as proud as my mum and dad say I am. Too scared or proud or both.

By the time my lashes are done, Nessa is dressed and she lies down for her turn. I look in the mirror and OH MY GOD THEY LOOK SO GOOD. I'm excited now to put my clothes on so I dance around as I'm pulling the things out of my bag: coconut body butter, a satiny pink vest even though they say gingers shouldn't wear pink, and striped black and white jeans and a mood ring and a Victorian cross choker. Nessa's wearing a Lycra dress with a plastic hoop round her belly button and clear tights that make her legs look shiny and the wrong colour. I put my chicken fillets in and put a few strokes of yellow hair mascara in my hair at the front to make it look sun-kissed.

When Nessa's mum goes downstairs, Nessa pulls a bottle of Malibu out of her bedside cabinet. We drink it from the bottle even though it tastes better with pineapple in it. We smoke out the window.

'What do you think about the sandwich then?' I say.

'For god's sake Sarah, it was just a sandwich.'

'Yeah but why was she giving it to him? How did she even know he wanted a sandwich?'

'Maybe she just presumed.'

'Seems like a lot to presume.'

'Yeah well people do. Anyway shut up about it now.'

Nessa turns on the telly. *Blind Date* is on and we have a good laugh at that and how old and sad they all are. There's one man who says his favourite song is 'Every Breath You Take' by The Police and I say, 'Stalker alert,' but Nessa doesn't get it and then I sit and think about that other Police song about magic and that makes me feel all good inside, despite the sandwich. When *Blind Date* goes off we say bye to Nessa's mum and go to get the bus into town.

We normally go to Royales but we've got to go to 42nd Street tonight because it's Nessa's brother's birthday – it's going to be shit indie music all the way. '42s, dirty shoes': they don't call it that for nothing. There's not even a door bitch here, just security. At Royales there's a snotty cow with a clipboard and a feather boa. Someone told me she was crowned Miss Cheshire recently, if not currently, and looking at her I'd well believe it. If you're on her list then you're truly honoured. But not here. Not at 42s. We just stroll straight in. They're desperate for girls as cool as us in here. We show our fake IDs to the woman on the till and pay our fivers. It's not so busy inside because it's early. We have another Malibu, this time with pineapple juice, and it's really nice. 'Blue Monday' is playing, which is like something your dad listens to when he's had too many Tennent's Supers. The men here are mostly minging but we ignore them. We dance for an hour or so and one of my chicken fillets falls out and we have a good laugh about that and dance round it like it's a handbag and no one knows what it is except a few people who go 'Ew'. A few men chat us up and we enjoy that, especially when one of them tells me he runs a modelling agency and I could be a model and he gives me a card with his phone number on it. The DJ plays one we like – 'Birdhouse in Your Soul' – and I imagine being admired by someone standing over by the wall, you know who, I'm doing special moves for them, seeing how I look in the mirrored walls. I imagine that the reflection of me is him watching me. I'm happy, dancing and spinning round when—

He

He's just

There

Like that

Like really

Like oh my god

Him

Him

Oh

My holy days

Like really and actually

He's

Coming over

And then he's

Just standing in front of me

He says, 'Jesus, Sarah, I didn't recognise you.'

Nessa's mouth is wide, like wider than I have ever seen it.

He's looking at me like he's really glad to see me. He looks so intense it's like he's wearing eye make-up but I can't imagine that's the case. His eyes are solid black and excited and his face is as handsome as ever.

'I didn't know you came here,' I say.

He says, 'Me, haha, I didn't know *you* came here. I come here lots, most weeks in fact.' He licks his lips. He's wearing a white T-shirt and blue jeans and he looks fit like an aftershave advert. He's sweating from dancing but I don't care, how could I, I love his sweat. Then I remember the sandwich, and Miss Kendall, and I feel my face go tight.

'Have you got a girlfriend?' I say. Because I've had five Malibus and I don't care.

'No,' he says. I smile. That sandwich meant zilch.

I say, 'Do you want a drink?'

He laughs and says, 'Sure, why not?'

His mate is dancing with Nessa. We go to the bar and he says he wants a beer and I get a beer and a Malibu and pineapple.

'Just like that,' he says, 'you ordering drinks.'

'What's so strange about that? You know I'm not a kid.'

'Hahaha,' he says.

'You look more relaxed than last time I saw you,' I say. 'I was worried about you, you looked harassed. I thought we were off.'

'Off?' he says. 'Me and you? Off? Never! We have a special connection.'

That's when I know everything is true, and real, and happening. We are back on. We've never been off.

'The truth is,' he says, 'I've had a wretched few days.'

'I'm sorry to hear that.' But I'm not. If he's wretched, he needs me. 'You should have told me,' I add, thinking he'll say his dad has died or he's moving out.

'Sophie and I broke up, it was a mutual thing.' I shake my head. He says, 'You know I was going out with Miss Kendall, right? I'm sure everyone in the school knew.'

I nod. There's no way I'm admitting I didn't know. I feel like I want to throw up. Why is he ruining this by talking about her? It takes all my power to focus on the past tense because the flood of images otherwise is too much to bear as I try to work out everything I thought I knew in the light of this information. I wonder if they fucked. I wonder how old she is – she must be in her late twenties at least. How do you even find a woman that old attractive?

'Yeah,' he says, 'I'm sorry if I haven't been myself. I knew it had to end, you know.'

Yes, I think, because of us. You can hardly elope with me while you've got a girlfriend, can you, you dummy?

'Oh, don't worry,' I say. 'You had to do it.' Which is when I realise this is perfect timing because he has got rid of her just before we go away together. It was only a matter of time, but the fact she existed hurts and I can't let my mind stay on it too long each time because it burns.

'Here's to the future,' I say and we chink glasses.

'Hold on to that optimism,' he says.

'I will.'

He takes hold of my hand and I hope he is going to lead me off somewhere but he doesn't, he just stands there staring at me, much closer than he'd ever dare in school, holding my hand like he never wants to let go. I think, fate has brought us together here tonight and he has chosen to tell me this now because he knows that I am a better girl for him than Sophie was and next week he'll be even surer of that and won't she be spewing when she hears about me. It's all become clear to him, I can tell by the way he's just staring into my eyes, like he's lost and found all at once.

'You do know that a relationship is a creative act, like writing or painting,' I tell him.

'Sarah, I think someone is going to fall very much in love with you one day and they won't deserve you.'

I don't like that so much. I go along with it because I think it's a compliment even though it makes me feel sick because it's one of those far-away-feeling things.

'I'm so glad to see you,' I say, and then I try it, 'Danny.'

He doesn't bat an eye. 'Me too,' he says, quick as a flash. 'You brighten up my days, you know.'

'You brighten up *my* days. You make me want to come into school.'

'You make *me* want to come into school.'

'You make me want to leave school.'

'You oscillate, Sarah Hudson, do you know that? You hum. Sorry, I shouldn't say that.'

'It's fine,' I say. And I can't even think straight for happiness. And then he leans forward and holds my face in his hands and he's about to kiss me, I know he is, right in public. And all my neck and back and shoulders are alive with nerves and needles and I think any minute now I'm going to wake up and be so sad because we'll be in denial again sneaking round unspoken and I've had this dream so many times but I also know it's real because how could it not be real because the truth is real and this is the truth, the truth of me and the truth of him, because all the truth ever really is is your feelings. Everything else is just paper. I remember what Nessa said about amateurs closing their eyes when they kiss so I keep mine wide open. I put my hands where they usually go, down on his hips and my bum goes all fizzy like it does when I'm on a rollercoaster. We just stand there in the dark and music of the club and I think any minute now, and when he doesn't kiss me I lean in to start the kiss myself. But he pulls back and I see his friend there – the one he's in a band with – next to us with Mr Keaveney's T-shirt sleeve in his fist, and he looks furious.

'Danny! Are you fucking mad? Her mate over there just told me, she's from— Tell me you're not. Tell me you're not . . .'

Danny (Danny!) opens his mouth to say something, but he doesn't say anything, he just shakes his head.

His mate says, 'Do you have any fucking idea what you're doing?'

'Look, it's fine,' I say to him. 'If you knew us you'd know that.'

'If I knew you, I'd be in prison, love. Dan, I told you you should've only had a half.'

I think Danny looks pretty far gone for a pint of lager and his mate takes his shoulder and before I can say anything he drags him to the exit and Danny – Danny – looks at me all the time they're walking away.

I could cry but I laugh out loud, just stand there laughing like a loon.

Nessa is next to me. 'Can you get over that?' she says. 'Oh my god wait till we tell everyone on Monday, what a loser. And his mate, what a saddo!'

'Did you see?'

'How much he was sweating? Mingadingding.'

'I sort of like his sweat,' I say and she looks at me like I've grown another head. I am not going to say any more because I don't trust her, which is new, and also I don't really need her now or anyone else ever again. I don't need Juliette, Nessa, anyone. I don't even really need myself. I just need him, and what we are together.

Skye

It was, Sarah told herself, the emotions of the trip. The pressure. She was hallucinating. Being around Juliette was triggering a regression; a wormhole dragging her into the vortex of their shared emotional history. Of course this was making things whirl into false shapes. It was general sibling guilt, childhood regret, all the things she'd not done for Juliette, all the ways she'd let her down over the years. You couldn't make it up in a week, but now her age and some kind of temporal panic was making her feel like she had to. Sarah had designed this trip so they could reconnect after drifting for so long and letting so much life get between them. But one trip would not be enough. There would need to be more. That's what her therapist always said: *You can't rush things, this kind of work takes years.* And her therapist didn't know the half of it. But she did know Sarah's propensity to rush. To always be thinking nextnextnext, nownownow. But you couldn't do that when you were still trying to find a place where your feelings met someone else's feelings. Someone you really loved, maybe more than anyone. The pressure was a killer. It was clearly making Sarah crazy. And Sarah never used that word to describe herself or any woman. But she was seeing people who were not there.

She reasoned with herself. How many times had she walked down the street and been convinced someone she knew was coming towards her, or sitting in a café, only to find, on closer inspection, that it was a wildly different human being she had mistaken for an acquaintance. That was what had happened here. And she'd been drinking! She was an unreliable witness. It wouldn't stand up in court.

There was just no way *he* could be *here*.

It was morning now. She'd barely slept. She'd escaped the ladies', and the bar, after hiding for what she assumed was around an hour.

Sarah boiled water on the little hob, made coffee and sat on the step of the van smoking one of the cigarettes that had caused all this trouble. Maybe the false sighting was a Freudian punishment for an outdated vice.

A robin, fluffed up in the cold, bobbed around on the gravel. It landed on the toe of her trainer, weighing nothing. A family of grouse scurried across the grass. A sparrow sat on a low signpost, staring back. It looked too fluffy, fluttery like a chick, but it wasn't the season for chicks. It was injured, holding one leg up beneath itself in a slack curl. She threw out some biscuit crumbs. Somewhere on the loch, a heron cronked. An early bee landed on a rock, its back end panting. In the sky, a plane left an impossibly long vapour trail, so long Sarah couldn't see where it began.

Juliette got up around nine. Sarah greeted her nervously – would Juliette judge her for smelling a bit of whisky right now?

But no, Juliette was a picture of positivity, of energy. It took Sarah aback.

'Hi!'

'Hi?!'

Something had shifted in Juliette, that much was certain. She looked lighter. It was almost as though she was trying a bit too hard with Sarah. Like if Sarah hadn't known better, and wasn't feeling as tormented as she was, she might have thought her sister was feeling guilty about something. There was an overcompensation in the way Juliette moved around Sarah in the tiny space.

They made a breakfast of eggs and soldiers and ate it at the table. His face kept appearing, and Sarah would shudder.

'So cold,' she said, covering for herself. She found herself looking down at the table pole for traces of blood.

Juliette nodded in agreement. 'Extra socks!'

'Hey,' said Sarah, 'I have to tell you something.'

'I have to tell you something too! Shall we do our tellings later? Like truth or dare?'

Sarah hesitated, then she nodded. 'Okay.'

Juliette said she'd take the pots to wash them in the scullery. Sarah dismantled the table, scouring the pole for smears, marks, any kind of evidence of the deer. Had Juliette given the pole a secret extra wash? Or had Sarah imagined the deer, too? She started unhooking the van from the electric and noticed the Aventura guy packing up too. She thought about waving, saluting, smiling, something – and then she'd thought too long about it and he'd gone, and she was just left with her fantasies of what a successful social interaction could have looked like. Her brain! This is why it wasn't good for her to be away from work. She needed structure, focus, hyper-stimulation. If any excess energy seeped around her focus she was doomed. Or everyone around her was. Or both.

Emptying the grey water was proving to be Sarah's least favourite thing about life on the road. It was even worse than the toilet. At least the toilet was quick. The grey water seemed to piss out of the van for ages. Sarah had to turn away and let the van finish in privacy.

*　　*　　*

They drove up to Mallaig, to the white sands they remembered from one of their favourite films, *Local Hero*, which they had watched over and over, but today Sarah felt too tired to quote. They took a tour on a fishing trawler piloted by a maniac who went charging into the swirling water. The sea boiled beneath them, slipping between shelves as the tide came in. The trawler jolted as it crested the waves. Sarah held on, trying not to vomit, convinced they were about to slip in and disappear into the cold grey.

They caught the ferry to Skye, and then drove to the Talisker distillery, where Sarah had booked a tour. Juliette put her arm around Sarah as the boat sloshed through the foam.

On Skye, the distillery was busy. They spent most of the tour trailing around after a stag do. The age of the barrels, the wood, the colours, it all had a library sort of feel. Academic. Sarah couldn't stop shuddering; she needed another drink. They had a tasting in a dark little corner of the distillery, where she necked two shots without even waiting to be told by the distiller what they were. Juliette looked at her, grinned catlike, and necked three. Sarah thought about trying to be restrained, to not go to a darker place. But then his face flooded her mind again and she knew the only immediate realistic solution was drink.

When they got back to the mainland, they drove on, further north, passing the iron tide of Loch Broom. Rocks, weed and water were strewn across the bay. A single rowing boat was stranded on the rust-coloured flats, lilting to one side like an abandoned drunk. Then the road descended sharply into Ullapool, the tarmac lined with a black and white barrier, segmented like a snake. Silver birches and skinny pines spiked the hillside. On a rock face, on the final bend, someone had painted: DEL <3 KELLY on the rocks. Tiny white houses perched on embankments by the side of the road. They drove past a small graveyard. As they reached the village itself, red and white boats bobbed in the harbour. They went up past the golf club and then, almost out of town again, there was the campsite.

They parked in a quiet corner, underneath a nut tree. Sarah wanted to sit in a pub. She was craving the comfort of fabric. Of other people. The everything-alcoholic on tap. They walked back down to the harbour. They sat outside a pretty little blue-washed pub and ordered white wine, red wine, whisky, dinner. Waiters came and tipped great steaming pans of fresh shellfish onto big white plates in front of them. They ate like they hadn't eaten for weeks, the alcohol hollowing their stomachs, the sea air sharpening their palates. Everything stung deliciously. As they ate, they watched the waves break – grey rolling into brown rolling into white. On the table next to them sat a woman in her sixties who looked like Jack Sparrow. Eyeliner, feathered jewellery, scraggy hair, torn tights. Props, thought Sarah. She watched the woman work her way through a formidable number of brandy Cokes. Sarah could smell them from where she was sitting. The pirate woman left and staggered down the high street.

In her place, a family came, cleaning the table with tissues before they sat down. The parents shared a bottle of wine and chatted away while the teenage girl sat in silence and drank a J2O miserably. Sarah stared at the girl. She couldn't help it. The girl saw Sarah looking and sipped her drink affectedly, pretending not to notice, pouting, but Sarah couldn't stop staring. She could remember seeing women her age staring at her, when she was that age, all those years ago. She used to think they were staring out of envy. Now, she knew it wasn't envy – it was incredulity. They were looking at you, thinking of the girl they'd been five minutes ago, wondering where the fuck she'd gone.

'You've been very quiet today,' said Juliette. 'Everything okay?'

'Yeah! You? What was it you wanted to tell me?'

Juliette shrugged and smiled. 'I'm enjoying this. Thanks. It was a great suggestion.'

Sarah squeezed her sister's hand, slightly confused. It was hard to ask even a simple question. Why did she feel like she was on a first date? She said: 'Was that really it?'

Juliette looked at Sarah and cleared her throat. 'No. Okay. So the real thing.'

Sarah sat up straight. 'If it's about the flat—When I—'

'I'm having an affair,' Juliette blurted.

Sarah felt for the edges of her chair, even though she was sitting down.

'An affair?'

'Mm-hmm.'

'But . . . but . . .' Sarah struggled. 'Affairs are . . . not for people like you.' Juliette made a face. Sarah continued. 'They're for . . . friends of our parents.' Sarah was aware she sounded eight years old – still she went on. 'They're for people in the 1990s. Or the noughties. Or people in Premier Inns.'

Juliette looked offended. 'It's not a one-off thing. I'm on a sex journey. I'm trying all the latest kinds of sex.'

At this point, Sarah could not control her facial gymnastics.

'You don't have to find it quite so unbelievable. I'm not quite so unattractive . . .'

'No, it's not that. It's just – I'm stunned. You and Johnnie? What's happened? I feel like I missed an episode.'

'I have a right to an erotic life!' Juliette stood up and declared it, glass aloft.

'Shh. Please don't say that. I mean, please don't be so loud. You'll disturb the grouse.'

Juliette flailed her arms around wildly. 'It's wild and I deserve a bit of wild.'

'Who are you on a sex journey with?'

'A dad from school. You don't have to laugh like that, you fuck.'

'I am so sorry for your loss, Juliette.'

'Fuck you. In the butt-butt. He's actually very hot. He's thirty-three.'

'Don't do this! If you're doing the affair thing, we can go on Hinge or Bumble or Feeld right now and find you someone cool. Even Instagram! So many people I know have met through successful DM slides . . .'

'This is real life, thanks very much. I did it all myself. And I like him.'

'Is he married?'

'Divorced.'

'And he's hot?'

'Hotter than Satan's ball-sack.'

Sarah looked at the optics behind the bar. The blended spirits and liqueurs. 'We are going to need to have a lot more of these horrible drinks, and I am going to need to see some photos.'

'He's a doctor.'

'I am also going to need to see some qualifications.'

Sarah got the drinks in while Juliette prepared the slideshow. When Sarah got back from the bar, Juliette presented her with the first pic. 'Aaron' – because that was his name – was relatively hot, as thirty-three-year-old dads went. He was a man who wore tweed flat caps and hairy scarves, like an extra from Mumford and Sons.

'He looks like a man who enjoys a kiwi vape but only outside the house.' Twenty years of dating gained you a lot of analytics. 'By the way, what exactly is a sex journey?'

'He googles things and tries them out on me.'

'That's very conscientious.'

'Johnnie hasn't ventured south for years.'

'It can get tiresome, for both parties.'

'Not if it's done right! After too long in the desert, I found myself fingering myself, thinking: will no other man taste this delicious fruit again? This mango? This peach? And I knew something had to change.'

'Yes, I think something does when you start referring to yourself as fruit.'

'I send him sexts.'

'You've never sent sexts before?'

Juliette went red. 'Well, yeah, obviously. But not as hardcore as these.'

'Are you telling me you're into young people's sex now? Pegging and choking?'

'It's not just a sex thing,' said Juliette. 'And it's not like I'm *completely repulsed* by sex with Johnnie.'

'Is it his keto breath?'

'There's still something exciting about *something* going inside me, *sometimes*. It's that basic, you know?'

'I feel like Johnnie only narrowly avoided being MeToo'd. Like only by virtue of his not being famous.'

'What?'

Had she said that out loud? Sarah swiftly continued: 'So where did you get it on with Hot Dad? Was it a case of . . . your eyes met as you handed over the Smiggle lunchboxes . . . ?'

Suitably diverted, Juliette smiled at the memory. 'It took ages for us to get talking. I am usually RUDE when I encounter people at the school gates. I am not a joiner, as you know. The last thing I ever want is to make *friends*. Do you know what my logline is on WhatsApp?'

'*Do not add me to your WhatsApp group.*'

'*Do not add me to your WhatsApp group.* So I don't linger at drop-off or pick-up. But we kept gravitating towards each other . . . and something about him cut through. Then we met by chance at a Matisse exhibition in the city centre.'

'Good old Matisse.'

'Molly isn't in his daughter's class so it's all legit.'

'Apart from the fact it's *an affair*.'

'I know him. That's what I mean.'

'I'm not judging you, by the way. I'm all for this, in fact. I think it's the best thing you've done in years.'

'I have a lot of love still, for Johnnie. He's a great father.'

Sarah nodded, gallantly. 'I'm so glad you found the energy for something.'

'Even though he does odd things. Did I tell you the other day he bought a foam nunchuck? No? Yeah. And he's been posting his personal bests from the gym on social media. I know. I just kept finding myself thinking, quite often: How did I end up with this moron I have nothing in common with?'

'Burn.'

'His penis is one thing . . .'

'I should hope so—'

'. . . but sometimes when he touches me, it's like . . . someone testing a steak.'

'Oh.'

'There's nothing natural about it. Nothing fluid or sensual.' Juliette exhaled. 'But it's a very strange thing to think about someone you've been married to for three years, and someone you've known for eight: *You just don't kiss me right.*'

Sarah made a grim face.

'I went to the doctor's late last year because I was worried about my hormone levels.'

'And?'

'She asked me if I had been having painful sex. I said, the thought of sex with my husband is painful, does that count?'

'Have you really been having painful sex, though?' Sarah considered it. Had *she*, at all? Even a little bit? Was her dwindling vim due to depleting testosterone? She was very testosterone-y. Or she had been in her youth.

Juliette was still lost in thought. '*Tidy that table.* That's how I talk to him. I wonder whether I'd speak to a friend like that. Or you, even. I don't think I would. It's like he's an unreliable member of staff. A shoddy intern. But that's what he feels like. I don't know where my anger comes from, but I want to kill him sometimes. I fantasise about his death. His funeral. He always gives himself the better-coloured cup of tea – do you think that means he's a Tory at heart? It doesn't matter. I don't mind if you find Tories sexually attractive. Often, you don't know until you've fucked them, I imagine.'

'I don't ask their political persuasion as a pre-requisite.'

'I think I stuck at it for so long because of something Grandma said. Do you remember? "The marriage with Grandad didn't start on my wedding day; it started the day he surrendered an argument just to make things okay. The conflict is the real marriage."'

'Depressing.'

'Yep.'

Juliette hammered another drink.

Their grandparents, Fred and Maureen, had lived in Bethnal Green, which was badly bombed during the Second World War. They bickered constantly. The story went that they were running to the bomb shelter late one night when their grandma stopped and yelled: 'FRED, FRED, WAIT, I'VE FORGOTTEN ME TEETH!' to which he replied: 'FUCK'S SAKE, MAUREEN, KEEP RUNNING – THEY'RE DROPPING BOMBS NOT SANDWICHES!'

Gran, who had come out in her mink velour slippers that time they took her for a day trip to Chester Zoo and only noticed when she was standing outside the alligator enclosure. Sarah couldn't help but admire that level of detachment. The last time she'd seen her, at the old folks' home, she'd been like a walnut with breath. The nurses had come to take her for a bath and Sarah had helped to lift her, like Jesus and John the Baptist; a scene at once obscene and sacrosanct.

Sarah felt like she couldn't get a grip on her feelings; like the whole day was a whirlpool.

Juliette called home again, and as Sarah watched her on the phone she saw yet another layer to her sister: a layer of protecting her children. Harpo and Molly must have no idea about where Juliette's head was at. 'Halfway there,' Juliette said. 'Home in three days.'

Maybe everyone needed to be having an affair with something. A person, a hobby, a substance, a political opinion. Maybe that was survival if you had half a brain. You needed somewhere different to live sometimes. It was basic sanity.

When Juliette was off the phone, Sarah asked: 'Do you think they know?'

'About the affair? Yes. The kids, probably. You think they can't understand you before they can speak, and then they remind you of things, later, of things that happened before they had language skills − and you realise they could. They're on to you, from the start. It's like a hardwired survival thing. They read emotions.'

'And Johnnie?'

'Not a fucking clue.'

'No time to think, amidst all those podcasts.'

'Do you remember reading D. H. Lawrence at school?' Juliette said. 'I know you do.'

'Vaguely.'

'I can't remember which book it is,' Juliette went on, 'but there's one where he writes about the "bone-deep" hatred you have for your partner, after child-rearing. It's true. As a woman, you do. It brings everything to a head . . . worrying about fertility, worrying about infertility, your ageing body, then the war zone of childbirth, the aftermath of inequality and self-abandon − the lot. And you throw it all on the nearest symbol of the damage you can: a man. And you think, where has all of my freedom gone? Where is the person who used to play with herself? Gone. Well, I'm getting her back. I'm pulling her back out from the inside of me.'

Sarah listened, afraid.

'He left me for dust in that fucking delivery room.'

'I wish I'd been there.'

'I have said "I love you" to many men and each time it has meant the same and also something different. I think sometimes we don't want to opt out, even when we know we should, because we've invested too much. We want to claw it back and make them see our greatness. Opting out feels like losing. Also because as women we're trained to think we have to save everything. We have to preserve, and nurture, and keep coming back. Well, fuck that. I'm done with saving things.'

Sarah thought of the table pole. The deer. Seeing *him*, in the bar. She wanted to puke.

'I thought you'd be pleased for me!'

'I . . . am.'

'I gave Johnnie the chance for an open relationship,' Juliette said. 'It was a hard no.'

'The problem with open relationships is that one person usually wants it more than the other.'

'He doesn't even care about what I want. That is the real problem.'

They finished their drinks and walked back across the campsite. Sarah looked up at the moon. She thought of their mother. Her attempts to run away had been aborted dashes to the bus stop. Angry walks around the park. Stomping out and returning, a few hours later, with a cake and a wet face. She couldn't do it, she couldn't run. There was a tenderness now, thinking of her in the stocks of domesticity. No, not a tenderness, an inflammation. It softened Sarah towards her mother. On the outside, Sarah was all smiles, but she didn't give her mother the time of day. All she ever felt was a deep, desperate need to run away from her. She didn't, couldn't, trust her. It had been chaos, with her, growing up. These things played out in romance. You were constantly seeking chaos, madness, instability. Then the second you got a whiff of it within a relationship you reacted. It was earth-shattering. All you could do was shut down. And so the pattern repeated. Sarah had tried to break it. She had really, really tried.

Back at the van, they carried on drinking. Unburdened, Juliette was giggly. 'Let's text Dr Aaron!'

'No!' said Sarah firmly. 'You are drunk. And you are not fourteen.'

'I'm going to.'

'Behave yourself!'

'Get off! It's my phone. I'm doing it.'

Juliette spoke as she typed. 'What are your current worries? Healthwise? He can help.'

Sarah shook her head. 'Give the poor man a chance to bed in. Don't let Mum get onto him about her creaky knees.'

Juliette was undeterred. 'Any suspicious moles?' She started to sing, '*We can't go on together, with suspicious moles. Suspicious moles!*'

'Okay, maybe a small one on my arm.'

'Fantastic. *Hey sugar-boo . . .*'

'SUGAR BOO.'

'*. . . my sister Sarah has a mole she's worried about – can we send a pic?*'

'I'm not sending a pic, Juliette.'

'He's replied – *okay*.'

'Man of few words. As well as a man of the people.'

Juliette took a photo of Sarah's mole and sent it, typing: '*What do you think . . . ?*'

Sarah scratched at the mole.

Juliette's phone vibrated. She squeaked. 'He says: *I think it's probably just a polyp. But she should also see her own doctor to be sure.'*

'Sounds reasonable.'

'Thanks. Sarah thrilled to have a polyp. Kiss.'
'Celebrating Sarah's polyp with whisky x'
'Wetting the polyp's head'

'Juliette, I think you should stop texting him now because he's not replying and you're going to start feeling rejected.'

'Puh.'

But Sarah liked this Juliette. The daft one. Juliette went to the toilet and Sarah did two lines of coke. She wasn't hiding it, she just knew Juliette would see it for more than it was.

Half an hour or so later, Sarah saw Juliette was nodding off. She got her out of the chair and into the back lounge, into bed. She covered her with a duvet and a blanket. As Sarah was tucking Juliette in, Juliette whispered: 'You've never called me "hun" before.'

'I know.'

'I didn't like it.'

'Yeah.'

'Don't do it again.'

Sarah nodded.

'What did you have to tell me?' Juliette asked.

'Oh, just boring work stuff. Never mind. It's not important. It's just hard.'

'Work?'

'Life. No one gets out alive.'

Newsflash

I've started smiling at strangers again. I stopped for a while but now it's back with a vengeance and I'm like a maniac in shops. I don't even care whether people smile back. I'm just doing it anyway. I'm that generous. I am a donator of smiles. Here you go, world, have another! That one wasn't even directed at anyone. It used to bother me when people didn't smile back. I think that's why I stopped, probably when I was about seven. You notice stuff when you're about seven. Now I couldn't give a shit. It's a great feeling, being this generous with my face.

I wonder if he's nervous about seeing me. I think if he doesn't walk through the door soon then I'm going to burst. The last two days have been a whirl. I've been living with the memory of that almost-kiss, and I haven't been able to eat or sleep or talk to anyone much with all the planning. I've been writing poetry. That feels like the only way to cope. I've replayed the moment again and again and again – him moving towards me, the way his eyes didn't leave mine. It's the best thing that's ever happened to me or the world.

He's five minutes late now. What's going on? Is he nervous about seeing me, is that what this is about?

Then the door twitches, the class quietens, but something's just not right, I can feel it.

Mrs Hamlyn walks in. But even she looks different. What is it?

Good morning, girls, she says. Mr Keaveney is off sick today so I'm going to be taking your class.

Sick?

I say, 'What's wrong with him, Mrs Hamlyn?'

'Some kind of stomach bug. I'm sure he'll be fine.'

Nessa whispers, 'More like hungover if you ask me.'

I think, thank god I didn't tell you, thank god.

Mrs Hamlyn isn't wearing any make-up, that's why she looks different. She normally wears lots of eyeliner but today she hasn't even got mascara on. I haven't seen her without eye make-up before and I don't like it, it makes her look young and weak.

After school Nessa says, 'I'm going to Matt's for a bit, you coming?'

'Nah,' I say, 'I'm going home to revise.'

I'm not bothering, she says, not when the teachers can't even be arsed to come in.

But I'm not going home. I wait until she is safely on the bus to Oldham and then I run and get changed in the interchange toilets where an old woman was murdered last year (don't think about it, don't look in the mirror) and then I get on the bus to Withington, where Mr Keaveney lives. In fact it's two buses. I have to get one to Manchester city centre and then another one out.

I get off the bus and go into a petrol station. I buy two bars of chocolate. I walk down his road. I've rehearsed what I'm going to say, I'm going to say: 'You need to not listen to what your friends say and I need to not listen to what my friends say, we need to bother less about what other people think in general, because this is our life, our one and only life, Danny, and our only responsibility is to ourselves, to be happy.' I think it's a pretty good speech. I reach his house and stop. My stomach is doing flips and flops, like there's things alive in there. I look at the windows, all the curtains and blinds are drawn. I'm standing at the end of his path, looking at his wall. Thinking, this is his wall. The path. This is his path. His feet touch that path every day. There's a crisp packet in his front hedge. I pull it out. I guess that the biggest window at the front is his bedroom window. I wonder if his dad is in – he doesn't work any more so he might be, and from what Mr Keaveney's said he doesn't go out much and that's part of the problem. Mr Keaveney is twenty-five though, so he really does need to get his own place, and his dad does have a point about that. I think I'll have achieved a lot by the age of twenty-five.

I was going to knock and offer him a bar of chocolate, like maybe we could eat them together somewhere nearby – not in the house, that would be ridiculous. I can't knock. I can't. But I want to do something. So I walk up to the front door – heart pounding, palms sweating – and slide the chocolate bars through the letterbox. There's those bristly things inside so I have to push extra hard. His dad can have one. When you're with someone, it's all about accepting their family too.

* * *

When I get home it's eight o'clock. Mum and Dad are sitting at the dinner table. There are gravy streaks on their plates and a few potatoes left on Mum's. She's had a drink.

'You should have told us you were going somewhere after school. This is it now, Sarah, you have to start taking life seriously. Your exams start in a few days.'

But they don't know how seriously I am taking life right now. If only they knew. Not long, not long.

Mum says, 'Nessa phoned. I said I didn't know where you were.'

Dad doesn't say anything.

I go up to my room and put my pyjamas on. Get into bed with Seamus Heaney. See? Revision.

I hear the phone ring in the hall. I know it's Nessa. She'll be on her own, bored, lonely. We used to be on the phone every night when we first made friends. My mum used to say, 'I should get a bloody payphone like Michelle down the road has got. It's a good job no one's trying to get through to me, isn't it?'

'SA-RAH.' Mum shouts up the stairs. 'SA-RAH it's NES-SA.'

'Where've you been then?' says Nessa.

'Nowhere.'

'You need to start giving me some answers, Sarah.' She's been watching *Cagney & Lacey* again. 'If you want me to cover for you on Friday then you need to tell me everything. I'm your best friend. You can't keep me in the dark like this, it's not fair.'

And I think, you're not my best friend, not any more; I've got a new favourite and I have had for a long time, but I say, 'O-kay.'

She says, 'Good, tomorrow you can come clean. And Candice is going to have your concert ticket so you don't need to worry about that any more.'

I go back to my room and pull out my best stationery and start to write. It's time to put the final preparations in place.

Ullapool

The next distillery on the route was smaller, a cottage affair, a
micro-distiller on the outskirts of Ullapool – two big copper kettles
in a backyard wood-shack. A husband and wife showing groups of
five people around at once. Sarah trailed behind Juliette, feeling
torn. She couldn't shake the thought of him. Should she go back,
try to find him? How could she do it without telling Juliette what
she was up to? She couldn't go into it with Juliette. She couldn't
believe he'd just been there, like that, a reality. If she wasn't going
mad? How many times had she googled him, scoured social media,
self-torturing, self-destructing, whatever you wanted to call it –
and there seemed to be no trace of him any more? Everything had
stopped when he'd reached a certain age. Had it definitely, certainly
been him? Sarah was a reliable witness, wasn't she? It had been him.
It had. She wasn't going mad. She was going to have to go back and
find him. But it was Juliette's birthday tomorrow. The point of the
whole trip was that celebration. Sarah felt sick with indecision.

After the distillery they parked up in a campsite near a pub.
Juliette was busy semi-quoting *Labyrinth*, when Sarah is warned by
the talking walls on the way to the Goblin City: 'Take heed, for this
path we are taking will lead to certain destruction!' The pub sounded

lively. Liveliness was what Sarah needed. Distraction. It was a shabby nautical place called The Green Oyster. A name that made Sarah feel even more sick. The sun was setting, and the bellies of seagulls flashed pink as they turned and wheeled in the sky.

They ordered drinks and stood by the bar. Juliette started to raise her glass to her lips and then stopped dead and froze. 'What's HE doing here?'

Sarah's blood ran cold.

She turned—

'Who?'

—to see:

The man from the Aventura motorhome.

'Oh thank god.'

'Thank god? Don't tell me you're planning on speaking to him. This is *our* trip.'

'Maybe it's a sign.'

'You're obsessed with fate.' Juliette paused to take aim. She fired. 'And men of a certain age.'

Sarah pretended to smile. She watched Aventura Man as he clearly deliberated whether to come over to them and say hi. The question presented itself and demanded to be answered: would she be game?

She would be game.

Aventura Man bravely drained his glass and took bold steps towards them. It was heartbreaking watching him be so pleased and proactive. Sarah tried to focus.

'Well, hello!' he said. 'The sisters on a sex tour.'

'*Well, hello*,' Juliette muttered under her breath.

It was all awkward but Sarah couldn't help but be glad of the distraction.

Steve, who was better travelled in these parts, suggested they move on to a live talent night at a place around the corner. He said it was always good for a laugh. People did am-dram turns, the locals went there. Sarah looked at Juliette. Juliette said okay.

'Are you sure? It's your birthday—'

'Not yet it's not. Look, it's fine. But you're going to his place.'

'What?!'

'You heard me.'

Half an hour later, the three of them stood together in the hot, crowded upstairs room of a different pub. The wine was good. This wasn't a locals' place, thought Sarah, although Steve thought it was.

A hype-beast leapt onstage, holding a mic: 'Evening, all! The Pig Sicks will be on at 10 p.m., folks, and they're going to blow you away if you haven't heard them before. They're basically anarchic but also literally schizophrenic and it's a totally destructive vocal experience.'

'What does that mean?' said Juliette.

'I think it means they're going to shout over each other,' Sarah said, looking at Steve's face. To see, satisfactorily, that his face was looking at her face. If alcohol wouldn't fully exorcise what she'd seen, then sex would. Alcohol and sex would rid her of the urge to run or fight.

'But first,' said the host, 'Amelia and Jemima Tinheart.'

Two girls climbed onstage, both dressed as robots.

'Feminism,' said Juliette.

One robot said: 'The thing about all of us, born in the twenty-first century . . .'

Sarah looked around, caught one of Steve's eyes. It was an okay eye, as eyes went.

'. . . the thing about us is, we used to dream of making our bedsheets into parachutes and flying away.'

Sarah laughed into her drink. Juliette did the same.

'. . . And I want to say, we never gave up. This poem is dedicated to everyone who never gave up that dream. Fuck technology!'

'WANKERS!' someone shouted from the back of the room. Everyone turned. It was a middle-aged man wearing a T-shirt that said 'CHOOSE CASK' on it.

One of the robots did a fake automated laugh. 'You . . . are . . . not . . . a . . . nice . . . human.'

'WANKERS!!!!!' came the cry again.

Steve stood a little closer to Sarah. Sarah knew it was on. Why wouldn't it be? This guy was on to a winner. Juliette swayed, her wine sloshed a little from her glass.

'Let's not get my sister any more white wine,' Sarah whispered to Steve. That was it. They were conspirers now.

'Why?' he asked, enjoying the whisper.

'She turns,' Sarah said, enjoying his whisper back.

'Into what?'

'A beast. A werewolf. A total fucking nightmare.'

'What, every time?'

'No, that's why it keeps happening. Because it doesn't happen every time, so we're lulled into this false sense of possible security. Then it happens again, and it's bad. Her cycle affects it. It's all chemicals. Someone told me that white wine contains oestrogen . . .'

He looked at his drink. 'You're telling me I'm going to grow tits if I keep drinking this?'

Ah. That was a shame. The word 'tits' didn't suit him at all. *Exotic*, Sarah reminded herself. Exotic.

'Yes. You'll grow tits and I'll grow horns.'

'I think we'll look great.'

'Sarah!' said Juliette. 'Pass me that bottle!'

Sarah did, reluctantly – a brief glance to Steve.

'Myself, I usually get home for midnight,' Sarah said. 'Since you asked.'

'Why? Will your carriage turn into a pumpkin?'

'My personality will. I'm at my optimum performance levels

between two and five drinks. Before that I'm anxious; after that I'm abusive.'

'How abusive?'

'Pretty fucking abusive.'

'Same again?'

Sarah looked at the time on her phone. Pretended to count on her fingers. Onetwothreefour. 'Okay.' She remembered about that stuff coming out of her.

The host came back onstage: 'Okay, guys, so the Pig Sicks can't make it. They've been detained at Edinburgh services for smashing up a bunch of Dyson Airblades' – a few small woos from the crowd then a fuck you, (no doubt from CHOOSE CASK) – 'Yeah, fuck you too. I love you, bro'

The host then read out some of his own poetry.

'Of course,' said Juliette, slurring now.

'FUCK but i HATE the WAY PEople READ conTEMporary POetry,' Sarah said, to Steve.

'Come out for a cigarette with me,' Steve said.

'Not right now,' said Sarah. 'Later.' She nodded to Juliette, her charge, who was lolling against the wall, on her phone, cursing unintelligibly. He understood, perfectly: the text, and the subtext, and the sub-subtext of the 'Later'. Could a man you were about to fuck have the same grasp of subtext as a sibling? It was highly possible.

He went out.

Juliette stood up straight to deliver her verdict on the situation. With one finger, wonkily, aloft. 'Buy condoms.'

'I didn't ask for your opinion.'

'He is fifty-nine, at least.'

'Sometimes you've just got to add something to your repertoire.'

'I get that older men are your thing, but they used to be preppy. Short. It was a fetish. Now they're just . . . old. You have to see that.'

'You can't have a fetish as a child.'

'You can when you are a sexual child.'

Juliette drained her glass, licked her lips and looked towards the bar for more.

Sarah felt shamed and went on the attack. 'Are you missing your lover?'

Juliette took the question seriously. 'He doesn't care at all. I bet he hasn't even looked at my Instagram once.'

Sarah turned to the stage. 'This guy is half demented already. The way he talks is so annoying.'

'The performer or Steve?'

'The performer. It's like he's running into his cave of secrets for two words at a time, running outside, setting them down and then running back inside again. I know we're meant to be spellbound but I just feel irked. I can't tell if it's dementia or if he's just a massive bighead.'

Juliette shook her empty glass.

Sarah shook her head. 'I think——'

'You think what?'

They went to the bar.

The barman was very young and very sweet. As Sarah's card beeped, he said, admiringly: 'I bet you used to be *so cool*.' Sarah stared at him. He stared back, his smile slowly falling, as it dawned on him that – rather than give her a compliment – he had said something terribly wrong. They took the bottle back to the alcove where they'd been sitting. 'You know what the worst thing is?' Sarah said.

'Yes,' Juliette nodded, filling her glass, 'he said it *so kindly*.'

Juliette sat down as Steve came back. She got her phone out again and started dabbing at it, frowning.

'She okay?' he asked. He smelled pleasantly of rollies. Sarah felt annoyed for some reason she couldn't put her finger on.

'You two really care about each other, don't you?' he said next.

'Yeah we do,' said Sarah, 'in our own way.'

'Have you always been close?'

'Not so much. I . . . wasn't very nice at school. I wasn't that thing people like to say they were. I wasn't a geek or an awkward artistic type. You know, the acceptable things.'

'What were you?'

'Oh, I was a bully. I was a bitch.'

'I can't imagine that,' he said.

'Maybe that suits you to feel that way, right now,' she said.

He looked at her quizzically. Don't fuck the vibe, Sarah, she reminded herself. She had been writing it on her hand in previous months, when the booze got too much of a grip – 'DTS' – in capitals, in black biro – three letters to look at throughout the night as a reminder: *Don't Talk Shit*.

She looked at Juliette, slumped, angry, eyes on the latest unfortunate act onstage. She started to plan the exit, for all of them.

She turned back round to face Steve. Her head was starting to pound with her own winey blood. He gave her a cigarette, and a look.

'Got a light?' she said.

'Oh, you want it all, don't you? Cigarette not enough, is it?'

Combative. Her ancient speciality. She could work with this. She felt the rise on the thermal of attraction.

'You know they last longer if you don't light them?' she said.

'How old are you?'

'Old enough.'

'Got kids?'

Now Sarah had dealt with this frankly fucking insanely impolite question in various ways. *I had a miscarriage this morning. I suffered early menopause. I have cancer of the womb. I had a baby once but I killed it, and prison was super boring – so I won't be doing THAT again!* Anything to shame them into considering their words and realising that this is a very personal, potentially pain-triggering question that you should under no circumstances ask a stranger.

She swallowed it all and shook her head.

Because this was . . . a moment.

Sarah let her leg touch his leg briefly and said, simply: 'We going then?'

'Yes,' he said, 'definitely.'

She insisted on walking Juliette home. Juliette was not happy about it.

'DON'T WALK ME HOME LIKE A CHILD.'

'YOU ARE DRUNK AND BEING STUPID.'

'YOU ARE BEING STUPID TOO REALLY.'

Sarah deposited Juliette at the Hymer and unlocked it, chucking the keys inside.

Juliette went in. 'Thanks, Mum and Dad – I mean Grandad!' she shouted as she toppled onto the back sofa.

'She's having an affair,' Sarah said. 'And she's a killer. She's got a lot going on.'

'Sounds like it.'

Juliette stared at Sarah, seething, as Sarah pulled the door snappily shut.

'Shall we?'

When they got back to his place, they went up the big shiny steps and he turned the lights on in his mansion on wheels. His Winnebago had a proper bedroom, with a permanent king-sized bed and wall lamps that you could imagine someone putting on to 'soften the mood'. He had a high standard of hygiene and a selection of mid-range spirits. Sarah realised the only way this was going to work was if she took the initiative – and straight away. Waiting for him was too much of a risk. She had to female-gaze the shit out of this situation. She went straight for him and planted a generous kiss on his mouth, parting his lips – not so easy, this man was no feminist – with her tongue. He let her in. She put her hands in his hair, digging her fingertips gently into the ridge of his neck, holding his face to hers as she loosened his tongue, felt him relax. This would do, she thought, yes this would do very well. Juliette was right.

She needed to stop thinking about Juliette.

He pulled back suddenly. She looked at him, concerned. 'Everything okay?'

'Pay no attention to my underpants.'

'Pardon?'

'When we get there.' He looked suddenly nervous, like he'd said something wrong. 'If we get there. I'm not – forcing you to do anything.'

Sarah frowned. This was all very much wilting her boner. Should she tell him she had an unidentifiable red discharge and *really* crush the mood?

'They're Homer Simpson,' he said. 'My son got them me as a joke last—'

'You need to stop talking now,' said Sarah.

He did.

'You don't have a pencil knocking about by any chance, do you?' Sarah asked.

He looked confused. 'I might have a pen?'

'Never mind.'

Sarah kissed him again and he joined in more earnestly, liberated from his terrible underwear secret, letting his tongue push into her mouth, thick and fast, showing some promise of things to come. He had a basket of sex toys in a bottom drawer – many still in their boxes, which was reassuring and also not. Sadly the Pleasuriser III didn't come with batteries fitted so Sarah discarded that on grounds of speediness. The Maude Vibe Hare looked promising, if a little worn, with its hot air outlet – Sarah had it on her in seconds. The hot bone of her pubis tightened with longing. Her pelvis was an iron ring on fire. Somewhere deep in her thorax, peony buds clenched and unclenched, like seasons on a time-lapse loop. Sarah unfastened his jeans – the button, the zip, easing them away from his arse and down his thighs. The boxers went too – Sarah made a point of not letting her eye catch them as she pushed. His cock was ready, saluting her, as her hand felt for it. She pulled him to the bed. Stand-up sex was for twenty-year-olds. She pushed him down – he liked that, now she could tell he was thinking of her as 'bossy'; that's what she was, a 'bossy little bitch' who was going to make him come whether he liked it or not. Sarah played into this, covering her fantasy with his fantasy. She enjoyed the attention he paid to her feet, and exploring the murky slot of his anus. She found his buttocks firm. His back was hairy like a mythical creature's. Eager to prove her youth, she finished them both by getting on top, a nubile starlet, enclosing his condomed cock and fucking him – hearing him cum as she disappeared him all together, and was just a cunt on a stick, pressing her own buttons. He was solid. Substantial. In that moment, everything she needed.

'Thank you,' she said as they lay there afterwards, and meant it. He squeezed her hand in response. He was a nice bloke. *A nice bloke.* Cursed words!

Sarah reached, smiling, for a drink of water from the bottle on the side and saw the Homer Simpson boxers on the floor, crumpled tragically. Homer was looking up at her, saying 'D'oh!' She lay back in bed and pulled back the covers, inspecting the potential damage, but only a little of the red water had leaked out of her and onto his bedding. She apologised and said she was probably due on her period. He made them both chai, in mugs covered with tiny wildflowers. She drank the tea, closed her eyes and slept.

The next morning, the anaesthetic of alcohol had worn off

long before the stimulant of alcohol, as always. She was wired. The memories were seeping back. Sarah wanted to get back to Juliette. When Steve offered her breakfast, she politely declined. Then she wondered if being a decliner of breakfast was a sign of spiritual bankruptcy. It felt like it. 'I have to get back to my sister, but thank you, this was so fun.'

Sarah knew this was bogus. It was bad script. But it was also polite. She caught a flash of sadness in his eyes before he said: 'Of course.' This was the awkward bit, maybe more so for the ones who had been married. Sarah experienced a bolt of insight. Steve was probably a younger brother.

As she put on her shoes, he picked up a flyer from a stack on the table. 'Come to my gig if you're around,' he said, handing it to her. 'I'd like to see you again. No pressure, obviously. If this was just a one-off for you then it was just a one-off for you.' Sarah smiled kindly. She took the flyer and stuffed it into her pocket, not looking at it. 'It should be a fun night,' he said.

'I'll mention it to my sister, see what she thinks.'

And I believe I can answer for her when I say: Fuck that.

'Great. Bye, then.'

'Bye.'

Letting yourself out of a caravan after a one-night stand was its own special kind of shame. Sarah closed the door behind her, then staggered back along the gravel path to the spot where the Hymer was parked – only to discover, with horror, that the van had gone.

Juliette had gone.

Dear Mum and Dad and Juliette,

15 May

I'm writing this letter in the hope of helping you understand. I know it will be hard for you at first, but I hope not forever. I can't tell you exactly where I'm going but know that I am safe and will be in touch soon. He is a good man and we are very much in love. You must not think you are in any way responsible. Everything that has happened is 100 per cent my doing because I know who I am and what I want out of life the most, which is True Love. I will be back in August and you will see how happy I am and how right we are for each other. Juliette, you can be a bridesmaid but I will be choosing the colour.

I remain your devoted daughter and sister,
Sarah
Xxxxx

Cape Wrath

Sarah blinked. Sure, she was hungover, rinsed out, post-shag and half blind in the early sunlight, but to just not be able to see a huge retro campervan?

She spun around.

Then she spotted it, glinting, parked down in a different spot, near the grassy part of the campsite. She ran to it.

The door was unlocked so she burst in. Juliette was sitting coolly in the back lounge of the van, sipping a coffee. She looked at Sarah.

'You moved the van? You? On your own?'

'It was the nut tree,' Juliette said. 'The nuts falling on the roof sounded like gunfire.'

The keys were on the table.

'Well done. It's not easy, is it?'

'Speaking of easy . . .'

'Oh, very good.'

Sarah started making herself a coffee.

'I don't feel well.'

Juliette looked concerned now. 'You okay? What happened?'

'No, that was fine. I'm just . . . feeling a bit like we should start heading home maybe.'

'But it's my birthday tomorrow!'

'I know. We could go for a treat meal in Manchester maybe. A hotel! Proper home comforts. Bit of luxury.'

'No no,' said Juliette. 'I'm getting into it now.'

She got up and came over to Sarah. She put an arm around her sister and pulled her in tight.

'Listen. Sometimes you've just got to put on a Breton top and a bit of lipstick, get behind a wheel and get the fuck as far away as possible from the person you shagged last night. It's basic science.'

Sarah nodded. 'I need a shower first.'

'Yes. Wash the sex off. Was it . . . good? At least?'

'It was okay.'

She went to wash.

Sarah felt like she was starting to have a grasp of what the answer might be, to the question that had puzzled her and Ginny the day they made their lists. Why is something defunct in our inward and outward gaze, as women? Why is there such a chasm between what we judge in others and what we appreciate in ourselves? We need someone to bridge that gap. To help us see how we already are what we want to be. To feel self-esteem trickle in from the feet up, and slowly – over years and years and years and years and years – settle in our bones. And for that, we need a friend. We need a sister.

When Sarah was clean, they unhooked the electric and sorted the grey water.

As she bent to wrench the tap, the flyer fell out of her pocket. Sarah stared at it.

She froze.

There it was.

His name.

His bold naked shouting shaking name.

Good god.

Sarah couldn't breathe. She hadn't been seeing things. That had been him in the bar. She picked up the flyer and held it, her hand quivering.

Juliette shouted to her from the window and she pocketed the flyer guiltily. Juliette would remember his name. Of course she would. Sarah couldn't believe he hadn't bothered to change it. Men were lucky like that. They didn't have to reinvent.

Juliette looked at Sarah curiously as she got back in the cab.

Sarah looked at the Aventura as they drove out of the site, the curtains still closed, knowing she'd probably never see it again. It knocked her sick to think that Steve was in regular contact with him. That they were friends, texted each other, touched each other's hands regularly, patted each other's backs. She stopped the van, pulled over and puked.

'Woah,' said Juliette. 'Want me to drive? Maybe we should leave it a few hours . . .'

Sarah shook her head. 'It's not a hangover. I think it might have something to do with the grey water.'

They set off on the road north.

'What is it?' Juliette asked. 'Are you angry with me? Was I too drunk? I'm sorry.'

'God, no!'

Then Sarah saw a sign – the Summer Isles. They both decided that sounded nice. The words were full of bright promise. Summer! Isles! A detour wasn't something Sarah had planned, but this was an adventure, wasn't it? A detour would lighten the mood. Sarah made her face slack, her eyes intense, as though something awful had happened to her and she was trying to be brave and almost failing. *If I can feel abused I'll weather this better*, she thought.

The drive there was magical – past Ardmair Point, where a woman was walking her sheepdog along a grainy shore pooled with piles of flat grey stones, and a seagull dangled behind the van for half an hour, like someone had it on a piece of string. Up on a hill, a solo house squatted like a toad. 'I wonder who lives there,' Sarah mused, thinking it looked nice.

'Probably a pervert,' said Juliette. They were back in joke mode. Sarah felt relieved.

The road ribboned around the peninsula, the low sun spilling over the mountains and glowing gold in the valleys. There was sunshine in the sky and in the shocks of yellow flowers at the side of the road. A rainbow. It was quieter, calmer. Then light rain fell from a bright sky. The land opened after skinny pines to rolling orange hills, gorse, churned mounds revealing dark earth. Wilder land now. Old wolf country. Netting on the rocks at the side of the road, things caught and held. The road surface was violet like the rocks.

'You sure you're okay?' Juliette asked. 'You look a bit florid.'

Sarah wound down the window and lit a cigarette. 'It's just a glow I got from the sun.'

'He's the son of someone. Although they're probably dead.'

Eventually they reached a tiny village called Achiltibuie, at the end of the track, past a series of log cabins right on the water's edge. The campsite stretched all the way to the beach, with only a wire fence separating the sea from the hardstandings.

'Look at that,' said Sarah. 'Sort of place you'd want to spread your ashes.'

'Or spread your asses. If you're Sarah Hudson.'

'Can we stop with the sex jokes? I'm done.'

'Oh, okay, she's done, ladies and gents. She's done.'

There was a pub at the campsite, the Am Fuaran bar. Sarah went in to pay for the pitch while Juliette hooked up the electric and made tea. It was a comfortable but cool family-run bar, advertising 'hand-dived scallops, every day'.

Sarah said she'd walk up the road to the post office for some supplies – milk, bananas and the like.

When Sarah returned, Juliette was sunbathing – sunbathing – in a camp chair, in a T-shirt and her pants.

'God bless the Gulf Stream!' she shouted, when she saw Sarah. Sarah could tell Juliette had had a few.

Sarah made herself a drink and they sat together, basking in the sunshine. That flyer! She couldn't stop thinking about it. Could he be here, now, in this campsite, on his way to the venue? Sarah looked around.

She thought of all the times she'd let Juliette down. Not going to her bonfire night party when she didn't know that everyone else had cancelled too. The thought of her there with all the food. All the food. All the food on the table. It gutted Sarah like a fish, still. Sarah had protected Juliette at school, just to lead her to that. Everything she'd protected her from, she'd also subjected her to. Was that the deep, twisted core of sisterhood? She was so fierce and loyal. She got in fights for her. She'd puked with fear the night before Juliette started at the same school. All over her bed. It was a yoke of responsibility she'd been hopelessly backing out of all her life. Life was just school played out in different rooms.

'What would you say to your younger self, if you had the opportunity?' Sarah said.

'Uh-oh,' said Juliette. 'Is this going to be like when you and Mum made me sit down and listen to "The One and Only" by Chesney Hawkes, whilst reading the lyrics and looking at me meaningfully?'

'It was an important message.'

'Cheesy. He was fit, though.'

'If I could say anything to my younger self,' Sarah said, 'I would say: never feel as though you don't have somewhere to be. Do not linger. Do not trail. You are better than that. You can be alone with yourself, in bed or on the road somewhere. You have somewhere to be.'

Sarah went to pee – in the toilet block. She was treating herself.

She made Juliette go too. Juliette waited outside. 'Remember when I used to make you stand outside the door and whistle while I was on the toilet?'

'Course I do. We'd watched *Poltergeist*.'

'We were too young. Blame Dad.'

'Did you know he's started wearing flatulence-filtering underwear?'

'They make that? What a time to be alive.'

Sarah shifted on the toilet and gasped. It was redder than ever down there.

'What is it?' said Juliette. 'You're hurt, I know it!'

Sarah sighed. 'Tell you when I come out.'

Sarah wiped herself, washed her hands and emerged from the toilet forlorn. She told Juliette about the red water and how worried she was. 'Thank you for sharing that with me,' said Juliette. 'Sounds really worrying.'

Sarah nodded.

'I genuinely think cancer is so unlikely though,' Juliette continued. 'It'd be deeper purple red, wouldn't it?'

'No idea. The internet offers different theories.'

'Infinite.'

'Yeah. But it's disgusting. I feel disgusting.'

'You're not disgusting. This is just something your body is doing. You should get properly checked out.'

Sarah nodded again. Good advice. Sound advice.

They sat outside. It was sunset. The mountains behind them loomed.

'I miss my babies,' said Juliette.

Sarah nodded. 'I miss home too.'

'You seem to be doing okay down there.'

'Yeah, I like it.'

'I think you've settled, haven't you?'

Settled. It wasn't a word Sarah often associated with herself. But who had told her she wasn't? Not her. Not her sister. She reached out and held Juliette's hand. Juliette enclosed Sarah's hand with her fingers. Neither of them spoke, they just watched the mountains and the sea and the darkening sky. Sarah felt the tension after five minutes, her hand itching, her arm muscles nagging.

She went to the toilet. The red water was there, again.

When she got back to the Hymer, Juliette was watching for her from the window. She opened the door.

'What news from town, sister?' she said.

'A pig has escaped, they've stoned another adulteress, and the Devil has been spotted down at Mulligatawny's Bar. Just another average day in the country.'

'I texted Aaron about your problem.'

'What? Why?'

'He's a DOCTOR.'

'Oh no! That was really private.'

'He replied . . . *She might have a cervical lesion. Someone should look up with a speculum. She needs a sexual health screening. Go to a GUM health. Tell her to get some swabs done.*'

'I didn't authorise that question! This is private business.'

Juliette ruffled Sarah's hair as she went past her to the loo, like she was five.

* * *

The next morning, Sarah woke Juliette with a card, a coffee and a pain au chocolat with a candle stuck in it. 'HAPPY BIRTHDAY!'

Juliette opened the presents they had brought with them, and then FaceTimed home. The kids sang and Johnnie said she had more presents waiting for her return. Sarah stood in the background, waving and blowing kisses to bookend the call. Juliette hung up with a sigh. Sarah didn't question it.

They packed up and set off, winding back around the peninsula, then north, up and up the country, towards Cape Wrath. The energetic sky above a rough moor, knuckled with bedrock. An hour or so later, the road turned into a single track. The landscape opened out into dry tundra, stretching to purple mountains dusted with snow, and beneath that, vegetation – the snow line, where snow became rain. The mountains looked otherworldly in their colour and composition and Sarah had the distinct feeling of being somewhere else entirely, another planet. The road passed through a U-shaped valley, curling around and then crossing a river. The sheep were impossibly clean. By the side of the road, the land had been cut and taken, in pieces, revealing welts of soft black peat. Sarah thought of lakes, the way the ones with the purest water look the bluest because they absorb every colour of light except blue, reflecting that colour back.

As they neared Cape Wrath, driving past the turning for the passenger ferry, the land became more ragged still. The very top of the country was close. Turning along the headland, strung along a rope, a line of green and yellow lozenge-shaped buoys led into the sea.

Cape Wrath's name was hideously apt. The landscape was moorland, thoroughly ragged moorland – it presented an elemental sort of excitement. Moorland, spreading wide on all sides. Long grass, a barber-shop lighthouse. Beyond that, a sheer clean drop down to the sea. The northwesternmost point of the landmass, so beaten by the sea that it was named after a deadly sin.

They drove through falling blossom that was pulled into the van's slipstream as though magnetised, flowing either side in mesmerising streams, like they were travelling through a time warp. A red-berried rowan tree only alive on one side. Brutal dam and reservoir towers, checkpoint Charlies.

Another ten miles or so round the headland and they reached Durness, the northernmost point of mainland Scotland. Sango Sands was a flat, wind-whipped campsite on top of a cliff. Down on the beach below, monolithic boulders broke the waves as the tide came in. They parked on a hardstanding and hooked up the van only to realise the electricity was off: the campsite was closed. They turned on the gas.

Sarah had an overwhelming urge to stand on the cliff and scream into the sea. She wanted to cut away her shadow where it met her body, like in *Peter Pan*. There was a light on a distant ship, like the neon of a club. *This way to the party.* Far away, the beach looked pale and there were grey boulders crouched like moons. The path down to the beach was well worn. Desire paths – the name for a path that people have made in grass because of where they wanted to go across a patch of uncharted territory. They start as one person wanting to go a certain way. Like one thought. Then another. Then another. Then another, until there's a track – a track it's easier and more tempting to walk down than stray from. A desire that has been designed.

Juliette was halfway down, on the phone to Johnnie again. Sarah could hear them arguing – their voices carried over in blasty gusts. Juliette looked as though she could hardly speak for wind in her mouth.

'Why is that fussing? That's not fussing. That's organising. Look, can we not argue in front of him? I can hear him saying his ABCs again, which is basically counting. We're stressing him out with our stress . . . And it's MY BIRTHDAY, JOHNNIE. And I have planned a whole week for you, with me going away. I have looked on fucking apps and found activities and batch-cooked and frozen homemade meals and when you go away, do you know what you do? NOTHING. No preparation. My fussing holds this family together. Did you forget to tell me how much the mortgage is? Or the service charge? That's your usual next line of argument.'

Sarah hated him. She watched the wind blowing the rain sideways in opaque slats, like someone closing a blind.

When Juliette came back, Sarah asked her how she was.

'Married,' said Juliette. Adding: 'Barely.'

'It sounds like it might be the right thing to get out of there.'

Juliette nodded. 'Or have I just made it the right thing? You know, everyone always thought I was the one who didn't run, who stuck at things. What, just because I got married and had kids? That means shit, deep down. You're more constant than me, Sarah. I know that's not your brand, within the family or the world or whatever, but you are a more consistent person. I'm the real flighty one. I've just got . . . stuck. I was going through old photos at Mum's the other day, and the thing that struck me was I looked like a different person in every single one, and not just age-different. If you lined me up over the years, these were not normal transitions over time – I was changing myself, over and over, to fit what I thought each man I was with wanted me to be. To fit *my own idea* of what these men wanted. Who was that multi-layered subterfuge serving, really? No one. I went blonde because my first boyfriend preferred blondes. I wore cargo pants because my second fancied Mel Blatt from All Saints. I got into emo music because the one after that was a bit of a goth. It went on. Each time, a bit more of me got chipped away; each time I was left wondering where the men ended and where I began, *if* I began, or if I was just a ball of wet clay waiting to be remoulded.'

'Have you texted . . . the doctor guy?'

'Yeah, he's ghosting me now, which is nice. I don't know what's going on. I daren't look at social media. Maybe all our medical questions put him off.'

Juliette cradled her phone, wounded.

'What you're basically telling me about the domestic situation is that you're a sub for your entire family.'

Juliette looked at Sarah and then her face cracked into a wide grin.

'That's what this is! I thought I was being taken advantage of, but it's just BDSM.'

'It's just BDSM.'

'Oh thank god. I'm a sub for my entire family. I should wear one of those necklaces. So other families know. In case they want me to sub for them, too.'

'Yeah, you might be missing out on loads of parties.'

'Thanks, sis. I think I can enjoy it a lot more this way. I didn't think I was having sex at home! Turns out I am.'

They hugged.

Sarah thought: it didn't matter who you fell in love with. What mattered was how you sold the inevitably disappointing resulting situation to yourself. That was real adult life. It wasn't growth, or success – it was *spin*.

Sarah felt the sudden urge for the toilet.

'Excuse me,' she said, and ran.

In the toilet block, she squatted, an ice wind blasting her backside. She felt the need to push. She pushed. She felt something strange around her fanny lips. What the—? Something was coming out. Something was coming out! She reached down. A soft, warm object eased into her palm. She looked. It was a tampon. Or at least, it had been in a previous life. Now, it was flat and purplish and stringless. Dear god. How long had that been in there? How far up had it been? Could it have been up her cervix? Instinctively, Sarah covered her mouth with her free hand because she thought she might laugh. It was too bizarre. It lay curled in her palm, like a stillborn mouse. She buried it next to the toilet block with her bare hands.

Then she walked back to the van. Juliette had laid out tea and biscuits.

'What's up?' she said.

'I just gave birth to an ancient tampon,' said Sarah.

'Con . . . gratulations?'

'It explains a lot. You know, the red stuff.'

'Good to know what that was, I guess.'

'Absolutely. I feel like things are really on the up for me.'

'I once had two in at once,' said Juliette. 'The Tampon Twins.'

'I should probably have a few days off the booze.'

'Or maybe you should just stop beating yourself up about it. And now the tampon's here, life is going to be very different . . .'

'So they say.'

'What are you going to call it?'

'Tammy. After Tammy Wynette.'

'Gorgeous. I'll knit.'

'And you'll share a birthday! Joint parrrrrrtiiies . . .'

* * *

They went for a walk through Durness. There was a shut lounge bar called Smoo's. A Second World War bunker in someone's front garden. Further along the road, a Nissen hut with a corrugated red steel roof, half smashed, a large hole in it. Deserted summer residencies. A swing horse made of ripped car tyres. Apple-green streetlights, awkwardly cluttered farm buildings, a collapsed caravan full of building materials on a driveway next to too many cars. They took a track that Juliette thought would take them back over to the sea, but when they walked up they found only empty farmland. Steel sheep compounds. A refuse, a tip. Concrete bases with rusting pins, old gun stations. A lone crow. And through and around it all, a bitter, bitter wind.

They walked back along the road to the campsite, looking down at the beach. Waves broke and split and stretched, and as each wave rolled onto the sand, a few tiny birds skittered away from the tip of the tide, returning as the waves retreated to see what might have been left behind for their delectation. They were oystercatchers. Sarah could just make out their shocking orange beaks. Trails of footprints from dog-walkers looped around the boulders. In the sky, a snow cloud advanced, fronted by a flock of sparrows.

They bought Orkney beers from a tiny shop. 'Wet the babby's head,' said Juliette. Sarah bought Juliette's favourite pizza, Hawaiian, and some bags of sweets and crisps.

They made a party tea and set it up on the back table, watching the sea through the window. Juliette raised a glass of cherry cola and bade farewell to her youth – an ironic act. A paradox. 'I can't have too much sugar, though. You know I have haemorrhoids,' said Juliette.

'From your exceptionally large stools?'

'No, from childbirth! They pop out every other week and I pop them back in, like Whac-a-Mole. I read that haemorrhoids are usually about your mother.'

'Really? A wonder I don't have them then.'

'For me, being a mother and having a mother are intricately interconnected. And you cannot do that with your eyes, Sarah, because I'm not saying *that thing*, I'm not *doing* that thing. But listen, hear me out. Boomer parents told their X-er and millennial daughters they could do it all, but they forgot to tell their sons to pull their weight as fathers. So you have all these burnt-out women. Fucked. Furious at their husbands. And their husbands have no idea why. They're fucking outraged, too. They weren't prepared for this. And THAT is why I have these fucking haemorrhoids.'

'I blame Mum for everything too,' said Sarah.

'You don't *engage* with Mum,' Juliette said. 'You zone out.'

'I know,' Sarah said.

'Maybe you should try to get to know her.'

'Why would I need to get to know my own mother?'

'Because what you think you know, you might not know. And you're a grown-up now.'

Sarah opened her mouth to comment. Juliette silenced her with a hand. 'No,' she said, 'it's my birthday so I have the conch. All day and night. Zip it. Listen to little sister.'

Sarah obeyed.

'You know what I realised?' Juliette said. 'I always thought Dad was the one with an imagination. The ideas guy. And Mum was just some kind of labourer. But maybe he got the luxury of feeding our imaginations while she did all the grunt work. Maybe she had a fire in her head that could never find a way out.'

'Maybe.'

'She's scared of you, you know. She is. I can tell.'

'Don't be ridiculous.'

'Shh!'

Sarah thought about this. She thought about it after Juliette had fallen asleep.

It wasn't a good night to be on a cliff. Gales howled around the van, buffeting it from side to side. Sarah lay awake wondering whether they should move it, whether they'd get blown off into the sea. She tried to imagine being a baby, being rocked in a big cradle by Mother Nature. It didn't work. She thought of the wind rushing round the cliff, like a ghost train, coming for them. She pondered the inner workings of handbrakes, imagined the mechanism loosening with every shake, and she got up and put the van into first. She googled the Beaufort scale and tried to calculate whether the Hymer, weight-wise, could survive a hurricane. Sarah stayed up all night listening to that wind.

In the small hours, the biggest thoughts came to her. She thought about the day she was born and how that must have been. Sarah and her mother in a tiny room, alone, staring at each other. Wonder, fear. A lifetime of unspoken things stretching before them, like a glacier.

The next morning, Sarah went to the shop for bread and milk, letting Juliette lie in.

And then she saw him. Again. Alone, this time. The young woman was nowhere to be seen. He was by the side of the road, near the shop, attaching a large caravan to a flatbed Toyota truck.

It was him.

It was definitely him.

He got in his truck and started to pull away, towing the caravan behind.

A teenage energy surged within Sarah. All the tiredness of the past few years lifted and she was recharged with pure adrenaline. She had to chase him. She had to. This was what she had been waiting for. She would chase him all the way to the gig and then — then she would think about the then-what.

Sarah ran back to the van, dropping the milk, not stopping. She ripped the electric hook-up out of the socket, turned off the gas, took out the chocks.

Juliette opened the door. 'What's going on?'

'We have to leave! Now!'

'Why? I haven't had a cup of tea!'

Sarah thought quickly. 'Storm's coming!'

'Okay, Sarah Connor,' said Juliette. *The Terminator.* One of their old faves.

'Now. Where are the keys?'

'Is it that Aventura guy? Is he bothering you?'

'No, no no no.'

Sarah found the keys. 'Leave the table. Just sit here and put your seatbelt on. And it's not your birthday any more so you have to do what I say.'

*   *   *

Sarah decided that three vehicles between them was the right distance. Three vehicles was enough to hold a visual but not enough for him to spot them, to clock he was being pursued.

The skies started to clear as they headed east along the coast. Sunshine hit the windscreen and lit up the van with thick golden shafts, like dusty searchlights. Now and then the caravan up ahead swayed and straightened, and Sarah wondered if he was drunk or kept falling asleep.

But then a timber lorry pulled out – and there was no way of not letting it. It positioned itself between the Hymer and the caravan. Sarah tried to peer around it, but the roads were so tight she couldn't. The lorry was slow. It slowed them down, so much that by the time the lorry turned off, the caravan had gone.

'Shit!' swore Sarah. 'Shit shit shit!'

She stopped the car at Scourie.

'What is it?' said Juliette. 'Why are you being weird? Look at this place! I like this place.'

It was getting dark. They would have to wild camp.

A post van drove past. Sarah got out of the van and walked round the back. Stood out in the wind and the rain. She stood there, standing her ground, watching the waves break. Grey rolling into brown rolling into white.

'Are you going to tell me what's going on?' shouted Juliette.

Sarah turned. 'You're right,' she said, 'it's perfect here. Let's stay.'

I tell Mum

I'm going to Nessa's for the night and I know it's the last lie I'll ever tell her.

'So I'm going to the 4Princes concert tonight with Nessa, remember? I'll be back tomorrow sometime because I'm staying over along with another girl who's called Candice – you don't know her.'

Does adding a true bit to a lie make it less of a lie? It sticks in my throat even though I know it's for the best. Juliette looks at me and I can tell she knows I'm lying, but what's she going to do? She can be a bridesmaid, she'll be happy with that.

'Who's Candice?' says Mum.

'Another girl from school. She's all right.'

'Is she getting friendly with Nessa, then?'

When she's not careful my mum can be so jealous it spills out of her and she ends up being jealous on my behalf and then ends up making me jealous too, even when I don't want to be. It's like jealousy is the time when she feels the most alive – like she doesn't know how to *be* unless she's under attack. Like a puffer fish that's suddenly all spines if you poke it. She doesn't even like Nessa.

'Dunno. It's all right though, cos me and Nessa aren't as close as we used to be.'

'Oh, and are you all right with that?'

Mum's had a coffee. She's all perked up and involved. But I do not want to spend another second at this table. I need a break. Fifteen years is enough for anyone of anything. Although I do hope to be married for longer than that.

'Fine,' I say. 'It's the way it goes sometimes, isn't it?'

Mum looks at me and for a second it's like she's scared of me. It's a look I've seen before and it makes me feel alone somehow but I like it because part of me wants her to be scared of me. Scared in an impressed way, I mean. Like when she came to see me play King Herod in the school nativity and I sang a song called 'I'm Not Finished Yet' and did a sort of jazzy tap dance that I made up on the spot to thrill the crowd and on the way home she said it was like I'd been keeping a big secret from her all those years and I clocked her crying in the wing mirror.

'You sound very grown up,' she says.

'Well, it's my last few weeks of school,' I say. 'I'm a sixth-form-college student in a matter of months. Official.'

It feels so bad to lie like this but I'm on a roll. There's no way I'll get a place at a college without any GCSE results. Don't think about it, don't. Like Mr Keaveney says, you can always figure everything out together.

I think of the poem and the letter, them finding them tomorrow when they go downstairs, like the mum and dad in that Beatles song my dad always plays, 'She's Leaving Home'. Them seeing the envelope on the mat and saying what's this, opening the letter and reading it and being sad and maybe a bit angry but then being pleased, maybe even scared-impressed.

'You be careful around that Nessa's brother,' Mum says now. 'I heard he's been in trouble with the police.'

'I'm sure he's just a person,' I say, 'doing his best. Most people are just people doing their best.'

I finish my toast and say, 'I'm going to get my bags and then go for the bus.'

The walk through the first zone seems longer than usual because it's the last time I'm doing it, and when you get near the end of anything it's like time speeds up so fast it feels like it's going extra slow, like it's stretching and thinning, like all your sense and understanding is getting compressed and compressed and compressed and you might die with not being able to deal with everything all at once. Like you're the heaviest thing trying to travel at the speed of light. A spacecraft on the edge of a black hole.

Anyway you've got to follow your dreams, haven't you. It's like Nessa with her plan for the concert. She's going to try to get backstage. She told me she was bringing a new dress into school and make-up and hair stuff and things to make a poster with and I thought, this is perfect, loads of girls will have bags in school for all sorts of reasons and I won't look any different, not suspicious at all. Then me and Nessa are going to get the bus together into Manchester and then go our separate ways. I think Candice will be coming too but that's all right. They're going to drink at the fort in Castlefield because no one ever checks there and it's not a long walk to G-Mex from there.

I leave Juliette at the school gates and I take a look at her face knowing it'll be months. If we were in a film I'd say I love you, and I do love her, but I don't say it because it feels forced. I say, 'See you in a bit.' Which isn't actually a lie. It's not like I'm never going to see her again. I go in and she goes in. I'll see her soon, I tell myself. I'll see her soon.

By the time I get to class, Nessa's already in and getting her shirt signed by the others. It's like everyone's decided to suddenly be friends now, like all the old wars have been forgotten and everyone's best mates. I even get my shirt signed by Emily Owen, although she writes 'She's Got One in the Oven' on it, which is an Oasis lyric and makes Nessa raging. CROSS IT OUT CROSS IT OUT YOU DAFT INDIE SLAG. Everyone puts the names of the bands they like on their own shirts and Nessa writes DAUBNEY across the back of her shirt in big letters like she's a footballer or a footballer's wife. It doesn't seem as though anyone is going to be working very hard today. The other ones who are staying on for the sixth form say things like, 'See you in September!' And I say, 'Yeah!' But I think, you won't. You won't see me probably ever again because even if they let me re-sit my exams I will be behind you all and probably actually be pregnant and loads ahead of you all in terms of real actual life, which is why I don't care about the exams because I'll be ahead in so many other ways.

Lessons pass in a blur. I don't see him all morning. Then at the end of lunchtime I'm walking back from the toilet and see the sleeve of his coat sticking out Miss Lawton's office like he's standing in the doorway. I slow down and go over, crouch down and pretend to tie my shoe while I listen.

He's being told off.

Miss Lawton is saying, 'I don't think it's appropriate to discuss these things in your lessons, Daniel. There are many parents who have expressed concern about your age and marital status.'

He says, 'I don't think that's really fair, Janet.'

She says, 'Still, you understand this is a fee-paying school, and more to the point an all-girls' school. And a male teacher – a young, male teacher – has to be devoutly focused on his conduct. We live in suspicious times, Daniel.'

He says, 'I did not and would not have a conversation about sex unless it was specifically contextualised within an analysis of the text.'

She says, 'I think let's avoid texts that require such analysis in future.'

He says, 'You want me to cut out all of Shakespeare and three quarters of the classics, Janet? I only go off the curriculum.'

She says, 'I'm very aware of the curriculum. Choose more carefully. Think of the implications. I also think you should be mindful of your absences this term.'

'My father is really sick, you know that.'

'We all have ageing parents, Daniel.'

His sleeve moves and I stand bolt upright. He comes out of the office and looks at me and I shake my head and smile and whisper, 'In trouble again, Daniel?' He gives me his warning look but then he walks down the corridor and looks back and he is grinning. And I don't care about anything other than that and that is a great feeling. It is magical. It is magic.

Not long now. Not long. Don't blow it at the last minute. Neither of us should.

By half three my shirt is covered in names of people I don't really like and who don't really like me but who cares, we are out of here out of here out of here! Nessa and Candice and me can hardly walk to the interchange so we run – run like we're horses that have been set free from their stable.

We do our make-up in McDonald's toilets and change into our going-out clothes. I twist my hair into short knotty tufts and put on some red lipstick. I drink two bottles of Metz from a carrier bag. We get on the bus to Manchester and sit on the top deck and smoke Consulate Menthols and have a little swig from a bottle of kiwi MD 20/20 Nessa's brought from home, from Lee's stash. I tap my cigarette and the end goes to a perfect point and Nessa says, 'Oooh, that means you're in love.' Candice is all right. We make a point of saying each other looks nice. When we get to Manchester I hug Nessa really hard and Candice says, 'Look at you two, it's like you're never going to see each other again.' And I whisper, 'August,' in Nessa's ear. Nessa says, 'Oh, I only told Candice but don't worry, she won't tell anyone,' and Candice is nodding and I'm not sure she's all that all right after all. Then they go down towards Castlefield and I go across the other way towards Oxford Street. There's loads of girls around in town even though it's only 5 p.m. They're all dressed up in crop tops and jean shorts and high heels and some of them have banners and posters they've made. Loads are for Matt. Nessa won't like that but she'll have to deal because that is the reality of the situation for now, for her. I smile at a few of the girls even though I don't know them, like I'm a little kid again. I'm feeling strong and happy and it's almost like people are moving to one side for me because they know the importance of my mission. I feel a bit like Moses parting the waves. Sometimes you walk down the street and feel like you know every single person you pass.

John o'Groats

Sarah woke at 5 a.m., switched on. Her breath was smoke in the air; the van was freezing. She sat up straight. Juliette was still asleep. Sarah brought her hand up to her mouth to chew her nail and jumped as her finger touched her cheek. It was like ice. She looked down. Her right foot was out of her sleeping bag and three of the toes were blue. Sarah panicked. She looked at Juliette – was she alive? Was she breathing? She was very quiet – not even snoring. For once, she wished Juliette would snore. Then a more terrifying thought struck her – what if the gas flame had gone out but the gas kept on flowing? They'd be gassed in their beds! Maybe she was dead! Maybe they were both dead, and this was like one of those high-concept dramas on Netflix where they had to now navigate their way through the afterlife while also working out they were dead, with flashbacks to all the bad things they'd done in their lives that they had to forgive each other for, which was actually what the drama was about.

Sarah hobbled to the door, opened it, hopped down and made her way to the gas locker. She opened it and checked – the gas had run out. The best of all the terrible possibilities.

Juliette shouted: 'What are you doing? Fuck it's cold!'

Sarah closed the gas locker and hobbled back in. 'I know! Look at my toes! They were sticking out of my bag. I think I have frostbite.'

'Oh my god. Can you feel them?'

'Nope.'

'Can you move them?'

'Nope.'

'We have to warm them! We should have brought those hand-warmers. Oh god, I didn't think. Mum would have had some.'

'Mum would have had some and you would have judged her and mocked her if she'd tried to give them to us.'

'I would. And now I see the error of that.'

'We literally have no power.'

They looked out of the windows. They were in the middle of nowhere.

'We have to get you to a hospital.'

'Shall we try rubbing them more first?'

Juliette began to rub Sarah's toes. But Juliette's fingers barely worked, being so cold.

'We have to drive.'

They quickly dressed and got in their seats, seatbelts on.

Sarah started the engine, shifted the gearstick into first. But as she put her foot on the accelerator, the van wouldn't move. The wheels were spinning. They were on ice. She turned off the engine. 'We need to melt the ice under the wheels. But how?'

Juliette looked at her phone. 'No reception.'

'This is bleaker than where we grew up,' Juliette quipped. But Sarah couldn't laugh. She was too busy thinking about the physio she'd need to learn to walk again with just two toes on one foot.

They got dessert spoons out of the kitchen drawer and tried to dig the wheels out of the ice, but they couldn't do it – the ice was too thick. They tried with pans – not sturdy enough. The pans were buckling, and the wrong shape to scoop. Why had they not packed a shovel? Surely these things should be standard? She hadn't even been offered a winter peril package at the hire place. They tried pushing the van, but it was way too heavy. Then Sarah thought of something – she hopped into the van and pulled out the foot mats from the driver and passenger sides, then put them under the front wheels and told Juliette to push at the back. Sarah revved the engine, and the van gained traction – and moved! She screamed. Juliette whooped and came running, diving into the van like they were making a getaway from a bank robbery.

They were elated for about an hour. The adrenaline coursed through Sarah. She put the heater on in the footwell and the hot air slowly brought her toes back to life. All was well. All was well.

*   *   *

They drove along the estuary, the wide sandy flats thinning to riverbed, the land narrowing and closing in around the road. These roads around the far north felt as though they were taking Sarah deeper into something, the winding single tracks dipping to meet dark lochs and rising to wastelands. She thought of the water in the lochs holding its own memories and the memories of the earth around it, the memories of the people who had tried and failed to tame this landscape. Memory worked like that, like a stone dropped in a pool, the ripples spreading, the stone descending. The Hymer swayed on the bends. The lochs, those memory pools, some darker and deeper than others. Sarah's dazed synapses made the landscape impressionistic.

The sea became dark grey, dark as wet slate, the breakers brilliant white. Sarah felt a knot loosen in her chest. Relief. Relief, and an intricate desire. Waves were battering the dockside and wheelie bins were tied up at parking points and to the gateposts of houses. There was nothing quaint about these fishing towns. The ragged lobster pots and beastly bungalows, the hard rain, the dog-waste bins, the rain rain rain rain rain. Driving through the driving rain. The rain hitting the tops of the fenceposts and spraying up like fireworks. There was a graveyard with five or six or seven graves in it. Vicious squalls, roads strewn with ripped tree branches and toppled wheelie bins. The Hymer was almost blown off the road. Sarah found herself gripping the wheel with both hands. She felt the wind pulling the van, wanting to take it, and she almost wanted to let go, wanted to let it. Sheets of wind blew up over the road and bonnet, covering the van, passing over them. Juliette was texting a lot – Sarah presumed to the school dad. At one point she thought she saw Juliette take a quick shot down her top.

They passed a village – an old red phone box weathered to almost orange. On the edge of a loch was a tiny ruin of a castle. The heather rippled like crawling skin.

There wasn't much in the way of overnight options, and nowhere to park. John o' Groats itself was a dull wasteland. There was a single inn they thought could be a good idea because they fancied using a proper bathroom and having a warm shower somewhere they didn't have to skid around in mud. 'That Glastonbury Monday feeling' was how Juliette described it. They parked in the car park and went into the inn, where the couple who owned it – Norma and Bill – invited them for a drink in the lounge.

Norma and Bill were the least suburban people ever. Or maybe the most suburban, Sarah couldn't decide. The inn was chintzy inside, with floral curtains. 'Daisy Daisy' was playing in the lounge. It made Sarah think of *2001: A Space Odyssey*. Hal, the computer that went rogue. She was fearful of robots thanks to Hal. She always said thank you to Siri. And Alexa.

Norma was in her late fifties with streaked short hair. She had a New Zealand accent and used the word 'critter' a lot. They had a noisy little dog. They served the sisters wine from a warm box of white on a radiator shelf. Sarah was horrified. She drank it anyway. So did Juliette. Perhaps the most terrifying thing about the situation, and there were several, was a stuffed brown bear, eight feet tall, dressed as Elvis, in the corner of the inn.

'You finding the Hymer okay to drive?' asked Norma.

'She's driving it,' Juliette deferred to Sarah.

'Yeah,' said Sarah. 'Sort of.'

'Great little vehicles.'

'It's just a rental.'

'You got a dog of your own in there?'

'No, just us.'

Bill grinned at them. Sarah couldn't work out if they were being nice or were just bored of each other. 'This is very nice,' Sarah said, about the wine.

'You like being on the road?' said Bill. He sounded like Pee-wee Herman, or like Sarah after too much coke. Sarah was starting to get freaked out.

'Mm,' she said, and then regretted her 'mm'. He might think that was her sex 'mm'. She was freaking out, it was official. Sarah looked at Juliette to save her. Juliette stared at a tasselly cushion. Sarah diverted, as she always did in times of great unease, to talking about the apocalypse. She found it very grounding to talk about the end of all time. Really took the pressure off the minutiae of life. Even when those minutiae involved potentially getting murdered.

'There's something so pleasing about driving along and having everything you need to survive in a few square metres of space. Makes me think we could survive the apocalypse.'

'Zombies,' said Norma. 'Bill's obsessed with zombies!'

'I've thought about zombies a lot,' Sarah said. 'And really all you need to survive them is a garage, a good combination lock, and a supply of irradiated milk.' She instantly regretted mentioning a place that could also serve as a location to hide captured women.

Now Juliette looked at Sarah desperately.

'So where are you headed?' Bill asked.

Don't tell him, he's a stranger, Sarah thought helplessly.

'Home soon,' said Juliette.

Norma poured more terrible wine.

Sarah stared at the eight-foot bear.

'Oh, him,' said Norma. 'Bill shot him in Oregon. And I'm a big fan of the King, so. He's been on the road with us ever since. Our daughter hates it.'

The word comforted Sarah. 'Is your daughter back in New Zealand?'

'Yes, she's at uni in Wellington.' She pointed to a picture on the wall, bolted with four brackets. It was a girl in school uniform, smiling, gap-toothed in an oval frame. 'That's our Fay. Years ago now.' There were other photos, around her, different girls in different frames. Nieces, maybe. Cousins. Or people they had killed. And chopped up and buried under the car park.

'We miss her, but you know, you have to let them live their own lives,' said Norma. 'Do you have children?'

'She's so pretty,' said Juliette. 'What's she studying?'

'Economics.'

'Wow.'

'Yeah, she's going to sort the whole thing out.'

'Someone needs to.'

Sarah drank her wine very fast. She regretted the fact that she had never learned any martial arts.

'Have you had your dinner, girls?' asked Bill.

'Um, we—'

'Because Norma's got a stew on and it's quite something. Do you like stew?'

IT'S GIRL STEW, IT'S STEW MADE OF GIRLS, shouted Sarah's brain.

Norma got up and stepped to the hob, lifted a pan lid. The smell of meat and gravy wafted out.

'It's Norma's best. Beef and dumplings. Have some.'

IT'S POISONED, IT'S POISONED. REMEMBER WOLF CREEK?? YOU'RE GOING TO WAKE UP IN BILL'S POLYTUNNEL, DUCT-TAPED TO A CHAIR.

Juliette said, 'If you don't mind, we're going to go back to the van after these drinks and get some rest. We had a terrible night's sleep last night and I fear we're not much company. But thank you so much for your immense kindness.'

Sarah loved her sister. She fucking loved her.

* * *

They ran-walked back to the Hymer, got in and bolted the door.

'Certifiable.'

'Complete fucking psychopaths.'

Juliette was howling with laughter, doubled up. Sarah looked at her and felt – a moment of clear, real joy.

Juliette stopped laughing. Her face went serious. 'Thank you,' she said. 'This has been so fun.'

I ask

Someone on a corner where is the Peveril of the Peak please and they say that way two minutes Victorian building in the middle of the road bright green tiling you can't miss it.

I get there and look at it for a few minutes, smoking. The thing I don't like about pubs is you don't know what you're getting until you get inside. It's not like a shop, is it?

I walk in and my heart is pounding. I scan the pub no no no no and then I turn round and see him coming out of the toilet and I say, 'Mr— Danny, here I am!' And he looks really surprised and says, 'Sarah?' I am surprised that he is surprised. Why is he surprised? Why is he not expecting me? This was our plan.

And I say, 'Here I am!' And he says, 'Let's go outside.'

We stand just outside and he looks nervous but that's okay because I guess I'm nervous too. Now or never now or never now or never. Sometimes you just have to do something that you know will make the world stop for a minute with the chance of it never starting again – it's like getting in a swimming pool, or pulling a plaster off. And I know I am the one who has to tell him the exact plan. You just have to do it have to do it have to do it go on Sarah just do it now now now now GO.

I open my mouth.

'I know you can't say this because of your position, so I've been strategic for both of us. I've got my things with me so we can leave now or as soon as you've finished your drink if you prefer. I was thinking Scotland because of Walter Scott but also we won't need to go through passport control or anything but we can still hide up there you know it's quiet and I've saved fifty pounds so we're all right for a few days at least food-wise, and we can just go in your car.' I point to his car, which is parked nearby. 'We can even sleep in the car tonight if we don't get to Loch Lomond in time – I've slept in a car before and I'm not afraid. I've planned it all on the map and we can take our time and just be together and then when I'm sixteen in August we can get married at Gretna Green and come back and be part of things again. I know you've thought about this too but I felt as though it was up to me to finalise things and put all the arrangements in place. I know you've been busy with your dad and your job and I've been busy too with my revision but I've not given that as much time as everyone thought because of this plan but I thought your job was more important than my exams for the sake of the other girls so I took it all upon myself so now we can just go.'

He goes white then green then white. It's a lot for him to comprehend, me putting it all out in the open like this.

He says, 'How did you find me?'

'You said. You told me this was your favourite pub and you came here every Friday – don't you remember? The book extract. The joining of Enlightenment and Romanticism.'

He shakes his head and covers his eyes with his hands, then uncovers them again, like he's playing peekaboo. Peekaboo! But his face isn't happy.

I wait for him to kiss me and tell me thank you thank you for being brave, one of us needed to be and I couldn't I just couldn't. But he just says, 'Oh god.' Like that. Oh god.

I can start to feel a feeling in my stomach. The butterflies in there are not happy. They're starting to swarm.

His mate sticks his head out the pub. It's the mate from the club and he looks angry, but not at me, at Danny. He says, 'Oh fucking hell, of course, nice one. Can of worms. Dickhead.'

'Shut up, Joe.'

'I'm having no part in this.' His mate shakes his head and goes back in.

Then Mr K— I mean Danny says, 'Sarah, I'm so sorry. I really didn't— I really don't know what to say. I am very . . . flattered.'

Flattered! I don't know why he's using that word. It's a word that puts space between us. It's a word that makes me feel like he's pushing me away from him rather than pulling me close.

I say, 'What? I don't want you to be flattered. I'm not trying to flatter you. I'm saying this because it's true. What do you mean, you're very flattered?'

Something happens in my stomach then like all the butterflies get together in a big ball and start rolling around. He is not kissing me yet. We are not leaving.

I say, 'All we have to do is walk to your car, get in and set off. That's all we have to do.'

He says, 'I'm not going to do that, Sarah.'

'Why not?'

'Because you're a very special girl but I've never thought of you like that.'

'Don't say I'm special – that is not a nice way to describe someone.'

I know I'm frowning in an ugly way I can't control, so I hold the frown and hold my face and when I can, I say, 'You can't tell me you don't love me.'

I want the dream to end. The bad dream. I want to wake up and this not be true. It can't be true.

'But that's exactly what I'm telling you, Sarah. I want to make that absolutely clear. I'm so sorry if you've got the wrong impression. I never meant to give you . . . that impression.'

He is talking so slowly and so carefully it makes me want to scream because I know it's just not real, it's just not him – it's some weird version of him he thinks he has to put on for his job or his mate or the world or whatever.

I say, 'Well, what about when you put your phone number and address in that book you gave me?'

He looks confused. Then he gasps. 'Oh that, oh no, I write that in all my books in case they ever get lost.'

I do not know what to do with this information.

'Well, what about the time you said you don't know what you'd do without me, and what about the time you said only you and I get that, and what about the time you said I oscillate I hum and I am in all ways beautiful, and all the times we looked at each other and when you said we've got something no one else has got, and what about the time you told me about your mum and we held hands for an hour and how you still thought about her some mornings and I reminded you of her in a good way?'

I'm ranting but I can't stop.

'I'm sorry,' is all he keeps saying, 'I'm sorry.'

'And what about when you almost kissed me! You can't deny that, I just won't let you deny that. It's a fact. You almost kissed me in that club, and people saw. Your mate saw. You're telling me that meant nothing? If you say that then I'll really know you're lying.'

His face flickers for a split second and then it hardens again – but I see it! Yes, I see you and I know you and I have you, and you are mine, you are.

'That was just a friendly thing,' he says. 'I was glad to see a friendly face. I was... intoxicated. I am so very sorry.'

'You're lying. But you know what, you can lie to yourself,

Danny, but you can't lie to me and you know you can't and you know I won't let you.'

'Listen, you can't call me that.'

He is white as a sheet. Whiter than white.

'Yes I can. You're not my teacher any more. You're just a person and I'm just a person and we are both just here looking out from our faces.'

He shakes his head again. 'I'm so sorry, Sarah, I hate to see you upset like this. Let me call you a taxi. I'll give you some money.'

'I don't want you to call me a taxi and I don't want any of your fucking money.' I can't speak for upset; stupid, stop it.

I feel like I'm going to faint. Like the light is growing dimmer, black coming in from all sides, like a tunnel closing up. He is at one end near the light, getting further away, further away, leaving me behind alone here in the darkness.

I want the sky to fall. I want the world to burn. I want to die. And while I'm dying, I want to watch him dying in a world that's on fire.

He says, 'I'm not leaving you here like this.'

'Come for a walk with me then to that park over there.'

'I can't do that.'

'Please.'

'I can't.'

'Why?'

'I can't. Oh, Sarah don't, oh god. Please let me get you a taxi.'

I'm running away and I hate myself and I hate him and I hate everything I'm wearing.

Loch Ness

The next stop was another whisky tasting: a distillery called The Singleton of Glen Ord, 100 miles south. Sarah didn't drink. Juliette barely sipped a few shots. Sarah bought her parents a bottle of whisky as they left. As she paid for the whisky, she pulled the flyer out from her pocket again.

There was the proof. He was up here. He was still playing in some crappy band. Still keeping his sordid little dream alive. The gig was the day after tomorrow, in Aviemore. The mountains down on the eastern side of Scotland, the Cairngorms: that was where they would find him. Why should he just be gallivanting around, enjoying his life? She bet he never thought about it once, what he'd done. She stuffed the flyer back in her pocket and gripped the bottle.

Back at the van, she got the map out and spread it across the table. Juliette was puzzled. 'What is it?'

'We have to go to Aviemore next.'

'When?'

'As soon as possible.'

'Okay, what's going on? Is this a work thing?'

'What?'

'Oh! Is *that* what this is, you chasing down a client? Is there someone you want something from?'

'No! How many times? It's your birthday!'

'Well, I don't want to go to Aviemore. I want to go to Loch Ness, like we planned.'

'Why?'

Juliette glanced guiltily at her phone.

'Okay, so don't freak out, but . . .'

Sarah looked at Juliette, aware for the first time that right now she was the definition of freaking out, although Juliette could have no idea why. At least, Sarah hoped she couldn't. 'So,' Juliette began, 'you know how this is my birthday trip and I'm a really hardworking mum of two with no time to or for myself ever.'

Sarah was waiting for it, waiting for it. A rain shower passed overhead. Hard on the roof, and then gone again.

'Well, I just wanted a bit of sex on this trip, and you guys got on so well over text, I've invited Aaron to meet me at Loch Ness for one night only – there's a posh new campsite there with glamping pods so I thought me and him could stay in one of those for the night and you could stay in this. On the same site of course. For literally one night. I hope that's okay?'

Sarah didn't respond. Instead she was silent. The silence filled. Juliette broke it.

'I feel like we've had our QT, haven't we? We've had some good chats? And I'm so grateful!'

Sarah nodded, processing.

'Is that okay? Please say it's okay. I feel terrible now, and . . .'

Sarah said: 'It's fine.'

'Do you really mean that?'

'Of course.'

'Do you mind? Say really if you mind.'

'It's cool. I just want you to have a nice time.'

'Thought I'd give you a break from me and my snoring!'

'That's really thoughtful of you.'

'I think he's stressing a bit about me being away. He went postal on the Year 2 parents' WhatsApp.'

'He sounds like exactly the kind of person we should invite somewhere remote.'

'He's a doctor. He's ideal!'

'I bring to the bar, exhibit A – Harold Shipman.'

'Harold Shipman was a real exception.'

'So is Doctor Death en route?'

'His train gets in to Inverness in a few hours.'

'Right.'

'He'll get a taxi from there to the campsite.'

'Very good of him.'

'You see, you do mind.'

'I don't!'

* * *

The road to Loch Ness was grey and wide and undulating, like the spine of a monster. Sarah put on some 90s tunes to lighten the mood. They caught each other singing together, harmonising, to Go West, 'Faithful'. It was an unexpected moment that made them both blush, then carry on almost shyly. It was a way to connect and not connect.

It was a new campsite, only open twelve weeks, with freshly cut wood chippings either side of the road and a Scandi feel to the whole place. As they parked up, Sarah saw six wooden glamping pods on the hill by the edge of the forest, huddled like megafauna.

The shower block was pristine. The toilets were sensibly in the same block, in a serene hut with wooden slatted roofs that sloped low. The whole building vibrated like a giant entity. There were solar panels on every inch of the roof.

Juliette went to check in to her sex pod, so Sarah decided to take a walk down by the loch. She put boot socks over her jeans and pulled them up. Her chunky running trainers made her feel purposeful. She wore a tweed overcoat and a waxed green Stetson, which she'd taken from her dad's fishing box once he'd stopped fishing.

Down past the reception, there was a little boat landing with five or six fibreglass boats. The *95*, the *127*, the *Kayren Amy*. A 'DANGER: DEEP WATER' sign. Then under the trees, a path snaked away, the same gravel as up at the campsite, the brand-new stones of a path recently made. On the other side of the path, sloping uphill, a second shore of auburn beech leaves. Further up there was a canoe rack, a sign saying 'Trailblazer Rest Site'. Sarah picked her way over roots to climb up to it, and found a shed on tyres, greening timber, with a rusted padlock. The remains of a fire pit, a triangle of logs that had served as benches for young bottoms, a ludicrously low cairn. She picked up a rock and placed it on top of the cairn and it fitted snugly, making a perfect peak, as though the cairn had been waiting for her to complete it.

A little further along, a pier made of caged boulders. On the loch, an abandoned pleasure craft bobbed incongruously. Boats came and went. The sky began to darken. She looked at the mouth of the river, up there, back into the mountains. How the river grass grew on the bottom, she could imagine it. How she had lain down in that grass and let water pass over her for so long now. The roar of a fighter jet startled her from her reverie. An ear-splitting roar, louder than Juliette's snores. The jet tore through the sky above the loch, the sound of it shaking her to her bowels. She felt it in her feet last, the ground vibrating long after the jet was out of sight. She was getting too far away. She started to feel uneasy, and began to walk back. Old as she was, she still glanced behind her sometimes when she was walking through dark hallways, or woods. As she left the shore she was sure she heard footfalls behind her, but it was just the gravel, just the gravel.

Sarah felt a need to eat that came and went. She smoked another cigarette. She got back to the Hymer and sat at the table, drinking whisky, and looked at the map of the Highlands. Aviemore. The word rose off the page like a phantom.

Juliette, freshly showered, buzzing with teenage romance, knocked on the door and came in. 'Hey!'

'Hey.'

'Listen, he's in a cab. Do you mind if he comes here first, for a drink? There's not really a bar . . .'

'We've not really got anything in.'

'There's whisky. A few beers.'

'I like to put on a buffet for cocktail parties.'

'Hahaha. You'll like him.'

Sarah felt as though it didn't really matter whether she liked him.

'Does he have a wife, or partner?'

'They're separated.'

'Still living together?'

'For the kids.'

'Right.'

Sarah felt as though she had the full measure of the situation now. She quoted *Labyrinth*. The talking stone walls warning the young woman on the wrong track: 'TAKE HEED TAKE HEED. For the path you will take will LEAD to CERTAIN DESTRUCTION!' Then, in an ultra-gravelly voice: 'SOON, it will be too late.'

'You're overthinking. Anyway, those talking walls were decoys. She was on the right path.'

* * *

As it turned out, Sarah did quite like him, this Dr Aaron. He was sweet and funny and seemed to be completely unaware of the fact he was having an affair and this was downright weird, to be sitting in a motorhome with a woman you were having an affair with and her sister who you hadn't met before and who were on holiday together. He was in middle-class leisurewear – a man who tackled peaks to mark milestone birthdays. He liked a craft ale, in its place. He no doubt had a National Trust membership sticker in his car windscreen next to a Glastonbury parking pass from 2019. He was, Sarah concluded, an alpha in sheep's clothing. Sarah had to admit – only to herself, of course – that she could see the appeal. That was the late thirties for you. Standards had slipped from grand romance to someone with a passable self-care regime who looked like they could reliably cook a medium-rare steak.

'Sounds like you've had an exciting time this week!' he said.

'I almost lost three toes,' said Sarah, going in with a medical anecdote. She clarified: 'To frostbite.'

'More likely frostnip,' said Aaron. Sarah liked him a bit less. 'I almost lost a testicle once when I was climbing,' he added.

Ooft. Juliette was going to have to delete that comment from the wankbank, Sarah could tell. She watched Juliette fumble with her glass. Was it odd that they were sitting next to each other, like a couple but not touching, or was that the norm with an affair? There was something very synthetic, very *suburban*, about the scene.

Aaron smiled. 'Thanks for letting me gatecrash. I've been working in sexual health all week so this is a real tonic.'

'So glad to know we're an upgrade from gonorrhoea,' said Sarah, smiling.

'I wouldn't say that,' he smiled back.

'Ha! Cheeky.' Sarah liked him well enough – as Jane Austen wrote. Well enough. Yes, he would do, he would do very well.

Juliette was dying, dying at the sexual health chat. Sarah felt her cheek warm with the heat of her sister's discomfort and disapproval.

'Do you have siblings, Aaron?' Sarah asked.

'One. A brother. Younger. They say it's the longest relationship of your life, don't they. With your sibling.'

'Do you get on?'

'Yeah, I mean we're not as close as you guys . . . You must be pretty close in age.'

'In some ways,' said Juliette. 'But in other ways not at all.'

'There's only two years between us,' said Sarah. 'I'm a millennial really.'

'She's on the cusp,' said Juliette.

Sarah nodded.

'You think that stuff means anything?' said Aaron.

'Oh yeah,' said Juliette.

Sarah said: 'I'll never forget the time I realised there might be a generational difference between us. We were on a hike, in our early twenties, and Juliette had a digital camera she was stopping constantly to take photos of everything with. It drove me fucking mad. The documentation. The narrative of the narrative. I could not understand the need for it.'

Aaron laughed.

'Sarah's all over the socials now,' Juliette said. 'She's caught up. She has more followers than anyone I know.'

'That's because I'm millennial with X-er rising,' Sarah said coolly.

'You've been worse on social media this week,' Juliette said. 'Rampant in my comments.'

'I don't use it,' said Aaron. 'WhatsApp is enough for me. I can't wait until AI can just manage all my messaging for me.'

'Seriously?' said Juliette. 'I hate AI. It's going to ruin the tablescape business.'

'So what?' said Sarah. 'No one gave a shit during the Industrial

Revolution when the looms took the place of the all the poor people sewing things. But now it's middle-class creatives getting their toes trodden on, the internet's up in arms.'

She went to the toilet. Juliette followed her.

'Do you think he likes me?' said Juliette when they were inside the safe wooden lodge of the eco-toilets.

'What? Oh god, no. No – I mean, I'm not doing this. It's bad enough I'm hosting the most awkward cocktail party ever, I am not doing the emotional overtime of reassuring you on top of that. We are not sixteen.'

'He wouldn't come all the way up here for my birthday if he wasn't into me, would he?'

'Juliette, are you listening to me? It's a hard no on this line of enquiry. I want the Juliette back who kills deer, please, not the one who faffs about whether a pipsqueak dad-bod with moobs and a Patagonia hoodie might want to motorboat her.'

Juliette started at this. The deer, she wasn't over it. 'Motorboat – that's an old-fashioned sex reference.'

'Sorry. Spitting. Gender play. Consensual non-consent. Whatever you do. With all of your two years on me.'

Juliette looked chastened. 'I didn't kill it. I put it out of its misery.'

'Shame you can't extend the same courtesy to yourself where Doctor Marcus Mumford is concerned.'

'He doesn't even have a full beard.'

'Oh, I don't mean that like it sounds. Just, be tough. Use logic. See this for what it is. It's meant to be fun! If it's not fun, what's the point, because you've got one like that at home. And . . . he is a nice human being. But he is not all that. I'm just saying. He is fucking punching. Which is why he got on a train today and wheeled his penis 400 miles up the country to stick it 400 miles up—'

'Gross! Unfair. That's the thing with X-ers, sexualising everything. I don't like to use the word "basic" but it's basic.'

'Says the woman who's spent fifty quid on a sex pod. I'm innocent! The thing with millennials is, you still sexualise everything IN YOUR HEADS, you just *pretend you don't notice the sexual stuff*. You smile like a Valium'd up suburban housewife. You're repressed. Strangled. Deeply resentful. The things you pretend are overt are just your shop sign. Your "sex journey" is just words you say – or better, post – to make yourself feel better about the fact you are very uncomfortable with the fact you're having enjoyable sex.'

'Mum said she didn't know what to do with you sometimes. You were always at it on the sofa in the lounge. Riddling away.'

Sarah hadn't heard that word for a long time. She felt smaller. 'I was a sexual child. Don't make me ashamed of it.'

'I would never—'

Sarah let out a long sigh. 'Ohhhhhh, Juliette. Don't come at me. I don't want to come at you. Men fuck us up. He's just next in the chain of something masquerading as a choice for you. You only ever got with Johnnie because you were lacking in self-confidence and accepted a man you knew could never hurt you but also one you knew you could never truly respect. And I'm so angry about that, Juliette. He's not your match. You know that.'

'You haven't met your match, either.'

'Maybe I met my match the day you were born.'

'You see, you say things like that, but you just moved out. You moved down south and left me. I'm not like you, I'm not enterprising.'

Sarah swallowed. She hadn't been expecting this. She had thought she would bring it up; had thought—

But: *enterprising*. What?

'What does that mean?'

But Juliette was away, back to the van.

'Why do men have nipples?' Juliette asked Aaron, back at the table. She was trying to turn herself on by making him be more doctor-y. Basic, Sarah thought. Basic.

'It's all about the way embryos develop . . .' Aaron began.

'Hang on! I think I know the answer to this one,' said Sarah. 'It's so they can be pierced.'

Sarah said: 'Do you ever use the phrase *At your cervix*, ma'am?'

'No I don't.'

'That's a wasted opportunity.'

He and Juliette went out for a vape together. Sarah could hear them whispering and giggling, between puffs of fruity vape. It wound her up.

When they came back in, Sarah was another glass down. She smiled at Aaron. He smiled back at her. Pleased. He was so pleased.

Sarah said: 'Tell me something: as a doctor, do you get many girls under sixteen coming in after they've had sex?'

Juliette's head snapped around.

'Yes,' Aaron replied, cautiously, 'a fair few.'

'How do you deal with that? Do you have to report them all as rape cases?'

'Woah woah woah, this is a bit heavy,' Juliette cut in. 'Can we chat about AI again?'

'No, not always,' said Aaron, matter-of-factly answering Sarah's question. 'Depends how old the male is.'

'That's interesting.' Sarah didn't look at Juliette.

'If the male is fifteen too and it was consensual, we wouldn't.'

'You're saying you think you can have consensual sex at the age of fifteen?'

He didn't answer.

'Sarah,' said Juliette. 'Please.'

'I don't mean to put you on the spot, Dr Aaron,' Sarah said. 'I personally think you can. I'm just interested in how the authorities deal with it. Off the record. Because it sounds like medicine accepts a grey area where the law doesn't.'

'There are no hard and fast rules. It's an individual doctor's opinion.'

Juliette said, 'Can I borrow you for a cigarette, Sarah?'

'Do you mean a cigarette or do you mean a vape?'

'Thank you,' said Juliette, holding the door for her.

When they were outside, Juliette said: 'You're freaking me out.'

'I'm just getting to know him. You texted him about my vagina. I'm playing catch-up on the whole inappropriate chat thing.'

'Please. Please, Sarah.'

Sarah could feel her rage building. But she couldn't bear to hear Juliette beg. Sarah thought maybe she was going mad with the altitude. What was she trying to achieve? Was this how it was all going to come out? Their historical truth? Here, like this, in a glamping pod with a man one of them was fucking out of desperation? Sarah felt dizzy. God, this was exactly why she shouldn't drink. She was falling, falling.

'Okay,' she said. 'I'll play nice.'

Juliette still looked fearful. Sarah squeezed her hand. 'Come on. Be all right.'

Back inside, Sarah suggested: 'Let's play a drinking game.'

'That's more like it!' Juliette said.

'Truth or dare?' said Sarah.

'I played a great one recently,' said Aaron, staking his claim in the chat. 'National treasures we secretly hate.'

They all agreed this could be fun.

'I'll start,' said Aaron. 'Tom Daley. Apparently he made his own wedding cake. Fuck off.'

Sarah thought. 'Monty Don. His soiled hands give me the ick.'

'Dr Brian Cox,' said Aaron. 'Don't understand why he's such a heartthrob. Why all the mums go mad for his floppy fringe and music credentials.'

'David Attenborough,' said Juliette.

'No, no, no,' said Sarah, 'you're not having that one. Sorry. No. He is the guardian angel of my childhood.'

Juliette cleared her throat. They looked at her. 'Safe space?' she said.

'Safe space,' confirmed Sarah and Aaron in unison.

'Okay,' said Juliette. 'Anne Frank.'

Sarah dropped her drink. 'What??'

Juliette looked away. 'I don't think she was very nice to her sister.'

This hung in the air.

'For shame, Juliette. It was . . . difficult times for the family.'

Juliette shrugged, unmoved.

'Well,' said Sarah, 'at least now I know I'm not just a ghastly Karen while you get to be a hopeless Becky.'

'Don't take it out on me!' said Juliette.

'What?'

'Your stuff.'

'I don't have stuff.'

'You're forty-two,' said Juliette. 'You didn't get what you wanted? It's too late. You didn't get what you ordered? It's your fucking fault.'

Sarah caught her breath. *What?*

Aaron was looking – for the first time that evening – suitably uncomfortable. Sarah gathered her words. 'Sad thing is, Juliette, I'm just a bit too clever to accept that.'

Unlike you.

Now it was Juliette's turn to imperceptibly gasp. There they both were, cut to the quick.

'I get it,' said Sarah. 'I get the dynamic.' She nodded at Aaron. 'You're the jock. She's the cheerleader. I'm the weird kid. It's been a blast but now it's time for me to put the head brace back on and go eat crayons in the corner.'

'You defined us all, Sarah. Good for you.'

'At least I'm self-aware.'

'You're not. It's a charade.'

The Fake. The Idiot. It all boiled back down to this. Their Greatest Hits.

Aaron said, suddenly: 'I was working in a hospital once and there was an object up an old woman's vagina that looked like a ball with hair. When we examined her under anaesthetic it turned out to be a doll's head.'

'A doll's head?' Sarah and Juliette said in unison.

'Yeah, it was the head of her sister's Barbie. They'd had an argument when they were kids and she'd run to her sister's room and shoved the doll's head up there out of spite. Then she'd forgotten about it. It had been there for sixty years.'

'Fair,' said Sarah.

'Did she give it back?' Juliette asked. 'After they got it out?'

Aaron shook his head. 'No, I think it was displayed in the medical museum.'

* * *

Sarah waited until Juliette and Aaron had gone to their pod, waited half an hour – counting down in five-minute blocks in her head:

Another drink. Music on.

Clothes off.

Foreplay.

Bit more foreplay as they're still new.

Sex. Etc.

Sarah took one of the attack alarms their mother had given them, crept over to the pod, pulled out the pin to set it off (Jesus it was loud; ear-splitting) and left it on the pod's sustainable slatted-birch patio. Sarah ran back to the van; she heard Juliette swear loudly, then the pod door open; the alarm was dropped at least once, and then silenced.

Sarah got into her bed. The table pole was lengthways down the side of her. If she moved her leg she could feel it, like the solid cold leg of a robot. Around her, inside the van, the air felt saturated, like she was being watched by a feeling. Her sister was fucked up, and so was she. Reliving the same painful patterns. Never feeling good enough. Never feeling sexy enough. Never being truly brave. Life had fucked them up, a long, long time ago. Sarah felt – maybe only for the second time in her life – as though the way forward was clear. No more running *from*. Time for some running *to*. They were worth it. And she knew what she was going to do to him. He deserved it. Because Sarah had been over false summit after false summit in her dreams, and she had reached the tower in her head, the only true height worth protecting. The thing all the other mountains had come and settled around. She had been inside the tower for a moment, then come out and locked the door again. The inside of the tower was decorated with Juliette's drawings of the family. On all of the drawings, Sarah was depicted as the third one along: the one in between Juliette and her parents. The one always next to her, holding her hand, because on the other side of Juliette was the void. Paper stretching forever. Sarah was the paper doll who stopped Juliette disappearing into nothingness. Again.

Get out the road

YOU STUPID COW! I'm walking fast wiping the snot from my chin trying to keep hold of my bags. Cars are beeping and drivers are shouting but I just flick Vs at them all and say fuck off fuck off fuck you yeah and you 'n' all. I cross the tram lines without even looking because part of me wants to get run over by a tram because then he'd have to come with me to hospital because he's the nearest person I know and I do know him.

I walk down past the Free Trade Hall where my mum told me Bob Dylan played and got shouted at and I like the thought of someone else being shouted at and feeling bad right now.

I walk down to Deansgate where there are loads of girls singing 4Princes songs and chanting all dressed up and I hate them all, I hate them. They all look at me like I'm sad, like I'm nothing. I walk along Deansgate until Castlefield and then turn left down under the bridge towards the fort.

I find Nessa and Candice on a wall drinking and smoking. They look all wobbly. I've never seen Nessa this drunk before. She's holding a big bottle of peach schnapps and doesn't seem to be able to stop squinting.

'SARAH!' she shouts, all glad and then her face drops. 'Oh fuck, oh mate.'

I drop my bags and run over to her and hug her even though I have to sort of hold her up as well.

I say, 'He denied everything, I feel like such an idiot – I'm fucking furious with him.'

She says, 'I'm fucking livid – is he still in that fucking shit pub?'

I get out my essay – *the* essay – and show Nessa the comments. 'How can he deny this, how can he?'

Nessa looks at the essay, reads his words, then looks at me, does a quick smile, reads again, looks at me.

'Tell me that's not real,' I say.

Nessa uses a voice so gentle I can't believe it's her voice. It's like she's talking to a tiny animal or a scared baby. She says, 'Sarah, I hate to say it, mate. I hate to say it, I really do. But these are just like normal comments.'

I thought Nessa was smarter than this.

'Don't be thick,' I say. 'They're not normal. They're code.'

Nessa takes a deep breath. 'Then he's using the same code with me,' she says.

'What do you mean?'

'He's just being a teacher.'

This hangs in the air. I snatch my essay back and look.

'He writes things like this on your essays too?'

She nods.

'Faithless bastard.'

Nessa shakes her head. 'No, no, no. It's just . . . regular teacher shit.'

'That's his phone number!'

Nessa looks. 'It just looks like some working out . . . maybe his big shop for the week? Isn't that bit the price of a pint of milk?'

'It's a phone number! Look at the numbers!'

'Have you phoned it?'

I shake my head. 'Not yet, but . . .'

I drop the essay to the floor and look at it there, lying splayed, like an injured bird.

Nessa tries to take my hand. 'Oh, Sarah. Have you based it all on this, sweetie?'

'Don't call me fucking sweetie like we're in *Ab Fab*.'

I drop her hand. I'm like, 'Get your lying filthy hand off me.'

It's quiet for a minute. Nessa is looking at me like she isn't sure where I am inside my own eyes. Like she's searching for a bit of me she knows. I can feel the heat rising up the back of my neck. I don't know what is going to happen when the heat reaches my face, don't want to know. Suddenly I blurt out: 'You saw the way he was with me in that club! He kissed me!'

'I think he was on drugs.' She pauses. 'Sarah, hon, did you actually kiss?'

My face falls. I have anger only for Nessa now, not the situation. 'Do you think I'm a liar? A complete fantasist? AND DON'T CALL ME HON. WE AREN'T THIRTY-FIVE.'

Nessa jumps a bit at this. She can see what this means to me. This is my life, my heart.

'I don't think you're those things. I think you're a clever romantic. And he might be a clever romantic too. And clever romantics always get a bit lost. That's sort of like their doom.'

I nod at this. This is more like it.

Nessa continues. 'But I think he's a mess. I think sometimes grown-ups can be messes too, and I don't want you getting messed up in his mess. You know why, Sarah? Because you're brilliant, and I know you don't feel it, but you are. You are, mate.'

'Don't say the notes are normal notes, then. Don't insult my intelligence.'

'Sarah.'

I shake my head. But I don't pick up my essay. Something about it is dead now.

She hugs me, holds me, whatever. Says into my hair, 'They are normal notes. It's all just normal stuff. It isn't code, it's the national curriculum.'

'It's poetry.'

'It's his job. I've had those notes off him. Well, similar.'

I feel like all the wind has gone out of me. Like I've fallen out of a tree. Can it be true? These lines he wrote weren't for me, he was writing them for everyone? He was just being . . . a teacher? I can't bear it. It's unbearable. That everything I have been feeling can be reduced to such . . . mundanity. And would I even know the word mundanity if he hadn't been such a good teacher and taken such good extra special care with me?

I let myself be held by Nessa for what feels like a long time. Four or five minutes, even. Candice is just lurking nearby. I feel cold with unspeakable things.

When that time is over, I feel Nessa twitch. 'Are you okay?' she asks. 'I'm sorry.'

I gather my strength and pull away from her, wipe the tear trails from my cheeks. I say, 'It's fine. I hate him and I don't want anything more to do with him. He's a liar and a wimp.'

Nessa laughs out loud. 'He's a drip, a feeble weed.' We both laugh at that but I know I'm trying.

Candice comes over and gives me a Consulate Menthol.

I say, 'I wish I could come to the concert with you two.'

Nessa says, 'What do you mean? Of course you're coming. Sorry, Candice, but you can see how upset she is and she is my best mate.'

'That's no way fair,' says Candice. 'That's well tight. I've paid you for the ticket and you said I was your best mate now.'

Nessa puts her hand in her pocket and pulls out a tenner and flicks it at Candice. 'There you go. Refund.'

'You're a bitch, Nessa Kunda, everyone says so. You're a user.'

'Am I? Is that what you're calling me, Candice? A user? Am I? Am I?'

Candice turns to me and goes, 'And she said you were well sad for going with a teacher.'

'You'd better fuck off, Candice, and you've got exactly five seconds,' says Nessa.

Candice stomps off across the cobbles back up towards Deansgate. Nessa goes in her pocket again and pulls out two tickets and hands one to me. I go in my pocket.

'No, my treat.'

'Thanks. Did you say I was sad?'

'Yeah, but I didn't mean it – they were just words, you know.'

'You were right anyway. I was sad.'

She passes me the bottle.

'Let's have a good night together, yeah?'

'Yeah,' I say, and smile. I'm so glad I have a new plan. The worst times are when you can't think of a single thing you're looking forward to. That was me five minutes ago. So I go hard at the peach schnapps and in about half an hour I have drunk a quarter of the bottle and I feel good. Then I start to feel really good like it doesn't matter at all what has happened today and like I can do anything and like he probably loves me for definite, he's just scared because of his position, and he's secretly hoping I won't give up and we'll see each other soon and kiss and have sex and I could even phone him with that number in that book in my bag.

'Fuck are you doing?'

'Going to find a payphone. Trying that number.'

'You're fucking not – what, to phone that dickhead? No fucking way. We're going to the concert. Don't you let me down a second time.'

'Okay.'

'Come here and I'll sort your face out. You look like shit.'

I leave the essay on the ground. I hope it sinks into the mud and someone finds it in a thousand years like a time capsule. Evidence of absolutely nothing.

At half six we set off for G-Mex, up past the Harley-Davidson showroom and along the tramlines. The streets are heaving with girls and we move among them. Now and then Nessa hisses at someone with a Matt banner but she doesn't properly kick off. We've lost Nessa's poster bag at some point, must have left it at the fort or dropped it or something. There are ticket touts everywhere and people sitting on the ground selling snide posters and T-shirts. Burger vans, ice-cream vans, fairground rides. Everywhere you look there's something. Nessa says, 'Our Lee says the MEN Arena's better than G-Mex but I'm not having it. This place has got soul. Is she prettier than me?'

'Who?'

'That one there. Blonde. Pink jeans.'

'Nah, there's just no way.'

'I just wish I knew which ones are here for him.'

'I know, mate, I know you do.'

'I've got to get backstage. I've got to get to him.'

'I'll help you.'

We've finished the peach schnapps now and everything seems possible.

We queue and Nessa hates being in the queue.

'I mean, how many of these lot have met his mum? How many have carried the shopping into his hall and seen his stairs? They're not true fans, these – there should be a separate queue.'

'You're right, mate, you're right.'

Once we're in there, the arena is roaring. There are glowsticks and whistles and there's all this hot energy; it's enough to make you feel sick. We have standing tickets which are best and we push our way down to the front, Nessa first, and sometimes people get annoyed and one time someone's mum tries to grab us, but we are too fast, like little ferrets, weaving between people and down to the very front. There are some big girls against the barrier and one of them says, 'No chance, we've been here since 11 a.m.,' and Nessa says, 'Shaking in my boots, Sarah, dunno about you,' and the girls move and we shove past and get a spot right on the barrier at the front.

And then I see her.

Juliette.

A bit along the barrier, with a girl from her year.

'Juliette!' I shout. 'JULIETTE! WHAT THE FUCK ARE YOU DOING HERE?'

She grins and makes her way over.

'Me and Amy saved up and bought some tickets off a tout. Don't tell Mum.'

'I won't. Stand with us!'

I feel a bit weird now with Juliette there, like I've got a job to do. But it's all right. Nessa is talking to them too. It's fine.

There's bouncers guarding a fire door next to the stage.

'That's where the dressing rooms are,' says Nessa. And she starts smiling at the bouncer on the door and he starts smiling back.

The concert passes in a blur. Nessa sings along to every word but I can't bring myself to join in. Next thing I know, the bouncer is over chatting to Nessa and she's saying, 'Listen, if you just let us back there for five minutes . . .'

'Nessa,' I'm saying, 'Nessa.' I don't like the look of this – he's got a tattoo of a naked woman on his neck and he keeps calling Nessa 'Tinkerbell'. She kicks me. Leave it. I leave it and watch the encore. Nessa is so set on this bouncer that she isn't even watching Matt. Then the band leaves the stage and Nessa says, 'Go on, go on.' And he nods at another bouncer and says, 'These two here, they're all right,' and I say, 'There's four of us actually, not two,' and I say to Nessa, 'We can't go without Juliette,' and Nessa looks annoyed but she's in a rush to sort this, and he opens the grey barrier and we slip through. I turn round and flick the Vs at the other girls all standing there like saddos and Nessa grabs my hand and I glare at her and she says, 'Fucking hell, Sarah, turn it in or we'll be out.' Juliette looks at me with her eyes shining like she can't believe it, like it's Christmas.

We go down a corridor and the sound of the arena gets quieter and there's just the clack clack clack of our shoes and the clomp clomp clomp of the bouncer's. We get to a door that says 'Dressing Room' and we go in. There's loads of people in there drinking and smoking and a big table of drinks and one of food and there's thick red curtains right the way round like we're onstage even though we're backstage.

'Don't you drink or smoke, Juliette,' I say and she laughs and helps herself to a beer with Amy.

'Gaz!' says Nessa when she sees him, because there's Gaz from the band in real life, smaller than he looked onstage and on the TV, and still sweaty from performing with his hair stuck to his forehead.

'What's this?'

'She says she's got a present for Matt,' the bouncer says.

Gaz smirks and shakes his head and says, 'He's in here.'

Gaz and the bouncer take us into another smaller room with the same thick red curtains and someone in there is crouching over a table and they stand up and spin round when they hear us. 'Fuck's sake.'

There are three other people in the room, Matt and Freddy and Theo from the band. Freddy and Theo wipe their noses and walk past us and out the door. I look at Nessa. She looks like she's been emptied out and filled back up again with little moving pieces like she's a beanbag.

She says, 'Matt,' in a stupid breathy way like she's in a film or a cartoon.

I look at Nessa and she's just staring at Matt from 4Princes. He wipes his nose and looks at the bouncer who brought us in and says, 'You're a bad, bad man, Twinny.'

The bouncer says, 'You girls can have a chat with Matt and Gaz if you like – I'll close the door.'

I have a bad feeling about this and for the first time in forever I want my mother to turn up in the car and drive me home. When the door is closed, Matt says, 'So what are you girls into then?' and I say, 'Shakespeare,' but it comes out quiet and he says, 'Shakespeare? Have you heard this, Gaz? Got ourselves a couple of intellectuals,' and that's when I want to run, like actually run. But I don't know how to get out and I don't want to leave my mate and I don't want to look sad. Nessa says, 'I don't like Shakespeare but I'm reading it to get ahead, you know,' and they laugh at this but not in the way we want them to laugh and I can tell Nessa is starting to feel weird too. Matt says, 'Do you girls do drugs?' And we say no. And Nessa says, 'Sometimes I have a bit of weed.' And he says, 'You should try this.' So he hands Nessa a rolled-up ten-pound note and points to some lines of white powder on the table and says, 'Just suck it up, suck it up with your nose and whatever you do, don't blow. One line, one line, that's it.' And she sucks it up her nostril and says, 'Ow!' and he laughs and says, 'That'll go in a minute,' and then he takes the note out of her hand and turns to me and says, 'Your turn, English rose.' 'Go on,' says Nessa and she looks more sober like it's done her good so I do it and it burns and it stings and I feel it drip down my throat and do a little retch. 'You all right? Drink some of this. It's beer.' I can tell Nessa just can't believe how well this has worked out. Like it's all gone to plan. She's sitting on his knee and telling him about how her mum did our eyelashes last week because she's a beautician and I'm sitting on Gaz's knee and reciting poetry to him and he's all, 'Have you heard this one, have you heard her?' and then I say to Nessa, 'Are you going to stay here then, because I really think I want to go and see you-know-who,' and she says, 'You're mad, just let that be why don't you?' and Gaz says, 'Yeah, whoever you-know-who is, you're sitting on my knee now, aren't you?' Nessa glares at me then and then she looks at Matt. So she says, 'Can I have your phone number, Matt? Don't worry, I won't ever ring it or give it to anyone else, I just want it to have to keep.' Matt and Gaz both crack up at this and we don't know what's so funny but we laugh too because that's polite and fuck it why not laugh rather than not laugh. Nessa gets some paper and a pen out of her pocket and says, 'Here, write your number down, I have to go home now but this has been lovely and I'd like to do it again sometime.' She's not herself. She looks younger than when I first met her. While she's doing this I lean over the table and steal one of the little white bags and flip it behind my wrist with my middle finger, nice and swiftly just like an eyeliner from Superdrug. 'Do you girls want another line?' says Gaz and I catch Matt give him a look like a little headshake 'nah' with his eyes slitted, and I think we might be able to leave and I was worried we wouldn't be able to so thank god for that, thank god. Then Nessa says, 'Sarah, I can feel the vom coming up my throat and I don't care really but I think I need to go to the toilet.' Matt says, 'Twinny, Twinny, get in here and take these ones to the bog, they're gonna hurl.' And the bouncer leads us off and we end up in a toilet somewhere and Nessa voms a bit. I try to vom but I can't. I never want to drink peach schnapps ever again but I might do that powder. We come out and say to the bouncer, 'Take us back, please, we're fine now,' and he says, 'Got a taste for it, have you?' and his top teeth hardly leave his bottom lip as he talks but then just as we get to the door Nessa starts to feel sick again and she puts her hand over her mouth and catches a ball of puke there. And the bouncer says, 'Fucking hell,' and opens the dressing-room door a nick and says, 'Matt, this one's gone, I'll take her out,' and I see in as the door swings open and I say, 'I'll take her, she's my mate,' and I take her along the corridor and when I look back I see Juliette being led into the dressing room by the security guy and she gives me a big excited wave. I don't know what to do. I wave back. But I feel worry in my stomach, like she's being washed away down a big river. Like I need to go and save her because she's too young to know what's going on and way too young for him to be into her really.

I go out the fire door and prop it open with my bag. I flag down a taxi and put Nessa in it and give the driver a tenner and her address. She lies down in the back. Then I go in the fire door and run back to the dressing room. When I get to the dressing-room door I push it open and see in and he's on top of her and they're kissing. I've never seen Juliette kiss anyone before, obviously. It's like she's not quite caught up with what he's doing, like someone who's dancing with someone who can dance a lot faster and a lot harder than them and is pretending to like it, but the trouble is if their sister was watching she would know that they don't like that kind of dancing, they are just pretending to. He starts unbuttoning her top.

She looks and sees me standing there. Our eyes meet and I hate her for a split second, then I want to kill him and pull her away. 'Get out!' she shouts. Like I'm not her sister. Like she's not someone who needs saving.

He looks up and sees me too. 'Fuck off, go on!'

Someone big and strong pulls me backwards and pushes me down the corridor. I am full of so many feelings and all I know is that I am going to puke them all out. I run down the long tunnel, towards the light. Then I run out the open door and down a street and down another and I'm shaking and hot and I stop and put my hand on a wall and I vom and vom and vom.

Aviemore

They arrived as they had driven there: in silence. Everything felt ghastly and cold. A heart and a homeland, turned to ice.

Aviemore was an old-fashioned ski resort, like an abandoned set from a 90s detective drama. It had a sort of hysterical tranquillity, a desperation that was barely veneered. It was the end of the season and the snow on the lower slopes was turning to mush. The last few ski lifts ferried a handful of skiers up to where the remaining white patches dwindled. Underneath it all was a world of dirt and rubble; a world admitting its imperfections: lost ski poles, Christmas trees, broken fences. Snow was a great trick. It covered all the mess, all the damage. The buildings, the things we constructed. It revealed the frailty of the human gesture against the void. And then it revealed its own frailty. Nothing was solid. Nothing was dependable.

They'd dropped Aaron at the station — he'd chirruped away about his most successful camping experiences, either oblivious to the tension in the van or motivated by it. As they'd waved him away at Inverness, he had worn an expression of wholesome erotic surprise. You had to give the medical community ten out of ten for effort on the people skills front, even when they probably wanted to die.

Sarah and Juliette hadn't spoken about the previous night's events and words, other than Juliette saying a simple 'Home tomorrow, yep?' after they'd deposited Aaron, and Sarah replying with what she felt was a damning 'You bet.'

This was the point it always reached, then. Wanting to go home. The excitement of any trip, any meeting, burned fast to a cold ash of desire to be alone again. Irritation, resentment. Sarah had never known whether she was an introvert or an extrovert but she knew her extrovertism was often alcohol-related and based on a childish notion of the importance of popularity. But this was the first time she had really wanted to get away from her sister. This was the first time that baseline of comfort, that bedrock of unfilteredness, had been cracked. Sarah had to be honest with herself. It happened on any occasion with any person, unless there were copious amounts of drugs involved, and then her detachment just seemed to double down the next day. But Juliette? Juliette had been her fallback. Her safe space. The one she would crave no matter what. The most interesting relationship of her life had, until now, also felt like the safest. But not today. Today, she needed to get away from her. And where would she go?

Juliette caught her staring out pointlessly at the softly drifting snow.

'Do you want to build a snowman?' tried Juliette.

'You don't mean that,' Sarah said.

Sometimes, not even the movies could save you.

This was it. Their last stop. So far from that optimism of a few days earlier. The excitement. The me too me too. Now they were both sick of it all, and each other. Weren't they? Always it came to this, was reduced to this. It was the dread of arrival. Of conclusion. Sarah had always been happiest in a car – in her father's car, on a Sunday, to be precise; the driving nowhere in particular. How many times had she begged him to go once around the block when they got home? Not wanting to arrive. Not wanting to go home. *You can never go home again*, the old psychology adage warned. Good, thought Sarah.

And now she felt further away from it, and everything, than ever.

Sarah was the wild one, the beast. Underneath, Juliette was the toughest. They all knew it. Juliette, when it came to it, had a skeleton of steel. She only looked like an animal; she was pure machine. On some shameful level, Sarah knew that in between loving Juliette, when she hated her, in those small moments, it was because Juliette had conquered her, long ago. The day she was born, in fact. Nature favours the new. And anyway, this was the patriarchy's classic death move, wasn't it? The grenade it threw into every relationship between two women: *There is not room for both of you.* Work colleagues, friends, lovers, sisters, mother and daughter. Whatever. Two women? *There is not room for both of you. Fight, fight, fight!*

Sarah put on her warmest things. Many layers. A jumper that itched but felt necessary. Two pairs of socks. She laced up her boots tight as splints. It was time to scope out the area, plan her route for later, figure out what she was going to tell Juliette about the thing she was about to do.

She set off walking, telling Juliette she'd be back later. Juliette said fine, engrossed in her phone. Or maybe she was just pretending. Sarah was losing her grip on what Juliette meant and what she didn't. She felt woozy like she did after waking from a nightmare, whiplashed from the hairpin bends of her dreams. Tiny licks of mania made her head hot and wet as she tried to focus on the trees beyond the boundary of the campsite – pines and oaks, hedgerows of beeches and balding conifers. The trees stood bolt upright, all of them the sturdy kind that doesn't mind the chill. The train tunnel, receding, the person silhouetted in light at the end, leaving, leaving. It was her mother, then it was her teacher – that stupid man, that pathetic moron, what had she been thinking! She'd be taller than him now, probably. And then she played out the same pattern to Juliette, didn't she. And she would, over, and over, and over. Sometimes you could choose the person you become and other times you got lost in her. But you couldn't blame yourself for all your bad decisions in the meantime. You couldn't think yourself out of the world. Sarah didn't trust anyone to love her, not even herself. That was the long and short of it. So she made herself ultimately untrustworthy, as a sort of neatening exercise. As a warning.

Sarah wanted to drink but knew she shouldn't. It was teatime, the gloaming; that most dangerous time of day for people with problematic habits. The time when you assess the day and decide what to give yourself as a reward or punishment before the night sweeps in and decides for you. That dangerous back-of-the-throat feeling, like when you fill your mouth too full and some of it tickles the hazard lines of your soft palate, threatening to choke you. Old habits die hard, Sarah thought. Or maybe they don't die at all. Maybe they wait like vampires, sleeping with arms crossed in the basement of your heart, waiting for some kind of night; some beautiful, terrible eclipse of reason.

Sarah stepped around a root-crinkled patch of tarmac. A teenage couple passed. They were holding hands and having a stilted conversation, their hoods up. Sarah heard herself go 'Ah,' removed from the moment for a moment. She let the sun shine on her face. It was a bit like a kiss. Then she pushed on, looking for his caravan. She was so distracted that as she walked past the reception, a woman flew round the corner of the toilet block and almost banged into her. The woman gave Sarah a dirty look. Sarah let it go. She might have regretted it, that look, as she walked on. The fact that you never got to feel another person's instant regret was a sort of daily tragedy. All these imagined wrongs, unrighted. All this mess, this carelessness.

When she got back to the Hymer, Juliette was on the phone, and quickly hung up. Like a hostage victim who was scared of being caught planning her escape.

'Hey,' said Sarah.

'Hey,' Juliette replied.

'I'm so sorry for leaving you and the cat.'

Juliette frowned, looked around. Sarah realised Juliette had no idea what she was talking about. 'The kitten. In Manchester. Mr Tumnus. I left you both and went to London.'

'Oh god,' said Juliette, 'I can barely remember.'

'You met Johnnie shortly after. And I feel like it was all one great big ricocheting bullet down the years, dooming us both to mad love after mad love, and never enough self-esteem.'

'So this wasn't my birthday trip. This was your confession.'

'No. Something turned up. And now I'm going to make it right.'

'What do you mean?'

'All of it. Our whole thing. The thing.'

'The thing?'

Sometimes, something so bad happens that your life stops and starts again; turns around. The past becomes the present and the present becomes the past.

Manchester

My teeth were gnashing, like I needed something more: something on my body or maybe even *in* my body. I got in a taxi and asked it to take me to Blackley. I wanted to be someone far away from everything, and there was also a small part of me inside that was going harder, saying: Fuck you Danny Keaveney, fuck you and fuck you Juliette too and Nessa and everyone.

I walked up the path and knocked on the door, not even caring if he was with anyone. I knew he'd let me in.

He answered.

'Hello, Macken,' I said.

'Sally?'

'Close enough.'

'What's happened?' he said. 'Where's Nessa?'

I smiled, tilting my head. 'Let me in and I'll tell you.'

He stood there, not moving. I tried a different tack.

'Hey, Macken, I've got some cocaine.'

His eyes popped. 'You've got cocaine? Where from?'

'Pop stars. Hahahahaha.'

'Hahahahahahaha.'

He looked down the street and then pulled me inside. We went up to his room where there was loads of United stuff on the wall and two football shirts hung up. I got undressed and he took the little bag off me and arranged two lines on a CD case. I didn't want one so he did the two and then he got undressed and his penis was erect, which was great, but then he kissed me like a washing machine, which was not so great. You know, exactly like they tell you not to: round and round and round. I tried to remember my learning. My reading. *Ten ways to drive him wild in the sack. Make a basket shape with your hands and rub it over the end of his penis.*

'Fuck are you doing?' he said.

'Is it not nice?'

'No!'

I stopped.

Then I remembered another one. *Drive him wild with this tantalising tongue move.*

'You seem a bit robotic,' he said.

I stopped then. I hung out the window, smoking a Consulate Menthol, offended.

He came over, pants back on. 'Sorry,' he said. 'I'll try some more foreplay with you.'

'Foreplay! That's offensive. If you don't want to get right down to it I'll just fuck off. I don't want to wait around because frankly, Macken, who has the *life*? Who has the *time*?'

'You're fifteen, aren't you?'

'Yeah, so I know what I'm talking about.'

He asked for something specific. I'd seen it. Position of the fortnight in *More!* magazine. Reverse cowgirl. 'I don't even want to sit on a horse the RIGHT way, Macken. Horses stink. I'm not doing that,' I clarified.

'Would you sit on a motorbike?' he asked. 'Think of it like a motorbike – reverse motorbike.'

'Maybe. That is helpful, actually. Thank you, Macken.'

I said this because I had actually met a person with a motorbike.

We got onto the bed. I told him to put on a condom and he did, then he tried to finger me but I had to help him and then it was the usual two fingers three fingers and he was moaning more than me. I did wonder whether I should moan more so he didn't think he was shit. I looked sideways at us in the full-length mirror and we looked like a raw chicken, legs and wings this way and that. It was boring, though. Maybe that was the cocaine. My vagina felt different. Colder. I held my jaw tight and counted the pumps and I estimated that by the time he got to fifty pumps it would probably be done. In fact, it only took twenty-nine.

Afterwards, I lay staring at the ceiling, smoking, and I thought: revenge is not sweet so much as it is sweaty.

'What are you laughing at?' he asked me.

'Nothing.'

'Did you have a female orgasm?'

'No, but don't worry. I think it's because I'm so drunk and on drugs.'

He nodded. 'Yeah, sometimes it gets me like that too. You do seem different generally though, Sarah. I dunno, sort of older than last time I saw you.'

'Must be the booze.'

'Must be.'

'They say it ages you.'

'Hahaha.'

I blew perfect smoke rings up into the dark and let the whole night sink deeply into me. He got up and took more cocaine and then played his handheld computer game and then he got up and took more cocaine and this happened until I heard him curse the bag for being empty.

After a few hours – around 5 a.m. – he turned off the light.

'Do you want to do it again?' I asked.

'Fucking hell, what are you, some kind of nympho?'

'Never mind. If you're not up to it . . .'

'I'm up to it. Look.'

We did it again. Only this time, the condom split.

Fuck.

Fuck.

Fuck.

'It's all right,' I said, 'I'll sort it tomorrow. Today, even.'

'Do you promise? I don't want to be a father yet, Sarah. I've got my career to think about.'

'Macken, I swear to you that there is no way on god's earth I will allow myself to bear your child.'

'All right, well you'd better sort it out then.'

He was in a huff then and didn't let any small part of himself touch me in bed. I flew off in my head to when Mr Keaveney would find out – the next time he spoke to me I would just tell him: *Yeah, pretty glad you binned me off that Friday because I got a top shag that night – no actually, make that two. He was a semi-famous footballer and he said I was the best sex he'd ever had. So your loss, mate.*

* * *

When I got home the sky was starting to get light. The letter, the letter! I rushed to get to it and – sing hosannas – it had been buried by a pile of junk mail. No one had seen it. Thank god. I dug through the pizza leaflets and other crap on the mat until I saw the stupid letter there in my stupid handwriting. I put it in my pocket and started to go up the stairs to see if Juliette was in her bed. But then I heard the sound of metal on pot, and I felt a sharp tug in my chest. I turned and walked through to the dining room.

And.

And.

She was just there.

At the dining table.

Eating a bowl of cereal — too much milk as always.

'All right?' she said. Calm as you like.

I couldn't speak. I looked at her for signs of damage, but she looked washed and dressed, her hair neatly brushed back and plaited, her sports kit on. She read my face. 'I've got netball practice at eight,' she said.

I tried to get something out. Before Mum and Dad got up. I was about to say sorry. I wanted to say sorry. I felt like I'd left something really precious and special out in the rain and now it was ruined.

'I had a great time,' she said.

'Did you—?'

'Yeah. We did. It.' My heart hurts when I hear this. It hurts so much I feel something snap inside. 'Sorry if that's not what you want to hear,' she goes on, 'but we did.'

'You did it?'

She stood and picked up her empty cereal bowl. She picked it up differently. Would she do everything differently now? Would she think she was equal to me?

Mum came in and looked at me. 'How was Nessa's? And the concert?'

I looked at Juliette. Juliette carried her bowl into the kitchen.

'It was all right,' I replied.

'You look tired, Sarah,' said Mum.

'I'm hungry.'

'There's some Hawaiian pizza left in the box.'

She pulled her dressing gown tight and went to put the kettle on.

I thought I might cry then, really hard, because I couldn't think of a single thing I was looking forward to.

A few minutes

Before 7 p.m., I set off for the Blue Owl – just like the flyer says. The flyer with his name on. I told Juliette I was going to grab some bits for dinner and she said she'd take a nap. So far, so stealthy. I close the van door quietly. I hid the table pole in the bushes earlier. Now, I pick it up and feel its comforting heft in my hands. I walk with it hanging like a baseball bat by my side. Just another happy camper enjoying the holidays.

Aviemore has become rowdier in the evening, people drinking and jostling, spilling out of bars into doorways. People savouring the last blast of the holiday season.

I hide the pole behind an electricity box outside the bar and chain a few cigarettes. I stuff my fag ends into a hole in the wall, among others. Mine have lipstick on; the ones around them don't. Lovers' wall, I think. Unrequited. All those little butt couples, snug in their crevices. Waiting to fall.

So much for that.

Inside the Blue Owl, I buy myself a cider and stand waiting by a pillar, hiding in the shadows. I don't want Aventura Steve to see me if he's around. On the ceiling, there is a still mirrorball and the limp green net of an empty balloon drop. I am twenty-odd feet away from the stage. A foot for every year.

To think now that I'd almost told my ex, Eric, about the thing. The thing that was soon to be standing in front of me. Six months or so into our relationship, a close, trusting night, when we were deep-warm drunk together; after dinner, wine, whisky – I felt the spiny anecdote lurch from my guts, but by the time it reached my mouth, it was just wind. Eric had looked at me, repulsed, and I knew that if he couldn't handle that, then . . . Well.

The area around the stage gets livelier, as the whole room bristles with anticipation of the gig. I wait.

And wait.

And then.

There he is.

The man who ruined my life.

Him.

His name has haunted me. His face has stared out at me from newspapers. His body has been the defining shape of every bad fuck, every phantasmic rejection.

Matt Daubney.

Matt from 4Princes.

Because that's who it is. Reduced to reality, to the present. Here now. In front of me. This sad middle-aged man who clings to a few traces of his former glory. A faded 90s pop star with sparks of dying energy coming off him as he burns out. His jumper stretches over his midriff. Aventura Steve is behind him, with two other men of a similar age, playing guitar and bass. There's a drummer with a long thin beard. Matt walks to the centre of the stage and takes the mic. 'Good evening, Aviemore!'

Then I feel a tap on my shoulder and I jump. Onstage, Matt launches into song. I turn and I see: Juliette. Juliette, my sister. Who has woken up and followed me here. Her eyes are wide, terrified.

'What are you . . . ?' Juliette is shaking, looking between me and Matt, the cosmic set-up, the horror of it, the horror. 'What *is this*?'

The band are playing one of the old 4Princes hits, 'Girl, You Girl'.

I shake my head. I need to get her out of here. 'You weren't meant to see this!' I shout, but she pushes me away. I try to bustle her out, but she smacks me. People look. Juliette's eyes are on the stage on the stage on the stage.

'My god,' says Juliette. 'Look at him.'

I look. We both look. Deer in the spotlights.

Juliette reaches to touch my arm. 'How did you know he was here?'

'I saw a flyer.'

'And you didn't tell me? Why – why did you want to come here? To see him?'

'Yes.'

'Why?'

I link my arm through hers and lead her towards the door. 'Come on, I'll walk you home.'

'Why, what are you going to do?'

'I'm going to come back and teach him a lesson.'

'What do you mean?'

'Exactly that.'

'Stop being mad!'

'I know what he did to you. That's why your life's a mess. I'm sorry for – leaving. I – I – wasn't well. I was out of it. Then I didn't ever know how to get back into it, with you.'

'He didn't . . . we didn't . . .'

We go outside the bar. Juliette looks down. Then she says: 'I exaggerated it.'

I shake my head. 'But I saw—'

She shakes her head in turn.

I sit down – I collapse, really – and light a cigarette. Juliette sits down next to me and puts her arm around me. She takes my cigarette from my mouth and smokes it – once, twice. Twosies. 'I want to go home now, Sarah. Like, *home* home. Back to Manchester. I can drive us. Come on.'

'No.' It's not what I want.

'Well, I'm not leaving you,' says Juliette.

We sit like that for a while.

When the gig is over, the crowds leave, and he comes out with them: lording it, holding drinks, regaling. We watch him pass. I put my hand on Juliette's knee. Then I stand up and pull the table pole out from the bush. I start walking, following the crowd.

'What the— Sarah! Fuck, no!' Juliette comes after me.

I keep walking, I'm like the Terminator. He goes into his caravan. Lights come on inside. Blinds are drawn. Music kicks in. He's having a party with his band mates and some people from the pub and some hangers-on. Young women. Aventura Steve. Juliette sees him.

'Him! He's the missing link.'

'In more ways than one.'

I sit down with the pole on a grass verge at the edge of the site.

'What are we doing?' asks Juliette.

'Waiting.'

She sits down next to me.

* * *

It is 2 a.m. before the party guests leave. We have smoked all the cigarettes. I have a numb bum. But as the last one leaves, I get up. Juliette follows. 'Sarah. Sar—'

I approach the caravan. Open the door. I have a flashback to that dressing-room door, to— But I don't want to look any more at that. This will help.

I look at Juliette instead. 'Why are you here?'

She says: 'I'm here to make sure you don't ruin your life.'

'Too late. Just like you said.'

Inside the caravan, the place is a tip. It stinks of must and stale ash. Dirty tumblers litter the surfaces. On a shelf by the TV there are two gold-coloured *Smash Hits* Poll Winners' Party Awards, in between cereal bowls overflowing with cigarette ends. A few Brit awards. An Ivor Novello. He lives in this van, I think. This shabby room on wheels. The gigs in largely seated tourist pubs. It's tragic. As is the evidence of coke on the table: the rolled note and streaked surface, the black credit card.

'Sarah, no!' Juliette hisses.

He is sitting in the back corner of the van, slumped over. His eyes are half open. As I approach, he starts to stir. 'Shona? Is that you, honey? I n– I need you.'

I walk to him.

'Hello, Matt,' I say.

He opens his eyes properly and looks at me. 'Who the fuck are you?'

'You don't know me. But I know you.'

'You and everyone else in the fucking world, baby.'

I sit down opposite him, holding the pole. 'You wish.'

He looks suddenly very unwell, like he is struggling for breath. 'I think I need a glass of water.'

'I think you need a lot of things.'

'Sarah,' says Juliette, who is frozen by the dirty hob. 'Please.'

'The cocaine is restricting the oxygen to your body,' I say. 'At your age, you're probably on the verge of a heart attack.'

'Are you one of those crazy ones from the past?' he replies. 'I've had a lot of stalkers. People have brought me dolls knitted out of their own hair, weird shit like that.'

'Lucky you.'

'Can you get me a glass of water?'

'No, I can't.'

'Why?'

'We are here to euthanise you.'

'We?' He peers behind me.

Juliette steps forward out of the shadows.

I say, 'Remember her? You raped her.'

'Er,' said Juliette.

Matt sits up. He says: 'I really hope I didn't, did I? You maybe said you were up for it? I never did anything to anyone who said they weren't up for it.'

Juliette looks at me, not at him any more. It's like he's not there. She looks at me. 'I said we'd done it when we hadn't. It was just some groping and stuff really, I can't really remember, but I know that didn't happen. Shortly after you left, I puked. He wasn't so interested after that so I left and went home. Someone there called me a cab.'

'You didn't have sex.'

'No. I mean, he still technically assaulted me. I was thirteen. But so was Juliet in *Romeo and Juliet*.'

'Yeah, but I think Romeo was thirteen too. He ruined your life. He ruined both of our lives.'

'My life is not a mess. I have children and a husband I love.'

Matt is trying to make a dash for it, towards the door. I smack him on the back with the pole and he cries out and falls flat. Juliette screams.

I turn to face her, brimming with rage. There is nothing between me and the livid fact: I had to keep quiet while she exaggerated. Feelings wriggle and belch within me. I scream back at her: 'Bullshit! You're having an affair!'

She's trembling. 'Fuck you, Sarah! This is about *you*. As always. Why do you want to do this? This is about who you think *you* should be, rather than who *I* am.'

'I've carried this for decades!'

'It was all your invention! Don't put this on me! It was your choice to be guilty. You love being guilty! You love the POWER.'

'You're right,' I say, holding the pole towards Juliette. 'This isn't mine to fix. This is your kill.'

'Woah, woah, woah,' Matt says from the floor. 'Please – I have children. I am told. Several. In various places. Please!'

We ignore him. I tell Juliette: 'It's for his own good.'

Then Matt gargles something unintelligible. We look at him. He's crawling for the door again. It's now or never. I raise the table pole aloft with both hands, though I am somewhat restricted by the caravan's ceiling height.

'No!' screams Juliette.

Matt shrieks weakly and tries to get up. I try to strike him around the head but Juliette intercepts and knocks the pole sideways. I keep my hold on it but it smashes his award shelf and his awards crash to the floor. Matt vomits. A foamy pile of pills emerges from his open mouth, triggering a realisation in me.

I grip the pole and look at Juliette, my blood pounding. 'You could finish him off now, Juliette. Just two swift blows to the temple. Kindest thing, really. He's done half the job himself with his pharmaceuticals. It's what he wants, too.'

Matt cries: 'It's not! No! No!'

'Too late. You think no means no? No doesn't mean no. Not for you.' I raise the pole again.

'No,' says Juliette. She pulls the pole to her own head, to her crown, and rests it there. I don't know what she's doing. Then she says: 'I know about the bus wanker. I know how you had to keep that inside. I'm so sorry, Sarah.'

I feel something break inside me. I drop the pole and start to cry, really cry. Crying like drowning, puking. For all the things I've lost, and all the things I've given away.

Matt is breathing heavily, probably with relief.

Juliette gets her phone out and dials 999. I hear her speaking to the ambulance service and declining to leave herself as a contact.

'We're going now,' she says to me after she's hung up. Matter-of-fact. Crisis-managing.

I grab a *Smash Hits* award, the only one that hasn't broken, from the floor. Then we leave, closing the door behind us.

* * *

As we pack up the Hymer, the ambulance arrives on the site. We watch through the window as he's put on a stretcher. The blue lights look like every shit disco.

The Brook

Nessa came with me to the clinic. We sat waiting for my turn, reading all the posters about smoking and sex and drugs and alcohol and whatnot. Nessa told me about how her cousin reacted when she told her about last night and as she was telling me she grabbed my wrist like her cousin did hers. I hate it when people re-enact anecdotes on me physically, like grab my body unasked, even friends. I shouted: 'DO NOT FUCKING DO THAT, NESSA, I HATE IT WHEN PEOPLE DO THAT.' Really I know I'm doing that thing where you're upset about something really big and your brain can't bear to think about that big thing so you get upset about all the small things instead. It's pretty useful actually.

'Fucking hell, mate,' said Nessa. 'Chill your beans. It's not even the end of the world if you're preggers. Macken's a good catch.'

'The last thing I want is Macken's baby, Nessa. I'm fucking petrified. Imagine having to know him my whole life and look at a little version of his face every day – I can't even think about it.'

'He's a better option than Mr Weedy.'

'That's not saying much.'

It still hurt. It did.

'Think of the parties you'd go to with Macken,' Nessa went on. 'You could be like the next Posh Spice. Except not posh.'

'Nessa, Macken can't hold a knife and fork properly and he's scared of prawns. He is not a proper man.'

'How do you even know that?'

'He told me. I said a prawn sandwich was the best thing for a hangover because prawns are like filters of the sea so imagine what they can do for your body, and he said he doesn't eat prawns because he's scared of them.'

'Sarah Hudson?'

I stood up. 'Yep, that's me. Can my friend come in?'

The doctor nodded. I looked at Nessa. 'Do you want to come in?' Nessa didn't need asking twice. She loved the Brook.

In the consulting room, I sat down and the doctor asked me loads of questions. I told her about the sex but not the drugs. I denied taking drugs when we got to those questions. Nessa whispered: 'Imagine if it was a crack baby.'

The doctor started to get cross. 'I'm not sure what's amusing you? Maybe it'd be best if your friend waits outside?'

'Sorry,' I said. 'It's nerves.'

Good one, that. Thanks, Mum.

'Yeah, I'm not even laughing,' Nessa said. 'I shouldn't have to leave.'

Nessa was enjoying the room and all the equipment. The formality of it, the ritual. The drama. She always did.

'And how old was the man you had intercourse with?' said the doctor.

'Sixteen or seventeen, I think.'

'Do you know which?'

'Does it matter?'

She nods.

'What if I said he was twenty?'

'Is he twenty?'

I looked at Nessa. 'I don't think so.'

Nessa shrugged. 'He's got money so it makes it harder to tell. He's a bit famous.'

'Shut up!' Last thing I needed was Nessa running her mouth off.

'He's fifteen,' I lied. 'He's actually a few months younger than me. So it was my fault probably. And I took the cocaine round.'

'You took cocaine?'

'One and only time. I found it on the street – I don't normally take it. I didn't really like it.'

'Please don't do that again. It's very dangerous.'

'Brownie's honour.'

There. She couldn't do anything with that. She wrote something down.

'Are you regularly sexually active?' she asked next.

'I'll say,' said Nessa.

'I've slept with two and a half people,' I clarified.

The doctor's brow furrowed.

'One didn't go in but I held it against my vagina when it was hard and then he came.'

'Your vulva or your vagina?'

'Huh?'

'Did his penis go inside you?'

'No. He came before we could get it in. Probably for the best as his mum came in the room two minutes later.'

'I see.'

Nessa said: 'Not as bad as what happened to me with Emir Tate – remember? His mum came in right as he was jizzing in my face.'

The doctor didn't flinch. She was a total pro. 'And you say the condom split last night, Sarah?'

'Yep.'

'Okay,' she sighed, 'I'm going to prescribe the morning-after pill. You've taken it before?'

'Yeah. Loads.'

'And I'm going to give you both some condoms.'

Nessa hooted. 'Fat lot of good they are. That's why we're here, doctor.'

The doctor ignored her.

'Have you considered going on the contraceptive pill?' she said to me.

'She does enough drugs, doctor.'

The doctor looked at Nessa with a look sterner than any teacher. It was such a hard look that Nessa looked down, and Nessa never gave up on a stare-out first.

The doctor came back with a small paper cup of water and two white pills in a pack. 'One now, one in five hours.' I necked the first pill; my throat was dry so it took all the water. Nessa started singing, 'Bye Bye Baby'. I said, 'There was never a baby, Nessa.' But we're laughing.

The doctor wanted us out, I could tell. She said: 'I'll give you some leaflets to take with you.'

Nessa said: 'Got enough to read, us, doctor. Revising for our GCSEs.'

The doctor smiled at both of us. 'Well, good luck.'

I grabbed the pill and the leaflets and flew out of the room, leaving Nessa to savour it a bit more before she followed me.

'So you're clean of womb!' Nessa said when we were outside. 'Let's celebrate.'

'How?'

'More booze. And then . . . tattoos.'

I knew she'd wanted to do this for ages – go to Rambo's in Manchester where Matt got the unicorn one done on his groin. You could see it on some of the photos where he was pulling his jeans down saucily. They had debated whether the photos were appropriate on Radio 4.

We went to Oldham Street and bought a quarter-bottle of vodka from the newsagent. I felt a bit lightheaded from the first pill but it was definitely better than gestating the child of a prawn-fearer.

We walked up to Rambo's Tattoo Parlour at the top of the Northern Quarter and looked at the designs in the catalogues and in the glass display cases on the walls. The man behind the desk asked us to fill in a form and we just subtracted a year from our birthdates. Easy-peasy. He didn't even ask to see ID.

Nessa chose a beetle.

'Why?' I asked her. Seemed an odd choice.

'I like beetles. I did a project on them.'

'How old are you?' said the man.

'Sixteen,' we said in unison.

I chose an Egyptian hieroglyphic. A swirly eye – the eye of Horus. It looked dangerous. Something they used to put on tombs to protect the dead.

Nessa went first. He wouldn't let me go in like they did in the Brook, which was annoying. I stayed in the waiting room feeling woozy. The machine sounded like a drill. I could hear Nessa laughing and then she screamed and then started laughing again. I heard the man say, 'Have you had a drink?' And Nessa said: 'NO SHUT UP AND GET ON WITH IT SLOWCOACH.'

She came out ten minutes later and showed me.

'What do you think?' she asked.

'Oooh, mate,' I said, 'it does look a bit like a dung beetle's crawling out of your arse crack.'

'Fuck off,' she said. 'Fuck off, it doesn't.'

'Ahahahahaha.'

'Come on then, coppertop,' said the man.

Nessa laughed then. I followed him into the little room. There was a black bed with a plastic sheet on it and a bin in the corner and a little stool for him to sit on. The radio was on quiet – Galaxy 102. He sat down and set to work. Bzzzzzzzz! It hurt but not much, like a cat scratch over and over. I counted three songs on the radio and then it was done. He took me over to a mirror to show me and it looked dead good and he said the red bumpiness would go away in a few days and told me to get some nappy cream to make it scab over right. I imagined Mr Keaveney seeing it and what he'd think. Then I reminded myself he would never see me again. Or my arse ever.

I went out to show Nessa.

'Woah,' she said, jumping up and covering her eyes, 'you don't need to get your whole arse out, mate!'

'Do you like it?'

'Looks like your arse has got an eye, dunnit. Like your arse is using a periscope to have a good look around. An evil arse periscope that spends all day looking in arses like an arse pirate.'

'Ladies,' said Rambo, 'that'll be thirty quid each, thanks.'

'Is your name really Rambo?' Nessa said, getting out her purse.

'Yeah,' he said, opening the till.

'Bet it's not though,' said Nessa. 'Bet it's something shit, like Nigel.'

I was still looking at my tattoo in the mirror. 'This will last forever, won't it?' I asked.

'Yeah,' he said.

I looked at the tattoo again, satisfied. 'I'll see you when I'm twenty,' I said to the tattoo. 'And thirty and forty and fifty and sixty, and—'

'She's weird,' I heard Nessa say. 'You can ignore her, Nigel.'

I said the next bit silently, in my head.

—and so will every man who fucks me.

We went to buy cigarettes and alcopops and then sat in Piccadilly Gardens, under the statue of Queen Victoria.

'Sarah,' said Nessa.

'Yeah?'

'I've got something to tell you.'

'What?'

'I never gave anyone a blowjob. Or a sixty-nine.'

'Me neither.'

'Really?'

'Yeah.'

We smoked quietly, our uninhaled gusts swirling around the dead queen's feet. Nessa handed me another lemon Hooch. 'We've got a lot of work to do.'

'Loads.'

'At least now we can tell the careers advisor what we want to be, next time she corners us.'

'What's that?'

'Dirty slags.'

We drive

Along the M6. Juliette is at the wheel and she takes it slow. We both feel the events of the week in our bones, hollowed out, sick with tiredness and adrenaline. I am poleaxed with fatigue.

We stop at Tebay services, which is the best service station in the world, because we think that buying cheese will be the best possible thing to do right now. They say cheese is a mood-enhancer. Know what I think? I think that presumes a lot about your current mood. And what you consider 'enhancement'. But what I do know is there isn't a lot that cheese can't cure. Okay, cancer. But it goes a long way to anaesthetising heartbreak. That's a scientific fact. I can forget about a lot when I eat cheese. There's something about getting back to safety, and buying things, and that probably makes me a horrible capitalist, but my emotions override my politics on this one and I just can't help what I feel.

We park the Hymer in the coach spaces.

'I need a wee first.'

'Standard.'

'I don't know it in here.'

'Oh, it's the best. I'll meet you by the cheese counter. You'll find it.'

I walk inside. Shops are comforting; food shops especially so. I walk past the cheese counter and look at the mounds of beige and yellow and red and orange, the most soothing sight, like a spread of candles; like the steps of the Sacré-Coeur. I take a basket. I'm going to buy a lot of cheese.

The cheese counter is busy. It's a hotspot. I walk into the adjacent aisles and look at the chutneys, the preserves and salamis. I hold some jars of expensive chutney, looking at the labels. People will always find a way of making a hierarchy, even with something as everyday as food. I choose a caramelised onion one. Juliette picks up some things for her tablescape business. Candles, napkins, star anise like a jar full of claws.

As I'm waiting in the queue for cheese, I hear a family arguing by the booze fridge – a mother, father and son – as they're filling a cool box. The father looks angry. 'We'll go for a pint when we get there, I said,' he says.

'We can't with our cases,' the woman says, to which he mumbles a response.

'Oh, all right then, Tommy. You ask a question and then answer it.'

'You should answer my fucking question right then.'

And like that, the whole thing, splayed, horrible. I wonder if she'll cry. She looks at the cider. Then he jokes about something and she laughs too much when he says anything else. I can feel the threat coming off him like animal stink. I hope he's dying of cancer, something like that – that would be the only excuse. Not that it's much of an excuse. Not for all the money in the world, I think. I choose to keep my power. I am not malfunctioning, I am adapting. Mutating. I text Ginny:

My darling we haven't bashed clits for a while - drinks tomoz? Btw I'm saying goodbye to her
Yes! (Who?)

261

You know who. The girl I was (vom)

Well done. Do you still need me to get your shades back from that carpenter?

Yes pls - altho he wasn't really a carpenter, that was just a fantasy

No such thing as just a fantasy

This is why I love you x

Juliette comes back from the toilet. 'There's a kids' playground at the back! I could hear it through the toilet window!'

'Yeah! There's a pond too.'

'A pond?!'

Juliette gets a little sad look and I know she's thinking about her kids. 'It won't be long,' I tell her.

Juliette says: 'You know every time I'm at a kids' playground it's your voice I'm listening for, among all the kids' voices? I realised the other day. Don't you think that's weird? There was a kid that sounded like you and I spun around and god, I was so disappointed it wasn't you because for a second I felt so completely at peace. Hearing you, as you were thirty years ago, my big sister, in a playground. That sounds mad. You've glazed over. Sorry.'

'No, no, it's fine. It's interesting.'

'Are you daydreaming? What chutney is that? I might get a chutney.'

'It's a wiring thing, I think. You know me, I get looped in my imagination sometimes. It's caramelised onion – it's just there, on the left. I've had it before. It's good.'

Juliette nods and reaches for the chutney.

I continue: 'I was actually thinking about what you said about me not having a transitional object. Well, you're wrong. My transitional object was you.'

'Johnnie will like this. The poor bastard. He will. I miss my imagination, you know. Motherhood took my fantasies away.

My daydreams. That's the real loss. The freedom of mind. The replacement of liberty, of free-shooting, joyous, sexual, charging, every-direction psychical metaphysics . . . with constant anxiety, like background radiation, affecting your every thought. Bog-standard, constant, plebeian, garden-variety anxiety. The only thing that gets rid of it is alcohol. And illicit sex, it turns out.'

I think about my fantasies, and the lesson of them. Everyone in your fantasies is you, like in your dreams. So the person you put in there to turn you on tells you about the parts of yourself you need to love more. The parts of you that don't turn you on are neglected. I have cocky, funny, powerful, in-control people in my fantasies to turn me on. That means the flipside – the vulnerable, the naïve, the unsure – is the part of me I need to love more. I know that. Doesn't mean I do it, but I know it.

'Maybe you should try cheese,' I say.

Juliette ignores me. 'It's a fucking outrage. I am still outraged. I fucking *love them*, you know. But I'm fucking outraged. Tell you the other thing motherhood did. It took away my instincts, repackaged them, and sold them back to me.'

'I think those two things can coexist in a person. Outrage and love. It's my modus operandi.'

'Whatever happened to Mr Keaveney?' Juliette asks.

I swallow. 'He lives in Essex.'

'How do you know that?'

'Facebook, obvs.'

'Did you message him?'

'Did I fuck.'

'Maybe you should. Bit of closure.'

'There's no such thing as closure. Only assimilation.'

I thought I was malfunctioning. But I'm not. I'm just catching up with myself. That's what all this has been. I haven't been waiting for Juliette. I've been waiting for myself to catch up with me. Now she's here, I'm calibrating.

His Facebook profile picture was of his kids. I'd looked at it for a couple of hours, finding his face in their faces, finding my feelings, finding my past self in myself, and then I never searched for him again. I could have looked at the picture of his kids forever.

He committed a crime. Many crimes. Didn't he? And yet he had won. Had he? Was he, out of all this, the winner? Did there have to be a winner? And why did being the winner have so much to do with babies? God, it's depressing. It is so hard to walk the walk of being a childfree woman. Everyone everywhere is talking the talk. It is cool and important to talk the talk. But walking the walk is a different matter. Every day is a fight against the rage and inadequacy put upon me not by reality or even my own deep true heart, but the world and all its fears of what women might become if we really were liberated from our bodies. When Juliette got pregnant, even though I was in London working my way up the corporate ranks, going on luxury holidays, treating myself to Liberty advent calendars and cases of champagne for New Year's, I was unable to deny the vintage victory I was sure she felt. It wasn't the truth of it, I knew. You couldn't change the natural order of things like that. But I had shrunk to our parents, to them I was suddenly smaller, and very far away. That was why I couldn't bear to visit.

'Why did you have kids?' I ask her now.

Juliette thinks. 'Because I believe love conquers all.' She says it faux-ironically.

'That's nice. For a long time I thought maybe it was just revenge on me.'

'I know, I thought that too. For uni. For London. For all the ways I couldn't seem to outgrow you.'

I tell myself not to say it. Don't say it. It's irresistible. 'But you remember I had that abortion when I was seventeen? So really it was me first anyway.' There is pain in Juliette's eyes. I want to be the one to take it away, after being the one who wanted to cause it. It's twisted, but it's true.

We buy ash-coated goat's cheese and fig biscuits. Children of our time. Our joint time. I also buy Chaource and Brie and a smoked Red Fox. And I think, no one can say I don't know how to look after myself.

And I don't feel as tired as I did a week ago. I don't. Maybe when I get my optimal energy back, I'll throw a party.

Juliette buys a selection pack of their most popular cheeses.

'A cheese journey,' I offer. 'For you and Aaron?'

Juliette laughs. 'I think a lot of the new cheeses are not for my palate.'

'When do you think you'll see boyo again?'

'God knows.'

'Well I am no longer enabling. Just so you know. Don't plan any sex tourism trips to my flat, thanks very much.'

'I won't.'

We walk out the back to look at the pond. The clouds chase each other across the sky.

I did therapy once, years ago – I know you're bang into it but it's never really been for me – anyway, all they wanted to do was take it all back to Mum, but in my mind you shaped me more than she ever did.'

I'm crying, crying and I don't have a tissue. We shaped each other, we did, and it is precisely because of this fact that as adults we find each other hardest to blame.

'I don't know who I am when I'm not putting up walls for you,' I say, between sobs.

'But I don't want the walls,' she says gently. 'I'm sorry.'

At the van, I pull her in for a hug. I breathe in Juliette, breathe her in hard.

'Are you sniffing me? Stop! I'm sure I stink!'

'You don't.'

'What do I smell of?'

I take another deep slug of Juliette-air. 'Nothing.' I smile. 'Nothing at all.'

'What shall we do for your fiftieth? Same again?' says Juliette.

'Let's just go to a spa. I already feel arthritic from the exposure.'

'You're obsessed with how old you are,' Juliette laughed. 'And you know what, Sarah?'

'What?'

'You're only getting older while you're fucking carping on about it.'

I look at Juliette, at the pond, Juliette, the pond. My stomach is full of oxytocin. I want to fall and cry and hug everyone. Juliette says: 'Thanks to you I'm smoking again, so we can die together, prematurely. Or you a few years before me, to keep things completely fair. I'm fucked if you get more time on earth than me. You already ate all my advent calendar chocolates and cut the hair off all my Barbies. You're not getting extra years, too.'

It's the order of things. The order of sisters. It's an order you cannot shake, or shift, or ignore; an order that will rule you both until your dying days.

Sarah had friends in their thirties and forties who'd looked into adoption. One of the most fascinating things about the process was a rule that if there were existing children in the family, then the adopted child had to be younger. An adopted child could not come in and suddenly be the eldest. Disrupting the birth order at the top was thought to shake the foundations of a family. Sarah had thought a lot about that.

London

It was sixth form at a different school in the end, and then after A levels, it was uni. Goldsmiths in Lewisham. Somehow it still felt like running away.

Sarah sat in her room in student halls and looked through the window at the quad, the trees turning brassy, the union with its tatty posters on the corner: Queens of the Stone Age, The Strokes, The White Stripes. Most afternoons she listened to 'No Scrubs' by TLC in her room on repeat, sometimes veering into other songs on the album *FanMail*, and then ended up in that sad, massive bar, ordering doubles and shooting pool with teenage boys who were her intellectual inferiors but social superiors – rich finance kids and from the City. One boy even said his grandfather had won the Booker. He asked her what it was like 'hanging out with proper writers'. She'd fucked him for that.

Her grades had slipped. No longer a straight-A student (her A levels had been a point she'd been hell-bent on proving), now she got essays that were marked in the high sixties – not shameful, but not what you could call excellent, either. Sarah knew the numbers represented a lack of attentiveness and care on her part. Something about the university environment made her feel less committed to her future and more committed to the present. Her parents didn't know and wouldn't find out – she was the first one out of both sides of the family to go to college, so she was now a beautiful distant mystery, or so she liked to think. At least until Juliette followed – and Juliette would because Juliette always did. But she was heading in the opposite direction: Edinburgh. Juliette was going to study Classics, which seemed a little pointless to Sarah, not to mention a surprise – when had Juliette ever shown an interest in statues, or pottery, or poetry? Sarah was the one with the hieroglyph tattoo.

Subject-wise, she had stuck with English. There wasn't much else that floated her boat. She'd made a few friends – her immediate neighbours in halls, girls she'd got talking to in the first few days, the people who sat near her in lectures and seemed to share her sense of humour – even just a raised eyebrow or a side-eye could speak volumes when you were on the hunt for new playmates. But Sarah's soul was untouched, untroubled, and that was the sad thing. She was friends with one girl because she admired her blusher.

Nessa said she was coming to stay in the winter. She was at college up north, doing her NVQ in beauty. Nessa seemed to have made a whole load of friends already and was on the verge of getting engaged. She'd already put her name down for a house on the estate behind the school. Nessa's life was moving fast, and Sarah didn't feel as though her place in it was as solid as it had been. They were at different speeds. Nessa didn't like it when Sarah told her things about uni or about the girls she was hanging out and drinking with. Nessa had mean things to say about people she'd never met. But Sarah had more in common with the girls who knew how to order Debutante cocktails and could quote Philip Roth or Philip Larkin, sometimes both in the same evening. They were her new tribe. But she was an outlander, a traitor in the midst, always looking to upgrade. She made eyes at her Early Modern Literature professor and even researched Alexander Pope to quote in seminars and impress him, and he flirted back – didn't he? She was sure he did – but he didn't bite. She settled for an MA student in the end, any port in a storm, after giving him her number at an extra-curricular lecture she'd gone to specifically to bag him. She spent the whole time with him in bed trying to convince herself she had achieved her dreams, but it was decidedly terrestrial sex – if she had to grade it, it was not even a 2:2, more like a low third. Scraping through. That five-year head start had clearly taught him nothing. He'd cancelled their second date saying he was going through some 'emotional shit', which she could only presume involved the female MA student who also taught undergrad classes and had been giving Sarah daggers in the refectory.

Sarah drank every night, trying to work out what was escape and what was fun. She shagged a few people after two-for-one spirits nights and in club VIP rooms on Mitsubishi pills. She had a threesome with two international students that involved absinthe and balloons. Sex felt like the ultimate aim of all the drinking, but it was a false summit – when she got to it, she realised that it wasn't it at all. So what was? Clouds. Smoking and breathing and fogged-up mirrors. Fuck knew. It was civilian or it was a mystery. The boys in halls and on her course had so much tenacity and yet so little actual game. Maybe the one last week – Chris, was he called? – was someone she could see again. He called every night around 7 p.m. on the hall's landline – he was a theatre director in the making (was that the appeal? His latent status?) and was head of the Drama Soc, putting on a production of *The Collector*, about the man who kept a woman in his basement. Sarah thought he was geeky but she liked the attention. The other night they'd agreed to tell each other their deepest darkest secrets, and he'd told her he'd put all his Sims in a swimming pool and taken away the ladder, leaving them to drown. In another lifetime, Sarah thought, this could be a connection.

There were live music gigs – indie bands, pop no more.

She became a tourist. There was frontman after frontman after frontman. In a way they were easiest to get because they were looking for the same thing, albeit to a different beat. She stood at the front, to the right-hand side, or by the sound desk, where they always looked. She was their critic, their soulmate, their best fuck. She woke up on tour buses, in hotel rooms, in different cities, in handcuffs. She travelled home in Mercedes people-carriers with aircon and mini Evians. The triple-A lanyards accumulated on her bedposts – notching her up, millimetre by millimetre, amounting to a ranking that somewhere, strangely, counted for something. Sometimes she even made it into songs.

When she thought about Mr Keaveney, it hurt. It still really hurt. Would it always? She didn't know where he was now and hadn't taken time to search the phone book, although it was only a matter of time before she used Friends Reunited. She changed her profile every day. Deleted messages. Her bio flipped from introvert to extrovert and back again. It was the same across all of her life – real, virtual, imaginary. She was struggling with herself, unsure whether to be a big personality or not. She couldn't let go because it wasn't safe. But she couldn't just stay small and quiet either. So she remained trapped, in a place between bigness and smallness, between riotousness and uncountability. A stage in a cave where a little girl messed with big guns. Without Juliette around, Sarah didn't know how to throw herself into relief. To find her own edges. Anything multiplied by anything always came back to Juliette, and Sarah couldn't change that. In a world of words, it was the maths she couldn't escape: Juliette was her zero. It apparently took ten minutes for the brain to die and maybe during that time you got played a best-of montage from your memories, like when you were leaving *Big Brother*. For Sarah, there would be so much Juliette. So much Juliette.

One night in halls she put on *Terminator 2: Judgment Day*. It was the first time she'd watched it without Juliette and there was no one to turn to her and say, '*Sarah Connor?*' in a robot voice. Now, Sarah had to be the robot. It was like she was trying to turn English into maths. To turn every experience and feeling into a story or a sentence. Into logic. But logic was slowly suffocating beneath the thing she really wanted to say to her sister, the thing she'd wanted to say for three years: me too. That man touched me on the bus as it went through Peel Underpass. She'd felt so ransacked, but she somehow *liked* being chosen by him, even though he hurt her. All of it somehow told her that she was doing something right – how fucked up was that, how fatal? Sarah wondered whether having a baby felt like that, too: a violence you were told to wear as a badge of honour. But it was too late to share. It was currency from a dead country. It was her birthday-candle secret now. Every year. Her face hotter, her heart thinner, she would blow out the flames and think, give me strength to carry this silently. Like all the outrages.

The sky outside was darkening. Sarah missed the sound of the motorway, although the leaves rustling in the trees would do. Everything would do. She was optimistic in that way. She started to get her make-up on, to head down for a drink, and who knew where the night might lead (alcohol, conversation, sex)? The London leaves in the London trees. She could feel the cascade of opportunities coming. She could either climb or float.

London: it was a long way from Manchester.

It was a longer way back.

MEDICAL NOTES

Sarah Hudson
DOB 01/08/82

13 November 1996 – Sexual Health Services, North
Manchester
14-year-old female. Broken condom <24 hours ago. No
other UPSI since last menstrual period 3 weeks previous.
Sexual partner similar age. Asked about coercion / no
coercion, voluntary. 'Wanted to do it, used condom but it
broke.'
GILLICK competent. No discharge or pain. No symptoms
infection. Swabs taken for chlamydia and gonorrhoea.
Emergency contraception prescribed.

28 May 1998 – Brook Advisory Centre, Manchester
15-year-old female. Broken condom <24 hours ago. Sexual
partner also 15. No suggestion of coercion. Had taken
cocaine several hours earlier.
GILLICK competent. Discussed with Child Protection lead.
Will enquire whether patient known to social services.

19 August 1998 – Brook Advisory Centre, Manchester
16-year-old female requesting contraceptive pill. Says has a boyfriend aged 16 with whom she is having regular sex. GILLICK competent – parents not informed.

15 February 1999 – Brook Advisory Centre, Manchester
16-year-old female came in presenting with discharge. Said she had used a glow-in-the-dark condom with boyfriend that she was later told had been used before, possibly several times. Swabs taken.
Clue cells seen on microscopy. BV treated with Flagyl. Parents aware.

2 January 2000 – GUM, Manchester
17-year-old female. Unprotected sex. Says at least one other instance a few weeks ago but can't remember clearly. Heavy drinking involved. Vaginal sex. Anal sex. Oral sex.
Emergency contraception refused. Patient said she would 'wait and see if she got pregnant'.

1 November 2000 – Sexual Health Services, Soho
18-year-old female student. Unprotected sex with university staff member. Seemed very proud of the fact and wanted to give all the details. Asymptomatic.
Query reason for visit? Reminded patient of staff/student power differentials. Patient replied, 'Don't worry, I'm not going to break him.'

27 July 2001 – GUM, East London
18-year-old female. Recently attended music festival. Concerned Glastonbury mud had 'gone up vagina' during sex in fields. Fears she has dysentery – reassured that

would be unlikely. Swabs taken. Obs stable. Orientated in time and place but slightly paranoid thinking.

6 March 2003 – Sexual Health Services, Dalston
20-year-old female, came in very upset. Unclear when/ if she had unprotected sex but she mentioned a bus a few times. And Manchester. Kept changing her story. Possible intoxication.
Referred to mental health services for counselling.

We run together

Me and my sister, down the path to the edge of the pond. She's already got her cardigan off and I pull my jumper off, too. The ducks fly away quacking. A few people are at picnic tables, braving the weather, smoking or vaping and drinking tins from the shop. They gawp at us. It's getting dark. As we take our boots off at the water's edge, Juliette says, 'You know this is why I had a second one. They will have moments like this. Forever. Even though the shit and drama will be there too. They'll have this.' And she grips my hand and it's the hand I've known the best for the longest and it'll always feel safe and dangerous and big and small and old and young and loud and quiet and lost and found. All of the opposites are in the space between my sister's palm and mine, as we hold hands. That's the space I can fly in. I don't know how to make it bigger, but maybe there is a way. I start to cry and drop her hand to yank off my socks and jeans. She tears off her dress and tights. Then I grab her hand again and we walk into the water. We are both in our underwear. It's freezing – I gasp as my chest tightens and every part of my body wants to get out. But I keep walking. We are laughing now – there's a lot coming out of me. I try and breathe. 'FOR SHAME!' someone shouts from the café but underwear is basically like a bikini, so they can fuck off.

The water is shiny and cold and I let it take my breath away because I take its energy back in return. It's all about give and take with bodies of water. I hear them shouting nasty things at us from the shore; all the old words, the incantations that have now lost their power, and I turn and flick the Vs, just one hand and straight fingers even though I am a professional now. You're never too old to do what you want with your body, every last little finger.

As the water passes her thighs, Juliette gasps. 'I think it's actually my vagina that feels the cold the most these days.'

'Is your pussy a pussy?'

'My pussy might be a pussy but yours is a twat.'

We go down to the stomach, to the chest, to the neck. Juliette says: 'Are you going to dunk?'

'I will if you will.'

She nods. I smile.

'Bye,' I say, and go under, holding her hand.

Bye.

Acknowledgements

Thanks

To Katie Popperwell, for the woman and girl.

To Sally Cook, for the sex and mundanity.

To Dolly Alderton, for hedonistic moderation.

To Julie and the Lovekins, for National Treasures We Hate.

To Ian Williams, for the legit doctor notes.

To Eden Keane, Jesca Hoop, Natalie O'Hara, Alison Taylor, Nicola Mostyn, Maria Roberts, Sarah Tierney, Gemma Dawson, Alexandra Heminsley, MK Trevaskis and Jessica Ruston for cheerleading and co-navigating the harder, faster years.

To Nikki Tattersall, for the best teenage friendship, peach schnapps debauchery, and all those Take That concerts. Mark and Robbie still don't know what they're missing.

To my book agent Clare Conville, evergreen, legend, riot, visionary, badass, guardian of my hopes, I do not have all the words but I am so grateful.

To the greatest screen agents in the land: Camilla Young, Katie Battcock and Becca Pearson at Curtis Brown. I am so lucky to work with you.

To my editor Suzie Dooré for extraordinary insight, psychic spark, patience, generosity, and for making it all make sense.

To Jo Thompson, Beth Coates, Jabin Ali, Sarah Foster and all the brilliant people at Borough Press.

To the cast and crew of *Below Deck* – every season, every spin-off. You (and cold showers) are my Ritalin.

To my parents, Frank and Lorraine. Thank you for letting me run to the edges. Thank you for lifting me high enough to feel the wind.

In memory of my grandma, Ann Unsworth: 1927–2024. Dance teacher, Bradley Walsh enthusiast, lionheart. Thanks for being the light in every room, still. For all the roses. I'm sorry I wrote a book called *Slags*, Grandma.

To Lucie: my sister, my hero. You had me at hello. You'll never know how much I admire you.

To Ian – I promise I will take a proper holiday soon.

To my little beloveds: F and A. I love you more than the mountains. Moon and back. Infinity to the power of infinity. I hope I make you feel as treasured, noticed and cherished as you make me feel, with you two in my life.

Finally, to all my wonderful readers – thank you for lending your precious time and supporting my work. It's never easy, but you always keep me going. Thank you. For me, novels are one-on-ones, tête-à-têtes, bistro tables in the pub, a safe place to play with dangerous toys. Thanks for being here and sharing yours with mine.

X